HOSTILE WITNESS

HOSTILE WITNESS

A KATE FORD MYSTERY

Leigh Adams

CROOKED
LANE

NEW YORK

Copyright © 2016 by copyright The Quick Brown Fox & Company LLC.

Published in the United States by Crooked Lane Books, an imprint of The Quick Brown Fox & Company LLC.

Crooked Lane Books and its logo are trademarks of The Quick Brown Fox & Company LLC.

Library of Congress Catalog-in-Publication data available upon request.

ISBN (hardcover): 978-1-62953-199-1
ISBN (ePub): 978-1-62953-212-7
ISBN (Kindle): 978-1-62953-659-0
ISBN (ePDF): 978-1-62953-670-5

Cover design by Jennifer Canzone
Book design by Jennifer Canzone

Printed in the United States.

www.crookedlanebooks.com

Crooked Lane Books
2 Park Avenue, 10th Floor
New York, NY 10016

First edition: February 2016

10 9 8 7 6 5 4 3 2 1

ONE

A man stood in the middle of the road, just inside the perimeter, and there was something wrong with him.

There was something wrong with him, but Kate's head was throbbing so badly, she couldn't begin to think of what it was.

She tried all the things that she usually did when she found herself in this position and found, also as usual, that none of them worked. The man was wearing black, and even at this distance, she could see that his earlobes were overly extended, as if he had done something to them that stretched them out. Was that what was wrong with him? Maybe he'd had those thick rings in them and then had taken them out. She adjusted her sunglasses. It wasn't a very bright day, but it didn't matter. She snaked her hand into her bag and grabbed her healing stone.

After checking to make sure there was no traffic on the road, Kate carefully pressed down on the brakes, then closed her eyes and counted to ten.

When she opened her eyes again, she thought the man had disappeared. Then she saw him, another three feet along, heading for the open maw of the parking garage.

That was wrong, too. This wasn't a pedestrian area. There were no sidewalks. There was nowhere to walk here *from*, and if you did walk here from somewhere, you wouldn't go through the garage entrance. You would go around to the side and enter the building at the front door.

It had been a long drive in from home, made worse by the throbbing inside her skull that just would not quit. Everything around her looked sharper and more detailed than it should have. Everything hurt.

The man was wearing a black suit that looked as if it cost five thousand dollars. His shirt was so white it caused glare. His tie was so black it looked painted on. Under the suit jacket was a vest, also black. Kate found herself wondering hysterically if the man was some kind of very expensive undertaker.

The car swung left as if of its own volition. She had been driving by instinct. She hadn't had to pay attention. Deep memory had been paying attention for her.

She jerked her mind back to the task at hand and stopped at the gate to present her identification. The interior of the garage was dark, silent, and still. She climbed carefully up the levels until she found one that was nearly vacant and pulled into an empty space. Then she turned off the car and waited until the engine noises stopped.

It was cool and dark in here. Nothing was moving. Nothing was happening.

Kate closed her eyes and put her forehead down on the steering wheel. Her headache began to subside. Her nausea—nausea she hadn't realized she had—began to subside, too. It was as if she'd been engulfed by a tide and the tide had turned and . . .

Kate gave it up. She'd spent most of her adult life trying to describe these episodes to everybody from lovers to doctors and back again. It never worked. When she was in the middle of an episode, she could barely speak. When she was clear of them, she couldn't really remember.

She thought back to her son, Jack, and the crazy fight they'd had this morning. The fight should have set her off, but it hadn't. Her head hadn't started to throb until hours later, when a traffic light had switched from red to green so suddenly it had made her shudder.

Kate took her keys out of the ignition and shoved them in her jacket pocket. She got out of the car, locked up, and looked around. The man had been walking toward the opening of the garage, but of course he hadn't come up here, if he had ever existed at all.

TWO

The Almador Corporation was one of those businesses that Kate used to make fun of when she was younger and that her son, Jack, made fun of now. Its premises were bland from the outside—but that was the problem, wasn't it? They were too bland. There was no way to tell, from the building's front elevation or from the parking garage entrance and exits, exactly what Almador *did*.

Nor could you form much of an impression once you got into the building. There was an expanse of blank walls and doors with people's names on them. The doors always seemed to be shut, even in the middle of the workday. Almador went out of its way to be as much like an evil corporation in some conspiracy theory movie as it possibly could.

She ran up the steps to the sixth floor instead of taking the elevator.

I am not wallowing, she told Jack inside her head. Then she pushed it all away. Things were always going to be a bit rocky with a teenage son, especially during puberty. It was bound to be worse when that son was a genius.

Kate pushed through into room 601. The morning bustle had already subsided. Kate was always careful to get in fifteen minutes late, just to make sure the noise and distraction of people piling in didn't set her off. Three of the assistants were plugging away at computer stations, all of them looking bored. Another one was fussing at the coffee maker, which was making the sounds a ferret would make if someone was strangling it.

The assistant at the coffee maker looked up and said, "Hi, Kate. I don't suppose I'm lucky enough that you don't want coffee?"

"Is there any alternative, Molly?" Kate asked.

"Well," Molly said, "there's that ginseng stuff you brought in a few months ago. You left a mountain of the stuff in the cabinet."

"Ah, well. I'm just not sure it will give me that jolt . . ." Kate started unconvincingly.

"Don't bother," Molly said. "I tried a cup once. It tasted like sawdust laced with cyanide."

"*That* would have quite a kick to it," Kate said innocently.

Molly snorted. "Go on in and get yourself set up for the day. I'll bring you coffee as soon as I can figure out how to make this thing produce it."

Kate turned for her office. Kate's office was also her perfect place. It wasn't that she was consumed by work and nothing else. She might not be the housewife type—Jack's father had had a lot to say about *that*—but she was much more concerned with the people close to her than she was with her client list.

Unfortunately, the people close to her were like people everywhere: they moved around suddenly, they started speaking without warning, they dropped heavy objects on the floor, and they did all the things that just might set off an episode. Her office was the only place where she could control the influx of stimuli.

She kept it dark. Only the computer screen glowed when she was there to see it. There were no lamps, and she always kept the overhead lights off.

Now she sat down at her station and booted up. The familiar noises came and went without bothering her much. Her desk was clear. One would never leave work lying around at Almador. Every document in the place was either classified by the military or an industrial secret. Her bookshelf was full of manuals for computer design and repair, including one thick one that was supposed to have the fixes for all the worst malware in existence. It didn't, but Kate did. There was also a smooth stone, polished until its surface looked like glass, sitting right in front of the malware book.

Kate picked it up and began to stroke it, deliberately and with concentration. A friend of hers had given it to her a few years ago, saying it was the most soothing ritual imaginable, something that could erase any tension anywhere. You held it in your hand and rubbed it until all your tensions disappeared.

Or they were supposed to.

Her desktop was up. She logged in. There were more of the usual noises, which actually helped instead of hurt. Kate opened her work e-mail and found a long list of mostly useless nonsense—the cafeteria menu for the day; chipper notes from human resources on "how to have a safe and inclusive workspace" and "developing trust between management and workforce"; and five announcements of various drives for canned goods, hats and mittens, and just plain money that would be counted as part of an employee's community involvement requirement.

Down at the bottom, she found an e-mail from her father, the subject line in all caps:

JACK UNUSUALLY UPSET THIS AM.

Kate bit her lip.

There was a careful, soft noise behind her. Kate swiveled in her chair to see Molly coming into the room with a Styrofoam cup of coffee in her hand.

"Hey," Molly said.

"That was faster than I expected." Kate held out her hand to take the cup.

Molly let the door snick closed behind her.

"I had an incentive," she said. "The office has been insane all morning. I'm going to be really happy when the trial gets started and there's some actual news going around."

Kate took the coffee. "The trial starts when? Tomorrow?"

"Tomorrow," Molly confirmed.

"And it's all about the boss's daughter," Kate said. "Corporate must be losing its marbles."

"I heard that Hamilton and Chan aren't speaking to each other at all," Molly said. "Chan's spraying emotion to the four winds, and Hamilton is being Hamilton, acting like emotions are for space aliens. You know how he hates publicity. This thing is going to run twenty-four-seven on cable news."

Kate took a long sip of her coffee and said, without thinking about whether or not it was a good idea, "I had something funny happen when I came in to work today."

"Funny?" Molly asked. "What kind of funny?"

"I thought I saw a man walking on the road leading up to the parking garage. He was wearing the kind of suit Hamilton always wears. You know, costs the earth, has a vest."

Molly blinked. "A man. On the road near the parking garage."

"That's right."

"But nobody walks there," Molly said. "There isn't even a sidewalk."

"I almost wondered if I was seeing things," Kate said.

Molly looked concerned. "Were you having one of your episodes? Do you think you were hallucinating?"

"I *was* having one of my episodes," Kate said, "but I've never in my life hallucinated anything. There's probably some simple explanation."

"Maybe you were having a vision," Molly said solemnly. "A lot of people who have second sight have a lot of trouble with, you know, headaches especially. I read about it—"

"I don't have second sight," Kate said firmly. "Half the time, when I have those episodes, I don't have any kind of sight at all."

Molly gave her one last long look, then turned and headed for the door. Kate had already turned back to her monitor when Molly stopped dead and said, "Oh, I forgot. Ballard wants to see you."

"See me?"

"See you personally. In his actual office. He said as soon as you got in. I'm sorry. The coffee maker disaster swept it straight out of my mind. God only knows what he wants."

★   ★   ★

Kate Ford could remember, with perfect clarity, the very first time she'd had an episode. It was also the very first time she'd been scared out of her mind to the point of freezing solid. There she was, on a cold, cloudless day late October, lying on the bench her father had built between two trees in their backyard. She was nine years old, and she had nothing on her mind but her two best friends and Halloween coming up. She was thinking with all the seriousness of youth that her life would be ruined if her mother didn't buy her the fairy princess costume that matched the ones Ann and Laurie would be wearing—that is, assuming Ann and Laurie could talk their mothers into the same thing, which Kate was sure they would.

Kate was having one of the days when everything was too sharp and too detailed and too much in focus. It was something that had happened to her all her life and that she considered both annoying and—when she found out that it was unique to her—lucky. Her powers of observation had always been much better than most people's. She could see and remember little things nobody else seemed to find important: the exact pattern on the brass buttons of Mr. Holliwell's blazer, the way Robbie Bellini's backpack bulged up near the top when he was stealing cartons of milk, the exact numbers Ann used for her locker combination.

Actually, by that time, Kate knew the combinations to almost everybody's locker in the entire fifth grade. She couldn't help herself. She couldn't stop herself from noticing. She couldn't make herself forget. It was as if her head were some kind of camera with a zoom lens. It was a good thing she wasn't interested in stealing other people's stuff.

There was only one real downside in all of this, and that was that Kate's head would start to hurt if the detail catching went on too long. The obvious thing to do about that would be to turn it off when she started to get tired, but she couldn't always turn it off. Sometimes she'd get thoroughly sick of the whole thing—who cared if Mr. Holliwell put pickles on his herring sandwich? Who cared what kind of sandwich he had at all? Then she'd close her eyes and count to twenty, and when she opened them again, the intensity of her focus would have subsided, and she would feel fine.

The problem was that it didn't always work that way. In fact, over time, Kate was finding herself with less and less control over the focus. She would be sitting in the middle of math class and her mind would start darting around the room, picking up random details and storing them. Tim Braves had bright-blue laces on his white sneakers. Carrie Holt was wearing black Mary Janes, and the strap of one of them had been broken and fixed very clumsily with duct tape. Louis Sanderson's brown Oxfords were scuffed at the toes. Mrs. Jackson's pumps were too big for her feet, so her heels kept slipping out of them when she walked across the classroom to write on the board.

By the time the break came, Kate would know everything about everybody's shoes and have no idea what the lesson had actually been about.

That day on the bench, she was just calm about it. She was looking from one of the trees to the other. She went from one brown leaf to the next, registering differences, registering similarities, allowing her mind to laser in as closely as it wanted to. She wished the sky wasn't turning that odd purple color.

No, she thought. It wasn't the sky that was turning that odd purple color. It was everything. Everything was bathed in a glow that was at first pale lavender, then violet, and then a deep purple that made it almost impossible to see.

It was also getting very, very difficult to breathe. The air around her was deep purple, and the purple was getting into her lungs and restricting her breathing. There wasn't any real air.

She was panicking. She could feel it. Her entire body had gone rigid, and no matter what she did, she couldn't make it move.

She tried to wrench herself sideways. Nothing happened. She tried it again. She thought she felt her body move against the bench.

And then there was a pain in her head as if somebody had thrust a knife through her skull.

The pain went down and down to the base of her throat, and she couldn't help herself. She wrenched one more desperate time.

The next thing she knew, she was off the bench and on the ground and vomiting—vomiting and vomiting and vomiting in big convulsive heaves that just would not stop.

Then purple turned to black and there was nothing.

It took her nearly a week to figure out what had happened to her after she'd passed out. "Fainted" was what her mother kept calling it. She remembered the air going black, but the next thing she knew, she was in the emergency room at the hospital and the lights were too bright and sharp. All the noises were too loud, too, and her focus was in overdrive. She could read the manufacturer's name etched on the side of a square metal box sitting on top of a wheeled wooden table. She could hear slippers shuffling against the floor in the corridor. She could see patterns in the overhead light.

Her mother was there, pacing back and forth in the little curtained cubicle. Once in a while, a doctor or a nurse would come in and pull her mother outside, but, oddly enough, Kate couldn't hear any of the details of that conversation at all.

After a while, her father came. Her father and mother talked in whispers in the hall, and Kate couldn't make that out, either. Then only her father came back in, and he brought one of the doctors.

"Kate?" he said.

"I'm all right," Kate said.

All of a sudden, her mother's voice boomed over all the other noises, coming from somewhere out in the hall.

"She had a *fit*," her mother said. "She had a screaming, frothing-at-the-mouth *fit*."

Everything in the cubicle went dead quiet.

"Is it true?" Kate said finally. "Did I have a fit?"

It hurt to talk. Everything was too sharp. It wasn't as sharp as it had been, but it was sharp. Kate wanted to go to sleep.

Kate's father was still staring at her. "I wasn't there," he said finally. "Your mother saw you. You were on the bench. She was looking out the kitchen window and she saw you. She said you weren't entirely conscious—"

"I was paying attention to the leaves," Kate said. She remembered it exactly. "There were these brown, dead leaves, and they had veins in them. I was looking at the leaves. And then I got sort of all tensed up. And everything was purple."

"Purple?" the doctor said. "Kate, can you tell me more about the purple?"

Kate looked at him. He was very small and sort of pinched looking.

"It was just purple," Kate said.

"Was it light purple or dark purple?" the doctor asked.

"It started out just sort of pale, like lavender chalk," Kate said. "But later it got to be very purple. And then it was black. All the air went black."

"Ah," Kate's father said.

The doctor shot him a look and shook his head. "There's no 'ah' about it. Too much of this still doesn't fit. We're going to have to run tests—"

"I've got nothing against running tests," Kate's father said.

"She was frothing at the mouth," Kate's mother's voice streamed in from outside.

The doctor turned on his heel and marched away. Kate's mother's voice stopped suddenly and irrevocably.

The doctor came back in. "That sort of thing is not helpful," he said. "I really must stress that, Mr. Ford. If we're going to understand what happened here—"

Kate was watching her father closely. He had turned toward the wall, looking at nothing, his shoulders hunched.

"My wife," he said, "is going to want to know if this was connected to, somehow, the other thing I told you about, the—"

"The hyperawareness," the doctor prompted. "It depends on the nature of the hyperawareness, and even then—" He veered around and looked straight at Kate. "Were you experiencing hyperawareness when this episode started?"

Kate looked blank.

"He means were you noticing every detail everywhere and remembering it?" Kate's father said.

"Oh," Kate said. "Not really. Sort of. I wasn't thinking about anything in particular."

"It doesn't fit the profile," the doctor said. "Epilepsy doesn't work like that."

"Daddy?" Kate said.

Kate's father cleared his throat.

"Epilepsy or not," he said, "my wife is going to want to know if the two things are connected. I'd guess we're all going to want to know that."

"I have never heard of a case in which hyperawareness resulted in convulsions," the doctor said. "I think at the moment, it's much more important for us to find out what happened here and why, and we can deal with the hyper-awareness issues at some later date."

"I like . . . the hyper thing," Kate said. But then she was tired. She put her head back onto the pillow and drifted off, drifted and drifted into a perfectly normal sleep.

After that, nothing was ever normal again. The one good thing was that months went by before Kate had another "convulsion." Other parts of the "episode" came back with increasing frequency, though. She got headaches so bad she could barely see. She got nauseated and sometimes vomited. She had less and less control of what the doctor called her "hyperawareness." At its worst, a slamming door or a dropped textbook could set off the symptoms, and then she had nothing she could do but wait the whole thing out.

Unlike the first time, though, not only did she not pass out; she didn't even need much time for recovery. The headaches and the nausea were there. Then the headaches and the nausea were gone.

And whatever it was that was wrong with her, it wasn't epilepsy.

What was wrong with her parents was another matter. Her father told her not to blame herself, but Kate knew there was no one else to blame. Before the convulsion, her mother had been standoffish and a little unhappy; after it, she was always just a breath away from exploding. And the explosions were always about Kate.

"I always told you something was wrong," Kate would hear her mother say to her father when they both thought she was asleep in bed. "I told you that right from the beginning. It isn't normal for someone to be like that."

"Like what?" her father would say. "She had an episode of some kind. She fainted—"

"She didn't *faint*. She was *frothing at the mouth*."

"All I can tell you is that nobody but you noticed any froth."

"You're delusional, Franklin. There's something wrong with her. There's been something wrong with her from the beginning."

Then she stalked off and slammed a door. She always seemed to slam a door.

Kate wasn't at all surprised when she came home from school a little more than a year later and found that her mother had gone—packed up her clothes, her wedding china, the Crock-Pot, her jewelry, and the very paintings off the living room wall and gone.

THREE

Harvey Ballard had been manager and supervisor of this division of Almador for longer than Kate had worked there, and in all that time, she hadn't been able to figure out what exactly his job was. That had been true on the day Harvey had interviewed her for this job, and it was true now, as she approached his door in the office he used on a floor above her own. Harvey stayed stashed away in his office. Kate stayed stashed away in hers. The two of them communicated by e-mail, as if they were in offices on opposite sides of the country. Kate couldn't remember the last time Harvey had asked to actually *see* her.

Still, Kate thought, as she marched up to the door and knocked as loudly as she could without hurting her hand, that didn't mean anything was wrong. She was almost certainly not getting fired. Her productivity was too high, and there were at least three government agencies who requested her by name whenever they had a computer security problem— which they almost always did, because for some reason, government agencies were completely hopeless at computer security, no matter what they did.

Harvey's voice boomed, "Yes? Who is it?"

Kate sighed. Not "Come in" or something else more pleasant. Harvey acted as if he thought managers were required to be rude just to maintain their authority.

"Kate Ford," Kate said. "Molly said—"

"Come in, come in," Harvey said, making shuffling noises just beyond the door.

Kate opened the door just fast enough to see him push a pile of papers under another pile of papers, as if he were trying to hide them.

"Molly said you wanted to see me," she said. There was a single visitor's chair. She sat down in it.

Harvey was a pudgy, harried, balding man just past middle age, the kind of person who sweats so much, the stains showed through the armpits of his jacket by the middle of the day.

The monitor on Harvey's computer was turned just far enough so that Kate could see what was on it. It was open to an article on CNN.com complete with a blaring headline about the trial and large photographs of Kevin Ozgo, Chan Hamilton, and, of course, Rafael Turner.

"I have asked you up here on a work-related matter," he said. He was trying to sound stern. He ended up sounding choked.

Kate nodded toward the screen. "Our boss's daughter gets herself involved in the most spectacular criminal case of the year and you don't think the entire building is curious?

If there's any connection at all between that case and our 'beloved' leader Richard Hamilton—"

"Don't be ridiculous," Harvey snapped.

"If there is some connection to the company," Kate pointed out, "we could all be looking for jobs in the near future."

"There is no connection to the company," Harvey said, "and implying that there is isn't improving your position here."

Kate stretched out her legs. "You said you had an assignment for me?"

Harvey looked like he was wrenching himself back from the abyss of God only knows.

"Well," he said.

"They asked for me particularly," Kate prompted.

Harvey started to shuffle the stack of papers Kate had seen him moving around when she came into the office. Then he seemed to realize what he was doing and almost jumped back in his seat.

Harvey found the papers he was looking for, pulled them out, picked up the messy stack, and hit them against the desk to square them.

"Yes," he said. "Well, the name of the company is Robotix—"

"Robotix?" Kate said. "I don't remember seeing that name before."

"You haven't," Harvey said. "As far as I know, no one at Almador has done work for Robotix before, and we in this division certainly haven't. They're a relatively new company.

Relatively new on the level that would require our services, I should say. They've recently become a serious player, and of course, that comes with major security problems. Specifically, they now have problems in one of their divisions. Four times in the last year, they've had their ideas suddenly appear in their competitors' product lines."

"But that sounds like industrial espionage," Kate said. "Not computer security. Especially if it's all coming from the same division of the company."

"I agree," Harvey said. "And I made the same point when I talked to Mr. Rose, head of the vacuum cleaner division."

"Vacuum cleaners?"

Harvey sighed. "*Robotic* vacuum cleaners," he said impatiently. "Everything Robotix makes is robotic. That's why it's called Robotix. Are you clear on that now?"

"Certainly," Kate said.

"Then let's get on with it. Somebody is leaking Robotix's vacuum designs to its competitors. It's almost certainly industrial espionage, but for a number of reasons, Mr. Rose does not believe that the problem is somebody inside the company getting ideas out. Why he doesn't think so is thoroughly covered in the material I am sending you. Robotix is convinced that they've been hacked. They seem to think that you're the best person to uncover that hack and get rid of it. That's what you are going to do."

"And they asked for me by name?"

"I already said that."

"Did they give us a time frame?"

"Yesterday was my general understanding," Harvey said. "And you can't blame them. This sort of thing can kill a company's profitability. Do you have something else you're working on?"

"I just finished the Markwell-Halliday job."

"Good. I thought you were off schedule. If you could take these," Harvey handed over the paperwork, "and get onto this right away, both Robotix and I would appreciate it."

Kate looked down at the thick stack of paper she held in her hand. "Robotix makes robots," she said.

"Yes, Robotix makes robots, Miss Ford."

"Are they run by computers or—?"

"I think that's the kind of information you'll find in the paperwork. And I've sent you the complete file of e-mails I've had with the company, plus some documentation."

"I'll get right on it," Kate said.

Harvey Ballard looked almost infinitely relieved, except that he was sweating again.

"Fine," he said. "Fine. You just get right on it."

★　★　★

Five minutes later, Kate was back in her office, the door closed, the lights low. She had her rock in her hands and was rubbing it rhythmically.

She went to her computer and checked her e-mail. There was an e-mail there from Harvey Ballard with attachments out the wazoo. She opened them up and started to download them.

And then she started counting the ways that this whole situation was odd.

First, there was the fact that the documents were here, right in her work e-mail inbox, just as if they were menus from the cafeteria or cheery motivational notes from human resources.

But the first rule of computer security was that you never used the same machine for confidential or classified material as you used for the general stuff. Hell, you didn't even use a computer on the same connected system or in the same room. Almador had a total of five secure rooms with computers that were entirely disconnected from the general network, two of which were for government work alone. It wasn't entirely impossible to transfer information from a secure computer to a nonsecure one, but it was difficult, and the secure rooms all had video cameras running twenty-four-seven. They also had no access to printers and no access to e-mail except (on the government ones) to the special system used only by the US Armed Forces and Intelligence Community.

But here she was with an assignment relating to what the client believed was a hack of his company's computer system with all the relevant documents in an e-mail file her thirteen-year-old son could access in half a minute flat.

The first thing she'd have to do on this job was find out whether Robotix was really this lax about its in-house digital systems and, if it was, try to get them to change over to something that had a chance in hell of being secure.

She'd run into that problem with other companies, and she hadn't always been successful in making the client see reason. Clients—at least commercial clients—often wanted speed and convenience so much that they refused to believe they couldn't have that and security, too, but that wasn't so.

Harvey should have sent her these documents in a way that could only be opened on a secure computer. But Harvey Ballard had not done that or anything like that. He hadn't even lectured her on maintaining the security of Robotix's confidential documents. He'd just jammed the whole mess into a ZIP file and sent it off to her, unprotected.

And that wasn't all he'd done.

Kate looked at her monitor and wondered if she should have downloaded these files, if maybe she should delete them immediately and forward the original e-mail to—where could she forward it to? There was no connection between this computer and the ones in the secure rooms. That was the point of the secure rooms. If she needed to use this material in a secure location, how was she going to get it there? She would have to send it back to Harvey, because one of the other things the secure computers couldn't do was connect to a flash drive.

A couple of years ago, one of Almador's biggest competitors had carelessly taken on a new client who turned out to be a front for ISIS operations in Western Europe. They ended up facilitating a hostage situation in Belgium and a bombing attack on the Eiffel Tower. The bombing had been unsuccessful, but all the hostages had been killed. And Almador had one less serious competitor.

Kate had no idea how sending files about vacuum cleaners insecurely could lead to hostage situations anywhere, but she wasn't about to let the whole thing go without checking it out.

And that was before she even started considering the *really* odd thing.

She picked up the papers Harvey Ballard had given her and rifled through them. The stack consisted of page after page of bold-faced type in deep, thick paragraphs that stretched relentlessly from one page to the other. She caught sight of a heading in all caps—"DIVISION PERSONNEL BY FUNCTION"—and then another: "DIVISION PERSONNEL BY LOCATION." She'd be willing to bet anything that the same information was in the files she was downloading.

She rifled through the papers again, more and more dissatisfied. Then she got up and went out her door and into the front room where the assistants were.

All the desks were filled now. All the assistants were sitting at their computer terminals, typing away.

She made a little coughing sound, and heads went up across the room.

"I just want to ask you guys something," she said. "Can any of you remember the last time that you or anybody else at Almador got information relating to an assignment on actual paper?"

It was Molly who spoke up. "Actual paper? We get letters, if that's what you mean, you know, for accounting and that kind of thing; sometimes people want the paper trail—"

"Not like that," Kate said. "I mean actual information relating to the assignment. Particulars about the client and the client's company. Things like that."

The young woman to the left of Molly—Rachel, the chubby one who always wore bright-red dresses—shook her head. She was wearing a tiny Star Trek pin just at the base of her throat. It was too small for most people to notice. It was the first thing Kate's mind connected with. "We're not supposed to put anything like that on actual paper," the young woman said. "Mr. Ballard says it's too easy to get paper in and out of here, and there could be a security breach."

"That's right," a third woman said. "And that's even more important if we're doing work for the government, because if that information got out, it could get people killed."

"Also, you don't want to get fired," Rachel said. "You'd be out on your ear in a minute if you put any of that information down on actual paper."

"I thought so," Kate said. "Thanks very much."

She turned away and went back to her office.

There were people, mostly older people, who believed that the old days of paper files had been much safer and less prone to breach than the new digital systems, but Kate knew they were wrong. You could put layers of protection on digital systems that you could never manage with ordinary paper. And paper, once accessed, was easy to conceal in clothes or shopping bags or any of a thousand other things. The old Cambridge spy ring that had devastated British military intelligence in the sixties had managed to get entire volumes of paper files out of their supposedly secure locations, and back again, without anybody knowing. It made no sense, with encryption and everything else that was available, to put the whole thing on paper and leave it lying around for anybody to get hold of.

And yet, Kate thought, here she was, with a thick sheaf of paper just sitting on the side of her desk, ready for anybody to come by and pick it up.

FOUR

Since Kate had always come into the office just a little late, she had made it a firm rule to leave a little later. She didn't really know which specific circumstances set off her episodes and neither did her doctors, but rush hour in the Virginia suburbs was just asking for trouble. It was a simple fact that her day was less likely to be derailed if she restricted her driving to times when she knew she would probably be alone—or close to alone—on the roads.

Today she was just too fidgety, and the longer she worked on the Robotix project, the more fidgety she got. On the surface, Robotix's problem was perfectly ordinary, the bread and butter of a computer security firm. The world was full of companies that were exactly what Robotix appeared to be: very good at what they did but completely clueless about the ways in which they were vulnerable to cyberattacks and hacking.

Every once in a while, there would be some big story in the media that would make everybody nervous. The 2015 hack of Anthem/Blue Cross had been like that, with hundreds of thousands of data sets—names, addresses, Social Security numbers, mothers' maiden names—scooped up in a massive identity theft operation that left everyone it touched open to total financial ruin. These companies would start to twitch, and Almador's offices would be jam-packed with new projects, all of them demanding rush results and total safety.

But . . .

Computer companies were *not* usually among Almador's clients. Granted, Robotix was not exactly a "computer" company, but it had to know enough about how to construct and operate digital systems to make its domestic robots function, and that ought to mean it knew enough either to protect itself from hacks or to have a security firm on retainer to protect from hacks.

She got out her standard checklist and started to work her way through it. She logged into Robotix's system. The password she'd been given wasn't bad, but it wasn't unbreakable either. If somebody really wanted to break it, they could. She looked around at the products section and found herself staring at all kinds of really neat stuff: robots that cleaned pools, robots that mowed grass, robots that zipped around your driveway and cleaned up gravel—even one robot that claimed to be able to iron shirts.

"Boys with toys," Kate muttered to herself. The prices were completely ridiculous. The pool-cleaning robot rang in at more than $1,800. The lawn mower topped $3,200.

So robots weren't exactly practical solutions for everyday maintenance problems yet. Anybody who could afford to buy these things could definitely afford staff.

By the time lunch came around, Kate was both starving and very tired, but she couldn't face going down to the cafeteria for the latest take on California rolls, quinoa salad, and gluten-free vegan wraps. She called Molly in and asked if she'd mind going down to the cafeteria and bringing her back something recognizable.

"A cheeseburger would be good," Kate said. "But I'm not expecting miracles."

"I don't think I've ever seen a cheeseburger in our cafeteria," Molly said.

"Just bring me back something resembling food," Kate said. "Oh, and ask Ben Jarndice to come in for a minute. I want to double-check something."

Ben was a very new hire. He was also very bright, dedicated, and considerably more skilled than half the people above him.

Ben got to her office before the food did. He came bopping in without bothering to knock and threw himself into one of those swivel chairs that dump most people on the floor.

"So," he said. "What's up? I don't believe you dragged me in here to find out the latest in the Ozgo case."

"Is that still all anybody's talking about?"

"It's all anybody's talking about, and it's all anybody's looking at on their computers," Ben said. "I tried looking into it myself, but I couldn't make any sense of it. Kevin Ozgo was in the army with Rafael Turner, who died in Iraq, and he was in love with Chan Hamilton, and Chan took Ozgo in and let him live at her place, and—it's like a soap opera. Nobody around here would even care if Chan wasn't Richard Hamilton's daughter."

"I know," Kate said. "But you're not going to get any help from me. I don't understand it either. And I've got a more practical problem at the moment."

"What's that?"

"I want to find out if this is as lame as I think it is."

Kate pushed her chair away from her computer terminal and gestured toward the screen. She had Robotix's commercial website and its internal system up, but she had logged out of the internal system so that it was now demanding a username and password.

"I'm not expecting you to actually give me the username and password," she said. "I just want to know if you can come up with the general rule."

"There's a general rule?"

"Oh, yes," Kate said.

"No randomly generated stuff that changes every forty-five days?"

"Not from what I can see from the material they sent me."

"Well, that's their first problem right there," Ben said.

The food came while Ben was still flicking back and forth across the commercial site, stopping every once in a while when he became intrigued by one of the robots and flicking away quickly when he saw the price. When the food came in, he looked over at it and said, "Why do you eat that stuff?"

The food was today's version of a gluten-free vegan wrap. It could have been rendered edible by the addition of bacon.

Ben had made his way to the "About Us" page.

"Here," he said. "History of the company."

"My thoughts exactly."

Ben sat back. "It'll have the name of one of the robots in it," he said. "My guess is that they've gone either for the first one or the best-selling one—or the first best-selling one. There will be Roman numerals that are some variation of the founder's birthday, or the day the company was founded, or—does this guy have a wife or a girlfriend?"

"Not that I know of," Kate said.

"Here's something I know," Ben said. "The first of these robots is the one that cleans walls. Goes right up them. It was invented by a guy named Trey Mitchell, and he probably still heads up this company. That means the characters will have at least one star in them, if not several."

Kate looked blank.

"Mitchell's got a side project going," Ben said. "Commercial space travel. He's a complete nut about space travel."

"That's something I should have known," Kate said. She looked up at the clock. "Do you know how long that took you? Given that set of assumptions, how long do you think it would take you to figure out the actual password for that system?"

"With decent equipment? I don't know. Maybe a day. Maybe less, if I got lucky. So I was right about the general rules?"

"You were exactly right," Kate said. "And it's been bugging me all day. This is a computer-based company. Can you imagine a computer-based company coming up with a password this lame?"

"Maybe it's a lucky break," Ben said. "Maybe this was delegated to somebody without a brain in his head and now we're going to be able to solve his problem in no time flat. Almador will get a lot of business from a new client. We'll all look like geniuses. When bonus time comes around, you'll get a nice big one."

"Maybe," Kate said. She'd given up on the gluten-free vegan wrap. She put it back in its wrapper as Ben stood up to go.

"I've got to admit, I don't see what you can really be worried about," he said. "The world is full of stupid. But you're twitching like you've discovered an attack on the Pentagon, and I just don't see it."

"No," Kate said. "Not an attack on the Pentagon."

"If you don't have anything else for me, I'm going to go back to this report I'm supposed to be doing."

"It's okay, Ben. Thanks for helping me. And maybe you're right. Maybe it's just a matter of the world being full of stupid."

★　★　★

Four hours later, Kate had finished her checklist and discovered that it was just as easy to get into Robotix's product development module as it was to get into any of the rest of the system and that the product development module provided unbelievably detailed information on all the new robots Robotix had in the pipeline.

This was the problem Robotix had come to Almador for. Somebody was stealing products Robotix had in development—products that were supposed to be secret. The more Kate tested the security of the module, the worse it looked, until she finally decided that it was a miracle Robotix had any new products left to develop.

Whoever had constructed this mess wasn't just stupid. He was almost criminally negligent.

At five o'clock, she came across the files for a robot vacuum called the Genvenix II. It was the oddest-looking one yet, with wedges at its sides as if it might be designed to fly. Drones were robots too, and they were big business these days. Kate leaned in closer to see what the thing was meant to do, and just as she did, the screen went blank.

She thought the computer had crashed, but a second later, the screen was back up, blue and forbidding, with nothing on it but big gold letters that read, "ACCESS DENIED."

Access denied?

First there was nothing but a sieve so worthless anybody could get any kind of access they wanted, and now there was a tripwire? For what?

Of course, Robotix had a lot of proprietary information it needed to protect, but it wasn't protecting it—except suddenly it was.

Kate started to hammer frantically at keys. She went back to the login screen and tried the username and password again. The Robotix system denied her access again.

She tried it again and, having hit the tripwire again, got a black screen instead of a blue one. The tripwire had shut down her computer.

Kate got up, left her office, passed through the assistants' office without noticing that the assistants had started packing up for the day, and headed for the closest secure computer room.

When she got there, she sat down, pulled herself up to the computer station, and started to plug in the information she'd been using in her own office and . . .

Access denied.

Access denied.

Black screen.

It didn't make any sense. It didn't make any sense at all. A tripwire should not have been able to shut down a computer on their secure system. The system was as fully protected against things like that as any military installation.

In fact, it pretty much was a military installation. Kate shouldn't have brought a commercial project in here at all. She wouldn't have if she'd been thinking, but she'd been so shocked by the tripwire that . . .

The next thing that happened didn't make much sense, either.

Harvey Ballard burst in through the secure computer room's door, his face so red Kate thought his head was going to pop.

He was yelling at the top of his lungs.

★ ★ ★

The ride home in the unbearable rush hour had not set off another episode, but it had taken damned near forever. Kate looked down at the car clock as she pulled into the driveway of her Merryhall townhouse and saw that it had been nearly two hours since she'd set out from Almador, Harvey Ballard's shrieks still ringing in her ears. She could have sat in the parking garage for half that time and probably gotten home earlier.

She flicked the garage door opener and waited a second for the door to rise before she pulled the rest of the way in. She was doing the thing she always told Jack not to do by blaming her problems on everybody but herself. But this mess was her fault, wasn't it? She was the one who had lost her cool and gone running to the secure computers as if her life depended on it.

At least, that was Kate thought had just happened. Harvey Ballard hadn't been all that clear.

She cut the engine, grabbed her bag, and popped open her door. The heavy inner door from the garage to the kitchen stood open, with only the screen door as a barrier between the kitchen and the garage.

Kate began to feel as if somebody had dumped a second bucket of rocks on her head.

"Dad?" she called.

A figure appeared at the screen door, but it wasn't her father, Franklin Ford. It was her son, Jack, the only decent thing that had come out of her marriage and now the local school district's resident child genius. One of Jack's teachers had actually called him that at a parent-teacher conference to discuss what to do about Jack's inability to sit still in math class when he knew all the answers.

"She keeps wanting me to 'show all my work,'" Jack had told Kate in the middle of all that fuss. "What work? I'm not doing any work. Anybody with half a brain in their head could look at this thing and know what the answer is."

Kate had tried to tell him then that most people could not look at even linear equations and just "know" what the answer was. But that had been two years ago, and she'd given up trying to impart that particular insight.

Jack opened the screen door and came into the garage.

"You look terrible," he said. "You look worse than usual."

"Thank you," Kate said sarcastically. And then, because something serious was going on, and because Jack would pick up on it, "I am worse than usual. I've had a very bad day."

Jack made a face. "You mean you had one of your 'episodes'?"

Kate could hear the scare quotes around the word. She gestured toward the screen door and the kitchen. "I take it Grandpa had a bad day."

Jack looked back at the door. "It was a weird day," he said finally. "It was one of those days when he talks about Grandma and about you when you were a kid. I put on music to see if it would calm him down."

"He wasn't calm?"

"He was sort of pacing up and down," Jack said. "He couldn't sit still. He wasn't violent."

"For God's sake," Kate said. "Of course he wasn't violent."

"He could get violent," Jack said stubbornly. "Grandpa has Alzheimer's disease, whether you want to accept it or not."

"Of course I accept it!"

"No, you don't," Jack said, his thirteen-year-old body seeming to fold in on itself. "You've got some idea that Alzheimer's is just about not remembering anything, and you didn't look at the material I sent you. I went to a lot of trouble to get you that stuff. I was on the Internet for days. Alzheimer's patients sometimes get violent. Some of them end up in nursing homes not because they lose their memories and forget who they are but because their families can't handle the—"

"He knows who he is," Kate said sharply. "We talked to the doctor. This is a very early stage."

"This was a very early stage a year and a half ago," Jack said. "Stages progress. I came home from school today and he was pacing back and forth in the living room and he didn't know who I was. He thought I was somebody named Billy. Do you know anybody named Billy?"

"No," Kate said, feeling suddenly deflated. "Listen," she said. "If he's . . . if he's not all right, we should make other arrangements for somebody to be here when you get home."

"I'm thirteen, not three," Jack said. "I can take care of myself for a couple of hours after school."

"Yes, sweetie, I know you can, but if he's, uh, if he's getting worse, maybe you can't take care of him, and you shouldn't have to take care of him. You're still a child."

"I'm not a child. And you don't have to worry about tonight, anyway. The music did the trick. That and a little occupational therapy."

"What do you mean, occupational therapy?"

"We're having hamburgers and French fries for dinner. I've got him peeling the potatoes."

"You cooked dinner?"

"No," Jack said. "I just got things out and started to get them ready. It gave him something to do that he understands. He remembers how to peel potatoes. I got out the rest of the stuff, too. All you have to do is march yourself into the kitchen and start cooking."

"I'll march," Kate promised.

Jack gave her a long, hard-to-decipher look. "You're going to have to do something about all this," he said. "I hate to sound like the grown-up here, but somebody has to. Grandpa isn't going to get any better. I'm not going to get any younger. You can't keep doing what you do all the time."

"Jack."

"Never mind," Jack said. "Come in and let's get things going before he goes off again. I hate it when he talks about Grandma. I never know what to think."

★ ★ ★

Franklin Ford was sitting at the kitchen table when Kate finally got inside, serenely and expertly peeling a potato. While she watched, he finished with the one he was holding. He picked up a sharp knife, cut the potatoes into long strips, and put the strips into the fryer basket at his side.

After a while, Frank looked up and smiled. There was nothing hazy or confused about his smile, but Kate knew instantly that he did not recognize her.

"Hello!" he said cheerfully. "Glad to see you. You should take off your coat and settle in. We'll be eating any minute now."

Beethoven's Symphony no. 3 played in the background, and Jack had been right to put it on. No matter what happened to Frank's memory, he never seemed to forget Beethoven. It always calmed him and often brought him back.

This information didn't make Kate feel better. He'd taught engineering at MIT. He'd been a war hero in two separate wars. He'd spent his retirement until very recently substitute teaching in the local high schools and volunteering with the Wounded Warrior Project. He'd helped raise Jack when Jack's father wasn't interested. He'd spotted Jack's intellectual abilities before any of the rest of them had known what was going on. And now . . .

Frank looked up from where he had just peeled another potato and said, "You ought to get settled in. It's not going to be long before dinner."

Kate looked down at the soft age creases in her father's hands, and all of a sudden, she couldn't face telling them both what had happened to her at work today. She turned away and headed for her bedroom.

The way things were, she would have to tell them both tonight and then tell Frank again in the morning. Jack was right. Kate spent too much of her time trying to ignore the fact that Alzheimer's was a disease that progressed over time, and sometimes progressed very fast.

She shucked off her work clothes and left them on the floor of her bedroom. She put on her most relaxed pair of jeans and a T-shirt that had come from the gift shop at CIA headquarters at Langley. She was very proud of that T-shirt. The CIA gift shop was inside the perimeter where only people with clearance were allowed. You couldn't just walk in off the street and buy what you wanted. She didn't think she knew another person who had one of these shirts. Or the CIA teddy bear, either. The teddy bear always sat on her bed.

When she came out to the kitchen, Frank was still sitting at the table, but Jack was on his feet and . . . cooking.

"Jack?" she said. "That's very nice of you, but I really can finish that. And I don't want you to start doing housework around here like you were—"

"If you're going to say the thing about me being a child again, I'm going to say the thing about throwing up again. Sit down. I've done this a million times. I just usually do it when you're not here."

"And Grandpa lets you do it?"

"You bet he does. *Especially* when he's showing no symptoms. He's not crazy. Why don't you get out the hamburger rolls and the ketchup and the mustard and that kind of thing? This doesn't take long."

"I'll never understand how you can stand mustard on your hamburgers," Kate said.

"There's mustard on McDonald's hamburgers," Jack said. "Why don't you stop bobbing and weaving and tell me what happened that's making you look like roadkill?"

"Oh," Kate said. "I think roadkill is a little harsh."

"I don't." Jack flipped three large burgers one after the other and then sat down at the table next to his grandfather. "You came home early today, too."

"Well," Kate said, "I won't be going in to work tomorrow morning."

"You got fired?" Jack looked honestly surprised. "Was it because of an episode?"

"It wasn't an episode and I wasn't fired."

"If it wasn't an episode, then what was it? We've talked about this, Mom. I don't understand how you have a job at all when you get those things, never mind a job that you have to have security clearances for. I wouldn't give you a security clearance. You could go off sometime and start saying things you didn't even know you were saying."

"I don't say anything at all when I have an episode," Kate said. "And last I heard, you didn't think they were real."

"I said I thought they were psychosomatic. That's not the same thing as not real. That means—"

"I know what psychosomatic means, Jack. They're not psychosomatic."

Jack got up to flip the burgers again. "Okay," he said. "Then what was it? And why aren't you going in to work tomorrow if you haven't been fired?"

The hamburgers were done. Jack picked up the spatula and started to transfer them to a plate.

"I am not going in to work tomorrow," Kate said, "because I have been suspended. For four weeks. Without pay."

Jack said, "Do we have enough to eat for four weeks without pay?"

"Of course we do."

The fries were done, too. Jack turned off the range burner and carefully transferred the deep fryer to an oven pad. Then he lifted up the basket and let the fries drain oil.

"So why are you suspended?" Jack asked again.

Kate hesitated only for a moment. Then she spilled the entire story, from the moment she'd first started to wonder about Robotix to her panicked rush to the secure computers.

"And the next thing I know, my manager comes bursting through the door saying he wants me off the premises and out of Almador for the next month. He went on and on, practically chasing me out the door. The only thing I can think of was that he was furious with me for using the secure computers."

"He didn't say that was it?"

"No," Kate said. "He didn't say anything coherent. But it would make sense. The secure computers are for military work almost exclusively. You know, I told you this. The military has its own version of the Internet, and it's important to keep it clean from outside influences. And using one for the Robotix thing might have jeopardized our contracts with the military."

"You'd think he would have said," Jack said. He got the ketchup and mustard Kate had forgotten and put them on the table.

"It's like I told you, he really wasn't being coherent. I thought he was going to have a stroke. And we'll know for sure in a couple of days. Almador will send me a letter with the particulars."

"Could you get fired at the end of the suspension?"

"I could," Kate admitted. "I'm not expecting to. Unless I did do something that lost us our military contracts. Then they ought to fire me."

"Wonderful," Jack said.

Kate took the rolls Jack was bringing over and picked up a knife to slit the first one apart.

"It was just the oddest thing," Kate said. "It was like a total lock-down of some sort. I've never seen anything like it. It was *worse* than a defense-grade tripwire. And for a company that makes pool vacuums, for God's sake."

FIVE

The first thing Kate noticed when she woke up was the noise.

The noise was coming from right outside her bedroom window, which faced the front of the house and therefore the street. It was tinny and harsh and hard to understand.

Kate turned over on her back and finally registered the sound as words: *Vote for Evans. District Attorney Reggie Evans for governor of the great state of Virginia. Vote for Evans. Vote for—*

There was a lot more of it, but it didn't make Kate want to vote, and it really didn't make her want to vote for Evans. She'd met Evans once or twice. She'd heard him speak. She liked what she'd heard him speak about. She even thought he'd made a very good district attorney.

She had to wonder, though, what kind of an idiot sent campaign vans streaming through neighborhoods at whatever hour this was in the morning.

She was about to turn over and find out what time it actually was when her bedroom door opened and Frank walked in.

Frank raised his hands and revealed a bugle. Then he put his lips to the mouthpiece and started playing "Reveille."

It was silly and as wonderful as anything could get until Kate remembered the night before and had a horrible thought. Maybe he was here to wake her up because he thought they were all back in her childhood, with her mother down the hall making breakfast and a stack of Kate's homework on the kitchen table so she would be sure not to forget it.

"I know you're not going in to work today," Frank said, "but you'd better get up anyway. Jack's got issues."

Kate let herself exhale. They were in the here and now. Frank was behaving perfectly normally.

"I've got issues, too," he said. "I'm supposed to give a talk on code breaking down at the senior center."

Frank retreated from the room, closing the door behind him. Kate got up and swung her legs over the side of the bed. It felt very odd to be in no kind of a hurry.

She got out of bed and headed for her small en suite bathroom. She threw herself in the shower and made the water as hot as it would go. It hit her scalp like needles. Then she got out and found a clean pair of jeans and a T-shirt and put them on. She half-expected that to give her a sense of purpose for the day, but it didn't.

As she entered the kitchen, Frank and Jack were sitting together at the kitchen table, looking through a war-gaming manual.

"I keep telling Jack here that war-gaming on terrain is a lot more realistic than war-gaming on those video games he likes so much," Frank said.

"*I* keep telling him he ought to learn how to play those video games instead," Jack said. "He might have fun."

Jack and Frank both had scrambled eggs, bacon, toast, and orange juice, and Frank had a cup of coffee. Kate got coffee and orange juice for herself and sat down.

"That all you're going to eat?" Frank asked.

Kate ignored him.

Jack was fidgeting more than a little. Kate looked at him and cocked an eyebrow.

"Well?" she said. "Your grandfather told me you had issues."

"Yeah," Jack said.

"I hate the word *issues*," Kate said.

"Yeah," Jack said again. He picked up a strip of bacon and examined it as if it were a very important clue in a very important murder mystery. "Here's the thing," he started. Then he stopped. Then he stared at the bacon some more.

"You're going to have to say something sometime," Kate said. "I'm not going to be able to figure it out on my own."

"Yeah," Jack said yet again. He heaved a big sigh and rushed into it. "You're not going in to work today, right? That means you're not going to have an emergency and have to stay late or anything like that?"

"Right," Kate said. "I thought we discussed that last night."

"Yeah, we did," Jack said. "But I didn't mention it up to now because I thought you'd have to be at work anyway, so it's not just last minute. I didn't just wait—"

"Wait for what?" Kate demanded.

"To tell you I had a meet this afternoon," Jack said. "It wasn't that I didn't want you to come. It wasn't anything like that."

"Ah." Here was a subject Kate wanted no part of. She could remember the last time she'd come to one of Jack's meets, and after that, he hadn't wanted her to again. "I see. Do you want me to come? I take it you're competing."

"In the relay, the fifty-yard dash and the hundred-yard dash," Jack said. "And of course I want you to come. I always want you to come. I just don't want, you know, one of those things."

Kate put her coffee cup down very carefully on the table. She rearranged her orange juice glass from the left of the coffee to the right.

"I really don't do those things on purpose," she said. "I don't plan for them. And I don't think I can stop them if they start."

"But they don't happen all the time," Jack said quickly.

"No, they don't, Jack. But they also don't come on a schedule. It's not like I can say that I'll only have them on Tuesdays, or if I had one yesterday, I won't have one today."

"But don't you get any advance warning? And they're not all as bad as that time at the swim meet. You practically passed out, and you don't usually do that, so there's got to be a reason."

"I agree there's got to be a reason," Kate said. "I just don't know what it is."

"I had to quit swimming because of the last time," Jack said. "I had to. You just fell over and the meet was cancelled and it was all I heard about for days at school. You wouldn't believe the things people said."

"So maybe you don't want me to come," Kate said.

"I think he definitely does want you to come," Frank said.

Jack had eaten his piece of bacon absent-mindedly.

"Yeah," he said. "I do want you to come. I've been doing really well, but most of the time, you're at work when we have track meets. So I want you to come. Because even if another of those things happen, there won't be a million people there. It won't get as crazy. So I think we should risk it."

"Okay," Kate said. Her chest was tight. If emotional upheaval brought on her episodes, she'd be having one right now. "I think you're right. I think we should risk it."

"So you'll come?" Jack asked.

"I'll come," Kate said.

"It's at four o'clock," Jack said. "You know where it is, right behind the school. You can just come and sit anywhere."

"Okay," Kate said.

"I've got to go," Jack said. "I'll see you there. Grandpa's coming too."

"Of course I am," Frank said.

Jack looked from one to the other, as if he were waiting for somebody to say something they hadn't said. When neither Kate nor Frank said anything, Jack leaped up from his chair and headed for the front door.

"See you there," he called back.

Kate heard the banging and rattling that meant he'd grabbed his backpack off the front hall table and then the sound of a door opening and slamming shut.

The silence that followed Jack's departure was so thick that being in it was almost like drowning. Kate stared at her coffee and thought about the kind of life she was giving Jack. His father was gone, and his mother was some kind of medical freak who couldn't be counted on to stay upright at a junior high track meet. Frank stared at Kate.

It was Frank who broke the silence. Kate could have sat where she was without a word for an hour.

"He's a good kid, Katie," Frank said. "He's a very good kid."

"I know he is."

"He's just worried about you."

"He shouldn't have to worry about me," Kate said. "I'm the adult. I should be worried about him."

"He's worried about me, too," Frank said. "I think we're all worried about each other."

"Jack thinks I can help this," Katie said. "He thinks I'm doing it on purpose. Not consciously on purpose, but on purpose."

"I don't think he thinks you're doing it on purpose," Frank said. "And I don't think he thinks I'm doing my thing on purpose, either. It's what I said. I think he's worried about you."

"And what's your thing supposed to be?"

Frank got up from the table and brought his dishes to the sink. "If you think I don't know what's happening to me, you're out of your mind."

"What's happening to you?" Kate was feeling very cautious.

Frank kept his back to her. "I don't always know when it's happening. I think maybe I almost never know. But sometimes I do. I knew last night."

Kate felt the excitement race through her. "But how is that possible? How do you mean you knew what was happening last night?"

Frank turned around to look at her. "It was like I was standing outside myself, watching myself. And the part of me that was standing outside knew who you were, and the part of me still in my body didn't, and I couldn't make the two parts connect."

Kate could barely make herself sit still. "Daddy, listen," she said eagerly. "That isn't like any kind of Alzheimer's I've ever heard of. I don't think that's Alzheimer's at all. We should tell the doctor. Maybe he made a mistake. Maybe this is something else and it's not so bad. Maybe we can do something about it."

"I've talked to the doctor, Kate. He said Alzheimer's manifests in many ways."

"But that's just because he doesn't want to change his diagnosis," Kate said. "He doesn't want to be made to look wrong, or incompetent, or—"

"No, Kate. You have to face reality. I've got maybe another year or year and a half when I'll know what's really going on most of the time. Before then, we're going to have to make some decisions. I'm not going to be able to go on looking after Jack, and I'm not going to be able to go on living here."

"I don't understand you anymore," Kate said. Her voice sounded like a child's. "You were never like this when I was growing up. You'd never have just sat down and accepted something terrible happening to you."

"I'm not just accepting it," Frank said. "I'm fucking furious, if you'll pardon my French. I get so angry, I could take off the roof. But it doesn't matter, Kate, can't you see that? You play the hand you're dealt. And this is mine."

"You seem to be feeling all right this morning."

"I'm feeling fine," Frank said. He came to the table and picked up Kate's now-empty coffee cup. "What's more," Frank said, "I was able to take in what was going on last night, and I was able to remember it this morning. You've been suspended from your job because your manager is some kind of jerk."

"I think he might have had a point to some extent," Kate said. "We aren't supposed to use the computers we have for our military contracts on anything else."

"All right," Frank admitted. "I know that. But it comes down to the same thing. You're not working for a month. You've got nothing to do but hang around the house brooding."

"I don't brood."

"Call it whatever you want. If you don't find something you can focus on, you're going to be hell on wheels, and he and I are going to be roadkill. You should try to do something with your time."

The kitchen faced the back of the house, so it took a while before Kate and Frank could sort out the noise that began to blare into the room.

Reggie Evans for governor, it said. *Vote for Reggie Evans for governor of the great state of Virginia.*

"For Christ's sake," Frank said. "That's the third time this morning. The first time was at six. Made me fall right out of bed. Reggie Evans, the district attorney, now running for governor. He is also the one trying the Ozgo case, as far as I know."

"Of course he's trying the Ozgo case," Kate said. "It's the biggest thing to hit Virginia in a hundred years. It's national news. Although, there is something interesting. A lot of people think the whole thing is a setup."

"You think the Ozgo kid is being railroaded?" Frank asked.

"It's Chan Hamilton that was kidnapped—Richard Hamilton's daughter. And Richard Hamilton is the guy who got Evans to run for governor."

"Is he?" Frank said.

"Maybe there's nothing in it, but it still looks fishy. Evans wins the case and Richard Hamilton does everything he can to make sure Reggie ends up in Richmond. It's just the kind of thing you could make a conspiracy theory out of."

Frank looked thoughtful. "*You* could make a conspiracy theory out of it," he said, "and that would at least make some kind of sense. Think about all the problems they've had.

They ditched the first detective team on the case. Then they lost a ton of forensics. Maybe Ozgo isn't guilty."

"Maybe," Kate said.

"You should pay attention to it," Frank said. "I think you should investigate it. Take your month and go find out what you can. You do detective work in that job of yours. You find out who or what has been messing with computer security systems."

"It's not the same thing. It isn't even close to the same thing."

"I think it's as close as you need to get," Frank said. "Jack and I are both right. If you don't have something to focus on in the next few weeks, you're going to go crazy, and you're going to drive all of us crazy. The Ozgo case is right there, right in front of you. The trial starts today. Go take your mind off Almador. Write an article. Publish it under a pseudonym if you think you've got a chance of going back to your job and don't want to make waves. Do something."

"You're out of your mind," Kate said.

Frank got up. "I'm very definitely out of my mind some of the time," he said. "But I'm not now, and I'm going to be late for the senior center."

"I could wear one of those Sherlock Holmes hats and carry a magnifying glass."

"You can't sit on your hands for a month, Kate. You're just not capable of it."

★ ★ ★

She spent nearly an hour doing purposeful things that she usually didn't have time for. She loaded the dishwasher. She walked through the townhouse picking up dirty clothes from wherever Jack had left them and then loaded the washing machine. She ran the vacuum over Jack's bedroom floor and then over Frank's. Frank had left clothes on the bedroom floor, too. Kate put those in the washing machine with Jack's things and then threw in soap and started the thing up. Then she went back to the living room and started vacuuming again.

Twenty minutes later, she was sitting on the living room couch, feeling at loose ends. No matter how she tried, she couldn't come up with a single thing to occupy her. She was feeling too anxious to read. She was feeling *far* too anxious to play games on her phone. Even solitaire was beyond her. She kept mixing up the suits. Red cards looked like red cards. Black cards looked like black cards.

After another twenty minutes, she gave it up.

She grabbed her jacket and headed for the door.

It was a bright, cold day and far enough from the usual rush hour so that there was not much going on except Evans's campaign vans still prowling from one street to the other and blaring their message over and over again.

Kate was a good ten miles into her trip before she admitted to herself where she was going: to the Fairfax County General District Court and the trial of Kevin Ozgo for the kidnapping of Chan Hamilton. Despite her destination, the project still felt ludicrous. Above all the other objections, there was the obvious problem: This was the first day of a famous trial. People had probably come from three states and farther just to see if they could view the spectacle. There wasn't going to be anywhere to park, and there wasn't going to be a seat left if she even got through the door.

"Making an idiot of myself," she muttered under her breath.

When she started to get close to the courthouse and the traffic started to get more and more snarled, she turned off onto a side street and went looking for parking. Most of the lots were packed solid.

Since Kate didn't want get towed, she circled, going from one side street to another, from one parking lot to another.

Kate was just thinking about giving up when a miracle appeared: a municipal lot—one of the small, cramped ones, tucked between two buildings that both looked about ready to fall down—nowhere near full. If she was ever going to start believing in fate, she was going to do it now.

The streets around this particular parking lot were deserted. Where the streets closer to the courthouse had been frenzied under the onslaught of the unusual volume of traffic, this street was so empty and silent it could have been part of an abandoned city.

Kate braved the spooky atmosphere and marched in the direction of the noise, the craziness, and the traffic. Once she got out on the main road, she could hear it. Horns were blaring. A lot of horns were blaring. Then she got closer and could hear people shouting. Whistles blew.

Another turn and another turn and another turn and there she was, turning onto the street in front of the courthouse itself.

The street was a solid block of people, cars, media vans, and police vehicles. Officers were on foot trying to direct pedestrian traffic. They had given up trying to clear the road so that regular traffic could get through. People were so closely packed together that they moved as units, with some people, mostly in suits, weaving their way through, trying to ignore the insanity around them.

This is where this ends, Kate told herself. *I'm never getting through that.*

By now, though, she had been caught up in the crowds. She was crushed in a crowd, but she managed to catch a glimpse of Evans by himself up near the courthouse door. The crews in the media vans turned their attention on him and began shouting. Cameras came up on shoulders. Photographers and cameramen rushed into the street and began whirring away in Evans's direction.

"Mr. Evans!" someone shouted. "Mr. Evans, do you expect to be successful in this prosecution?"

"Mr. Evans! What do you say to the rumors that you've been bought and paid for by Richard Hamilton?"

"Mr. Evans!"

Kate watched as Evans went his way without giving any indication that he had heard a thing, but when he got to the courthouse steps, he climbed halfway up and then stopped, turned around, and faced the cameras.

He had a politician's face and a politician's smile, more so in person than he did on billboards and television.

She was now all the way up to the edge of the courthouse steps. She had no idea how.

"Mr. Evans!" someone was shouting. This turned out to be a woman reporter in a red dress and red high heels, holding a microphone up to her mouth. "Mr. Evans! The defense says that there was a third person in the house on the night of the fire and you're not pursuing that because Richard Hamilton wants a quick conviction. Do you have anything to say to that?"

"Ozgo is guilty in this case, and I will prove it in the next few days."

"Do you expect to get a conviction?" somebody else shouted.

"I expect to get a conviction."

"Mr. Evans! What do you say to the rumors that you've been bought and paid for by Richard Hamilton?"

For the first time, Kate saw a flicker of real emotion on Evans's face. The man was furious. A single vein that ran along the edge of his jaw swelled as if it was going to burst.

"I have," Evans said, "the best conviction rate of any district attorney in the history of Fairfax County. Part of the reason I have that rate is that I have always been very careful about who I charge and when I charge them. The evidence in this case has been thoroughly examined on every level of law enforcement. The forensics have been checked and double-checked, both by our people here—and our people here are excellent—and by Dr. Henry Lee, who graciously agreed to come down from Connecticut and look them over. There is no doubt whatsoever that we have the right person on trial. And there is no doubt whatsoever that Ozgo will be convicted in this courtroom and that he will go away for the longest possible sentence. What's more, I consider what I have just said to be a promise to the people of the great state of Virginia, and I'm willing to stake my life, my reputation, and my future prospects on it. And that's all I've got to say."

"Mr. Evans!" six people said at once.

Evans had turned his back on the lot of them and resumed his ascent of the courthouse steps.

From Kate's vantage point at the foot of the courthouse steps, she was actually in a better position to see him than some of the reporters. And the steps were right there. There was no reason she shouldn't walk right up them.

But there probably wasn't any point. The seats would all be full. Most of them must have been reserved, and the few left for ordinary citizens had probably been snapped up hours ago.

At just that moment, there was another stir in the crowd and then noise that went beyond insane. The media had been eager to interview Evans, but this was more than eagerness. This was bloodlust.

Kate turned back and saw what the rest of them had seen before her. There was Chan Hamilton herself, and she was not alone. Her father was with her, and with her father was a security detail that would have been too much for a visiting dignitary with a price on his head.

The security detail managed to keep the crush of reporters and camera people away from Chan and Richard Hamilton. It was probably a good thing, because the crush was getting closer, even if getting closer meant they would smother their quarry to death. Kate backed up onto the first of the courthouse steps, appalled.

"Mr. Hamilton! Mr. Hamilton! Miss Hamilton! Mr. Hamilton!"

"You'll notice," a voice said in Kate's ear, "that there's no sign of Kevin Ozgo. That's because Ozgo wasn't able to make bail."

The man standing beside her was good looking but a little strained. He had a tiny scar on the right side of his nose in the shape of a crescent moon. He was staring at Richard and Chan Hamilton and the circus.

"Excuse me?" Kate said.

The man pulled his eyes away from what was going on in the street. "I'm trying not to be cynical. It's very, very hard at the moment."

"I don't understand how they think. These media people, I mean," Kate said. "They get so crazy, and what's the point? They're not going to get any closer than they would if they'd taken their time about it, and I'll bet people don't say anything except what they intended to say anyway."

The man turned his full attention on her. "Do you really think so? That people only say what they mean to say in these situations?"

"Richard Hamilton isn't going to say anything else," Kate said. "He never says anything unless he wants to.

And he isn't going to let Chan say anything at all, if you ask me."

"True," the man said. "But not everybody is Richard Hamilton, and not everybody has Richard Hamilton to look out for him. There is, for instance, Ozgo."

"Has he been talking to the media?"

"Not on purpose, no. He's been quoted in the media quite a bit. I take it you haven't been following the case?"

"Not really," Kate said.

"That's a little odd, isn't it? Here you are, in the middle of the frenzy, and you're damned good at getting yourself into strategic places. Most of your fellow spectators were rounded up and penned in half an hour ago."

"Yes, well, I'm not really sure how that happened."

"You didn't come here to see if you could get yourself a seat to watch the trial?"

"Not on purpose," Kate said.

This was at least half the truth. And, yes, the man was very good looking. He got better looking the longer Kate watched him.

The man had turned his attention back to the circus. Richard and Chan Hamilton and their circle of protectors had reached the courthouse steps. None of the media people had gotten any closer to them than they had been before.

Chan and her father mounted the courthouse steps without haste and without hesitation. They stared past everything as if none of it was there. Richard Hamilton looked like a very cold man. Chan looked practically catatonic. A moment later, they entered the courthouse doors at the top of the steps. The reporters fell away from them and returned to the street.

"How about this," the man said. "I happen to have two reserved seats, and one of them isn't going to be used today. Why don't you come along and sit by me?"

SIX

Kate didn't know how long it had been since someone tried to pick her up and didn't know how she felt about it. The man was attractive, and he wasn't being too pushy. On the other hand, Kate hadn't been interested in getting involved with someone for years. A bad marriage and a life with little room to breathe had taken care of that.

Kate tried to brush it all away. Nothing was going on at the moment but some good luck. She could tell, as soon as they had approached the doors to the courtroom, that if she hadn't run into someone with reserved seats, she would never have gotten in at all. The reserved seating was toward the front, but it only took up two rows of seats on one side and one on the other. The rest of the seats were up for grabs for the first people who could get to them, and there were an infinite number of people who wanted them.

"It's the speedy and public trial thing," the man said, watching Kate watch the crowd.

"What?" Kate asked.

The man held out his hand, formally. "I'm Thomas Abbot. People call me Tom."

"I'm Kate Ford." Kate shook Tom's hand.

Tom looked behind them at the already filled seats. "The Constitution says an accused person must be afforded a speedy and public trial. Trials are public events. They can't be closed to the public, and they can't be closed to the press except under very, very unusual circumstances. So when a trial starts up, seats in the courtroom are open to any member of the public who wants to come and watch."

"They'd have to hold the thing in a football stadium if they wanted to let in anybody who wanted to come and watch."

"I don't think they necessarily want to let in anybody who wants to watch," Tom said. "It's just that they have to, as far as they are able. And there's no saving your seat once you get it. At least not for the next day. All members of the general public who got in today and want to come back tomorrow have to go through the same waiting up and camping out they did today."

"And will they do that?" Kate asked, looking behind her at the crowd.

Tom shook his head. "No," he said. "In my experience, the first day or two draws crowds who are not members of the press. But no matter how sensational the trial is, the crowds drop off after a while. They don't come back again until the jury goes out. Everybody wants to hear the verdict. But, not to put too fine a point on it, most trials, even most dramatic trials, are largely dead boring. There's a lot of technical detail. There's a lot of nailing down small points that are hard to connect before the prosecutor or the defense attorney sums up the case at the end. Even the juries start to nod off after a while. That's why judges always make such a point of telling them that they can ask for clarifications any time they want."

Kate shook her head. "Do you really think this trial is going to get boring?"

"Sure it will," Tom said. "Reggie Evans has a lot he has to establish. He's going to have to call arson experts. He's going to have to go into the nature of accelerants, their chemical composition, how they're used. What effect the accelerant used in this case had on the course of the fire. Then there's the ransom request, the way it was transmitted, the identifying marks on the paper . . . Anyway, most people don't care about that sort of thing. They're not even all that interested in what goes on with dead bodies. The technicalities of determining time of death and cause of death. You've got to have something dramatic to get the public's attention. Maggots and worms. Sex after death. Something."

Kate shuddered. "At least there's no sex after death here. I don't think I could handle that."

"There's almost everything else, though," Tom said. "Money, power, sex, drugs, and rock and roll. I've been watching this case from the beginning, and it's always bothered me."

"Because it's so sensational?"

"No," Tom said. "Because it feels stage-managed."

"Stage-managed? But I don't understand. Do you mean you don't think it's real? That somebody made it all up?"

"Not stage-managed like that," Tom said. "Obviously the house burned down. And somebody tied up Chan and put duct tape on her mouth. There's even an unauthorized video up on YouTube to prove it. But there's something wrong here. I just can't put my finger on it."

"Are you a reporter?" Kate asked. "Is that how you got assigned seats?"

"I'm a cop," Tom said.

Kate was startled. "Are you a witness? Are you going to testify?"

"No."

"But then what—?"

"That's the bailiff," Tom said, pointing to an elderly black man with a voice as deep and resonant as the voice of God.

"All rise," the bailiff said.

Kate got to her feet along with the rest of the crowd.

★   ★   ★

Tom's assigned seats were better than anything Kate could have hoped to snag on her own. They were in the second row behind the prosecutor's table, which gave her a clear view not only of Chan Hamilton but of Richard Hamilton sitting beside her. Kate looked back and forth between the two of them as the judge and the lawyers droned on and on about the seating of jurors and other things Kate had to admit were just plain boring. She let herself focus in. Chan was wearing three charm bracelets going up her right arm, each crammed full of silver charms, each with a theme: musical instruments on one (piano, violin, drum set with drumsticks); animals on another (bear, deer, elephant); and stars on the third (Star of David, five-point star, eight-point star). Richard Hamilton's fine silk suit was grey but with a navy-blue stripe so thin and so widely spaced that it would have been invisible to most people. Richard Hamilton was a man who did not like to be conspicuous, but Kate already knew that.

Meanwhile, her initial impression of Evans was being confirmed. He was striding back and forth in front of the judge's bench, raising his voice here, dropping his voice there. It was an act—that much was clear.

Richard and Chan Hamilton didn't seem to be putting on an act, but what they were doing made Kate very nervous. Their body language was just . . . wrong. Richard Hamilton had brought his daughter in to court. He was sitting right behind her, lending her public support. Kate was sure there would be comments on all the news programs about how he was standing by her. And yet . . .

It's like they hate each other, Kate thought. Enemies stood like that when they were forced to be together. Every time they accidentally bumped against each other, Chan jumped. It was a tiny jump, less than a hiccup, but it happened every time.

She turned her attention to Ozgo, and instantly she knew who she would be sympathizing with in this case. She'd seen pictures of him in the papers and on television, but those were still just pictures. Photographs had two emotional tones: very happy or dead-eyed zombie. In the very happy ones, the person was smiling. In the staring-zombie ones— well, anybody would look like a serial killer in one of those.

Ozgo in person was far more human, and he wasn't emotionless at all. His face was round, and his expression was completely guileless, as if he were a child. A very unsophisticated child, Kate thought. Jack hadn't looked that clueless since he was five.

How could anybody believe that this person had done— well, all the things they said he had done? Kidnapping. Arson.

Ozgo looked both confused and frightened, and Kate recognized at least some of his fear. Every time Evans raised his voice or slammed his fist on the prosecution table, Ozgo jumped, and every time he jumped, he became less and less able to control himself.

Kate recognized the signs. This was classic PTSD. She'd read a hundred articles about returning veterans with just these symptoms. There was sweat on Ozgo's forehead in tiny little dots. His shoulders were pulled back and stiff in an uncomfortable-looking twist Kate was sure had to be painful.

Kate was suddenly aware that she had risen slightly out of her chair and that she was as rigid as a board. She made herself sit back down again and go through her ritual to calm herself down. This was when she needed her soothing stone.

I really can't do this right here and now, Kate told herself frantically. *I really can't.*

She tried to concentrate on Ozgo. His whole body was twitching. His head was moving from side to side. When it moved far enough in her direction, she could see his eyes. They were rolling. Everything on Ozgo's body was rolling.

And this room was hot.

It was very, very hot.

The lights were glaring. Everything was too bright. Everything was too loud.

Loud, loud, loud.

The room had turned a very light shade of lavender.

It was a question of taking control now while she still could. The room felt claustrophobic. She'd be better if she could get some air. She stood up and moved carefully toward the aisle.

She went to the ladies' room. She was sure there would be fewer people there so that if something bad happened, it wouldn't happen in public. She was right. The foyer was full of people milling. The front steps probably still had media people. The ladies' room was empty.

It was also beautiful, one of the old ones with a little room off the side so women could lie down if they had cramps. She sat down on the little cot, closed her eyes, and then lay back.

★　★　★

"Fainted," a voice she didn't recognize said. It was an older man's voice, thin and querulous. "Happens every time. They get too hot. They faint."

"I don't think she's fainted," another voice said. That one Kate knew. It was Tom's voice.

"I told you not to call the ambulance," the older man said. "No point in calling the ambulance. Causes a fuss nobody wants, breaks up the work of the court, gets everybody mad as hell even if they won't say so."

"I wasn't the one who wanted to call the ambulance."

Kate still had a headache. It was a dull one, not the piercing, jagged knife that hit her in the middle of an episode, but it still hurt. She raised her hand to her forehead and rubbed it. She kept her eyes closed.

"She's fine," Tom said.

Kate opened her eyes.

"Do you want to sit up?" Tom asked her.

"I can sit up myself," Kate said.

She did just that. She even managed not to wince when the upward movement made her head pound.

"Give her some of that water you brought," the older man said. "Got to be dry as a bone."

Kate's throat did feel scratchy. So did her eyelids. So did her tongue. Tom reached up to somewhere behind the couch and came back with a large bottle of Dasani water. "Thanks, Talbot," he said.

"Know what my definition of stupidity is?" Talbot asked as Tom twisted off the cap and handed her the bottle. "Paying for water you can get for free out of any tap."

"I never thought of it that way," Kate said weakly. She tilted her head back and drank the water in a full, long stream. Her throat felt better. Her head felt better. Even her eyes felt better.

"I think," Tom said, "you'd better skip the rest of the day in court."

★ ★ ★

In all reality, the episode hadn't been a really bad one, but laying on that couch in the courthouse's "ladies' retiring room," Kate had been convinced that she was out for the rest of the afternoon. Her head would ache. Her limbs wouldn't work right. Her hands would twitch. Her arms and legs would be too weak to handle ordinary things.

"That weakness you keep describing really bothers me," one of her more conscientious doctors had said around the time Kate was in college. "It doesn't fit the rest of it."

Kate had liked that doctor, Dr. Parker. He was one of the few doctors she saw over the years who took her completely seriously. The rest of them were like Jack. They thought whatever was going on was psychosomatic. She was either playacting or her subconscious was producing the episodes as a way to work out some inner psychological conflict.

The episodes always started with the lights around her getting brighter, but that didn't explain anything either. Kate had always been sensitive to bright lights. They hurt her eyes and made her fidgety and anxious even when there was no episode in sight. What was more, she didn't automatically go into an episode when bright lights were flashed at her or when she was subjected to strobes or other things that brought on seizures in epileptics. Lights didn't trigger her episodes; they were just a product of them. There was no rhyme or reason to any of it. There was no pattern she could hold onto.

Of course, if there had been anything like that, Kate would have had a medical diagnosis by now instead of increasing numbers of people who believed she was seriously addled.

At some point, she must have taken her jacket off. She spotted it on the windowsill, and when Tom saw her looking, he grabbed it and brought it over.

"I think maybe I should drive you home," he said. "You still look a little rocky."

"I'm all right," Kate said.

"You ought to take it easy and get a little sugar into you. You don't have diabetes?"

"No," Kate said. She flexed first her arms and then her legs. They felt fine. "I'm all right," she said. "I think I really am. I'm hungry, but it has to be about lunch time."

"I'll buy you lunch."

Apparently, Tom was looking after her. Kate thought she should be flattered by that, but all she wanted to do was get away.

"You want to watch the trial," she said. "It will be going on all day. You need to get back."

"Nothing is going to be said in that courtroom today that I couldn't miss," Tom insisted. "At least let me take you to lunch and make sure you feel better. I don't like the idea of you driving in the state you're in."

"Am I in a state?"

"You were in a state," he said.

Kate made up her mind. "No," she said. "Thank you, but not now. I left my car in this little municipal lot on this side street somewhere. I just want to find it and get myself home."

"You're sure you're going to be all right?"

Kate nodded. The nodding was just a little too much. The throb in her head got larger. It felt like a balloon with too much air in it.

"I really just want to find my car," she said. "Then I want to go home and lie down for a while."

It was easier to find Kate's car than she'd thought it would be, but Tom insisted on coming with her, and halfway through their walk, he darted into a little hole-in-the-wall restaurant and grabbed her an ice cream cone. And she had to admit it made her feel a lot better.

The little parking lot looked even more deserted than it had when Kate had first parked in the morning. She spotted her car near the front and strode over to it. Kate rummaged inside her purse to find her car keys and then she just stood there awkwardly. She could have been thirteen and back in junior high. She had no idea what to do next.

"Well," she said.

She tried to remind herself that she was talking to a man she barely knew. He was a very attractive man. He was a very nice man. But he was a man she barely knew.

"Well," she said again.

"You're absolutely sure you don't want me to drive you home?" Tom tried again.

"Absolutely sure," Kate said.

"How about this," Tom said. "Tomorrow, I'll pick you up and drive you out here. I can park in police spaces. It'll be more convenient."

"I'm going to need the car later," Kate said. "I mean, there's the day, things to do—"

"Okay. How about you drive back here and park the car, and I'll be waiting for you. And you can use my partner's reserved ticket again."

"Isn't your partner going to want to use it himself?" Kate asked. "You're with the police. You must have some serious reason to be attending the trial."

"That's a little complicated. And my partner doesn't really want to attend the trial at all. He thinks I'm wasting my time. So you come. And when the court recesses for lunch, I'll buy you more ice cream and tell you what I'm doing here. And then you can tell me what you're doing here."

"I told you before," Kate said, "I'm just curious. I was at loose ends and thought I'd check it out. I never thought I'd actually get inside."

"Maybe," Tom said.

Kate shook her head. "There's no maybe about it. That was it. And I feel like an idiot."

"And you don't want to go back?"

"I do want to go back," Kate said. "And that makes me feel like an idiot, too."

"I'll see you here tomorrow morning, then. I'll be here before you, I promise."

"Okay," Kate said.

Tom leaned closer to her and put his thumb and forefinger on the front of her jacket. Kate looked down at what he was holding and saw with surprise that it was her Almador security pin, the one employees used to get into the Almador parking lot through the building.

"I'm really interested in this," Tom said before walking away.

★   ★   ★

If Kate had headed for Jack's school as soon as she'd left the parking lot, she could have made Jack's track meet. And that was exactly what she would have done if she had remembered that Jack had a track meet, but she didn't. She was far more shaken than she had admitted to Tom, even if she was far less shaken than she would normally have been after an episode.

She started driving with no idea of where she was going to go, and once she started, she couldn't make herself stop.

It was nearly seven o'clock by the time she pulled into her own driveway, close to fully dark. The lights were on in her townhouse, and she could see somebody moving back and forth in front of the window: Frank, carrying things. Kate instantly felt guilty. This was later than it usually was when she came home. She was supposed to make dinner. Jack and Frank must have made dinner for themselves again.

She shut off the car and grabbed her bag. Now that she was here, it felt urgently necessary for her to get into the house right away. She climbed the two steps to the garage entry and went inside. When she got there, she found that she had guessed correctly. A dinner of hot dogs and potato salad had been made and consumed. The remains of it were strewn across the kitchen table.

"Sorry," Kate said. "I forgot the time."

Jack looked up from where he was sitting. "We looked for you on the news," he said.

"Oh," Kate said.

"It wasn't a big deal," Frank said. "Jack thinks you had another episode, but I've been arguing against it."

"I don't know what it was," Kate said, not realizing she'd just admitted to something they would have had no other way of knowing about. "It didn't feel like the usual thing."

Jack was not looking at her.

Kate was just about to ask him what was wrong when he abruptly rose from his seat and began to collect plates and utensils.

He turned to look at her, up and down, and then he shook his head.

"I placed in two events."

SEVEN

The next day, Tom was waiting for her near the entrance to the little municipal lot she'd parked in the day before, leaning against the ticket booth and conversing with the attendant. He saw her pull in to the ticket booth and straightened up. Kate waved at him.

"You're even early," he said after she'd pulled her car into an empty space and gotten out.

"I don't feel early," Kate said. "I overslept."

"Court never starts before nine," Tom told her. "Sometimes it doesn't start until ten."

"I like the suit," Kate said.

He brushed his hand against his suit jacket. "It'll do," he said. "But it's a little tight in the shoulder with the holster."

By the time they got into the courtroom and to their seats behind the prosecution table, Kate had managed to get over that line about the holster. She didn't take her sunglasses off when she sat down, but if Tom noticed, he said nothing about it. Chan Hamilton was already in her place, as was Ozgo. Richard Hamilton was at his place, too, his face set, his expression murderous. Chan's face was much softer and just a little befuddled looking. But it was still Ozgo that Kate felt the most sympathy for. He really did look like a child. And like a child in a dangerous and bewildering situation, he looked terrified.

Tom leaned close and whispered in her ear. "Take a careful look at Chan. They've gone the pharmaceutical route."

"What?"

"You've got to balance the danger of a full-blown public breakdown with a demeanor so blank, the jury will think you just don't care. They've given her tranquilizers. They've opted for 'just don't care.'"

"You'd think they'd let her have a breakdown," Kate said. "Wouldn't that get the jury to sympathize with her?"

Tom laughed loudly enough that some people turned to see who he was. "It would probably make the jury think she was faking," he said.

"Really? But I thought you said yesterday that juries liked to see emotion."

"They like to see the right kind of emotion at the right place and the right time. Juries think they know how guilty people behave and how innocent people behave. They think they can tell just by watching. And they're usually wrong."

"But," Kate said. Then her eyes went to Ozgo again and, behind him, a thick, heavy woman dressed in a blue cotton jumper with tiny roses all over it. Her hair was thin and held back in a rubber band. She turned her head to look around the courtroom, and Kate saw that her eyes were very blue and very bloodshot—and also very young.

Kate had not been in the courtroom long enough to hear much of any importance yesterday. Now it felt as if the court was in the middle of something that had taken place out of her sight, and for a few moments, she had a hard time catching up.

Evans was strutting back and forth in front of the judge's bench. There was a tiny, heart-shaped grease stain on his green rep tie, just above the lapels of his jacket. He gestured toward the jury box, which was now filled with jurors. The jurors were a motley group, mostly middle aged, mostly white, mostly women.

"Interesting jury selection," Tom said cryptically.

Evans took a big breath and bellowed, "Detective William Flanagan."

There was a short line of uniformed police officers one row back. Detective Flanagan was tall and red faced. He walked to the stand and sat down abruptly, without being asked.

The judged cleared his throat and said, with considerable annoyance, "Please remember that you are still under oath."

Kate couldn't imagine that Flanagan could get any ruder than he'd already been, but he managed it. He behaved as if he hadn't heard the judge at all.

"Meet Wild Bill Flanagan," Tom whispered in Kate's ear. "The biggest fraud in law enforcement in Fairfax County."

Kate would have asked him what he meant, but Evans had approached the witness stand.

"Mr. Flanagan," he said. "When we left off yesterday, you were telling us about your experience as a criminal investigator. Let me go over that once more to refresh the jury's memory. How long have you been a police officer in Fairfax County?"

"Thirty-two years."

"And how long have you been a detective?"

"Twenty-one years."

"And in that twenty-one years, you have investigated homicides?"

"Yes."

"A great many homicides?"

"I have been a detective on the homicide squad for ten years."

"The last ten years?"

"Yes."

"What were you doing before those last ten years?"

"I was a detective on the arson detail for eight years."

"And before that?"

"I was the department's liaison to the FBI for abductions."

"So you therefore have extensive experience in investigation of all the types of crimes involved in this case."

Flanagan shifted a little uneasily in the witness chair. "I wasn't an investigator for abductions," he said. "I did do some investigating on a couple of cases, but, technically, I was a liaison to the FBI, and they did the investigating."

"Let the clarification be noted," Evans said. "Now, you were a homicide detective on the night of April twenty-fourth of last year?"

"Yes."

"You were on duty and in the station at eight fifteen of that evening."

"Yes."

"And what happened at eight fifteen on that evening?"

"I took a phone call from a woman who identified herself as Chan Hamilton."

"You took this call yourself?"

"Yes," Flanagan said. "It was directed to me by the uniformed officer who first picked it up."

"Did you in fact identify this caller as Chan Hamilton?"

Flanagan hesitated. "I was more convinced than not that the caller was Chan Hamilton. I couldn't be absolutely sure until—"

"Never mind," Evans said. "What did the caller tell you?"

Kate sat forward. Had Evans really said "never mind"?

"She said she was Chan Hamilton, daughter of Richard Hamilton, and that she was being held hostage in her house on the Hamilton estate by a man named Kevin Ozgo. She said she thought he was going to kill her."

"Objection!" the defense attorney said, jumping out of his seat.

"Objection overruled," the judge said. "We discussed this yesterday, too, Mr. Brayde."

Evans looked like he wanted to hit something.

"Mr. Flanagan," Evans said. "Did you investigate the accusation?"

"I sent two senior detectives out to investigate," Flanagan said. "Thomas Abbott and Kyle Lord."

Evans tugged on his lapels. "No more questions at this time, but I will be recalling this witness at a later date."

The defense attorney jumped up and began hammering at Flanagan. Kate thought he looked familiar.

★ ★ ★

When the court finally broke for lunch, Tom was suddenly swarmed by uniformed police officers. He managed to untangle himself, and he and Kate got out of the building after only a few minutes and headed straight for the same place he'd bought her ice cream the day before. Then he ushered her into one side of a booth.

Tom took the menus from the waitress and handed one over. Kate looked at the menu and opted for a hamburger with avocado with onions and a glass of water.

"I was worried you would be the kind of woman who counts calories," Tom said. "That's some serious not worrying about calories. I approve."

"I want you to explain it to me," Kate said. "Just what went on there?"

The waitress came back with Kate's water and Tom's Coke. "Tell me something first," he said.

"What?"

"Why is an employee of Almador attending this trial?"

"I'm not an employee of Almador," she said. "I mean, I am, but not exactly. I was working there two days ago, and then I made a mistake, and they put me on a month's unpaid leave. So I am, but—"

"What kind of mistake gets you suspended from a place like that?" Tom said.

Kate launched into an explanation of what had happened and why. "I know better than to use those computers for anything but what they're there for. The government departments go completely ballistic if you do that, and they should. It's really hard to keep security tight enough so that we don't all blow up. As far as I know, when this month is over, I'll never work for Almador again. I may not work for any security company that does work with the government."

The waitress was back again. She had Kate's hamburger. She also had Tom's order, which included not only a hamburger but a large order of French fries that glowed oddly red under the bright lights.

"Cayenne fries," Tom said. "Want to give one a try?"

Kate took the fry Tom was holding out to her. It was very, very red. She bit off half of it. Her tongue felt as if it had been sliced by a razor blade.

"Oh," she said, swallowing quickly.

"That's what most people say," Tom said.

Kate put the uneaten half of the fry on her plate. "I think that may be a weapon of mass destruction," she said. "Are you going to tell me what's going on? I promise you I'm not going to report back to Richard Hamilton."

Tom was contemplating his burger. "How much do you know about the night Chan's house burned down?"

"I know what everybody else knows," Kate said. "Chan phoned the police. The police went out to investigate. Between the phone call and then, Chan got tied up and gagged with duct tape. And then there was the fire."

"Do you know who Kevin Ozgo is?"

"He was some guy who had served with Rafael Turner in Afghanistan," Kate said. "Chan was in love with Turner and he was killed in combat, and this guy showed up and she gave him a job because that would be doing something to honor Rafael. But Ozgo was always in really bad shape, right from the beginning. Odd, you know, and off."

"PTSD," Tom said.

"I guess," Kate said. She thought back to Ozgo in the courtroom. "You can see what he's like now. That's definitely PTSD."

"You never saw them before?"

Kate shook her head. "Chan never comes to the Almador offices. Never. Even Richard Hamilton only comes every once in a while, usually for meetings. Ozgo would never have a reason to. If he was anything like what he is now, I would have remembered him."

"I never saw him before this, either," Tom said. "The first time I laid eyes on him was the morning of the fire. He was a mess."

"You mean you saw him in jail?"

"I saw him in an interrogation room at the department," Tom said. "Through one-way glass. I never got into the room to talk to him, and I've never spoken to him. They switched Bill Flanagan onto the case almost immediately."

Kate considered this. "That isn't all that strange, is it?" she said. "He must have had a lawyer by then, right? He wouldn't be talking to anybody."

"He didn't have a lawyer at the time," Tom said.

"So why didn't you talk to him?"

Tom started eating French fries one after the other, as if his mouth were made of tin. "That's a very good question," he said, "and the short answer is because I wasn't the assigned detective on the case. But that's the kicker, because I *was* the assigned detective on the case."

"That doesn't make sense."

"No, it doesn't. I was next up on the roster. The captain called and told me I was going to head that investigation. When I got down there, though, I wasn't. The decision had been rescinded. Flanagan was going to head that investigation."

Kate frowned. "They did that without telling you?"

"I think they probably tried to get hold of me before I came in," Tom said. "At least, they say they did. My cell phone was unnaturally silent. So I showed up, I asked where Ozgo was. I was told he'd been brought up to interrogation room B. When I went up there, Flanagan was already in there with him."

"Did they give you any explanation?"

"Sure they did. They said that this was a very high-profile case, that they already had Richard Hamilton on their necks. Flanagan was the ranking homicide investigator and already a public figure, so they thought it would look better if they had a known entity on the case."

Tom had actually finished his enormous hamburger. Kate wasn't a third done. "It must have been infuriating," Kate said.

"It wasn't just infuriating. It was maddening. You don't put Bill Flanagan on a case if you want to get the damned thing solved. The man hasn't run a case for at least a decade. They pair him up with people who actually know what they're doing to make him look good in public. He's also pretty good at handling the press. He looks good on television. He's glib. He can give a press conference that takes the heat off for days. But he couldn't solve a murder, or an arson, or a kidnapping to save his life."

"Did they pair him with people who knew what they were doing?" Kate asked.

"No," Tom said. "They gave him a team of junior officers, every last one of them wet behind the ears. At least two of them I can almost guarantee you aren't going to last a full year as detectives. The uniforms are going wild. They're convinced that the whole thing is a setup."

"What kind of a setup?"

"Ah," Tom said, "now we come to the sticking point. The best guess in the department is that Reggie is hauling Richard Hamilton's water. And that Hamilton wants Ozgo's scalp, whether he kidnapped Chan or not."

Kate had pushed her plate away. It still had two-thirds of a hamburger on it. Tom reached across for the plate.

"Do you mind if I—?"

"Go right ahead," Kate said.

Tom took the hamburger and went at it. It kept him quiet for a few moments. Kate was amused by the blissfully happy look on his face.

EIGHT

Sometimes, things go right.

It had been days since Kate had felt that her relationship with Jack was anything but erratic, troubled, and heading for disaster. Sometimes she'd felt as if she was spending more time feeling guilty about Jack than loving him. Sometimes Jack appeared to be closer to forty than fourteen.

And then, for no reason, it was all right. Jack was home when Kate got home herself, sitting in the living room with Frank playing Risk. When she called out to him, he responded cheerfully, and Frank responded with no trace of vagueness or confusion.

Kate was early enough to cook dinner herself. She ended up staring into the refrigerator for a minute and a half without coming up with a single idea.

She walked into the living room and said, "Maybe I should order pizza."

Jack and Frank barely looked up from their game. Jack had the dice in his hand. "Make it two pizzas," he said. "Make them extralarge."

"He's a growing boy," Frank said. He was staring at Jack's hand.

Jack tossed the dice and crowed.

"Exactly. Exactly what I was looking for."

Kate had never understood Risk.

She did understand pizza, though, and she called their favorite place and put in a delivery order for two extralarge pizzas with everything on them.

"You should have heard the kids at school today," Jack said, sitting down at the kitchen table when the pizza came and taking enough to feed Kate for three days. "Grandpa gave a talk at the senior center this morning. Clarice Mortimer's grandmother was there. She texted Clarice at lunch that she shouldn't be allowed to talk to me because Grandpa was probably teaching me all this stuff about hand-to-hand combat and how to kill people efficiently, and you never know what's going to happen, so—"

"Don't tell me," Kate said. "That awful woman in the school psychologist's office, Mrs. Carlson, wants to talk to me."

"Nah," Jack said. "She called me in for a fishing expedition, but it didn't go anywhere. I mean, I don't know anything about hand-to-hand combat. And Clarice is an idiot. I did point out that she can't go around saying she supports the troops if she thinks the troops shouldn't talk about anything they did as troops. Grandpa was a troop."

"Some time ago," Frank said.

"You know what the real problem is?" Jack said. "Mrs. Carlson thinks smart people are psychotic."

In the last two years, Kate had come to hate her. To say that she didn't get Jack was like saying that rutabaga plants didn't get algebra.

$\star \quad \star \quad \star$

After dinner, Kate told Frank to take his cup of coffee out into the living room, and she cleaned up the kitchen. Considering the day she'd had, she ought to be exhausted. Instead, she felt restless and moody. She loaded the last of the glasses into the dishwasher and went into the living room.

"I'm going to go play on the computer for a while," she told Frank.

He barely looked up.

The room where she kept the computer had been advertised as a "study," and at first, Kate thought she would use it to do some work at home. Instead, it was Jack who mostly used it. He had his own laptop, but he liked to use the study's desktop and the workstation with its expanded surfaces when he had a large project. Kate found Jack's debris everywhere.

She picked up three empty cans of Dr. Pepper and eight empty cardboard boxes of Hot Pockets. Then she sat down at the computer and booted it up.

Once the computer was up and running, she opened Google. Then she paused.

She cast her mind back over the day. The thing that struck her most, the thing that she couldn't get out of her head, was Ozgo's face. There he was, looking so terribly alone in the courtroom, looking so lost.

Kate typed "Kevin Ozgo" into the search, and it returned 22,566,471 hits. The first results page was mostly stories about the kidnapping, the arson, and the trial. Kate added "bio" and tried again. She looked at pictures of Chan's enormous "cottage" on fire and of Chan and Ozgo in front of the blaze, Ozgo in handcuffs and Chan off to the side being tended to by an EMT. Chan looked blank. Ozgo looked as shell-shocked as he had in court. There was another picture, an inset, of Chan and Turner together, back when they were first seeing each other and Turner was not yet deployed. Turner was wearing a dress uniform.

Kate went back to looking at the pictures of the fire. There was one that looked like nothing but a crowd of rubberneckers milling around the front lawn. Something at the edge of it caught her eye. She enlarged the picture as far as she could and leaned closer to make sure.

There was a man, all in black, standing very still. Kate was ready to swear he was the same man she had seen on the road near the Almador parking garage on the day she ended up getting suspended.

Kate clicked back to the web results. The first site up was Wikipedia. She passed over it.

The next site was the *Washington Post*. She clicked on that. What came up was a page with multiple pictures and multiple links, apparently one of a set of pages devoted to reporting on the crimes and the trial. The byline read, "Mike Alexander," and Kate filed the name away to check up on later.

Born in Balfour, West Virginia, on May 23, 1993, Kevin Ozgo was the seventh of nine children to Cassie Lee Ozgo. His father is unknown.

There were pictures, including one of the mother and all nine children sitting at a picnic table. Kate recognized Ozgo, but she also recognized one of the other children, a heavyset girl with her flat hair in a rubber band. She was the one who had been in court this morning.

It made her feel a little better that Ozgo had at least some family with him. It also made her feel miserable. Here they were, people who had no damn luck at all, as her father would have put it. Even the army, the one thing that usually provided an escape for people born in circumstances like this, hadn't provided it for Ozgo.

Kate went back to the text.

Enlisted in the army at eighteen. Deployed to Afghanistan almost immediately after basic training, where he met Rafael Turner. Turner, being from West Point, was an officer. Returned to the United States injured. Six months recovery. Deployed again.

Kate finally found the information about the last deployment, the one in which Ozgo had been injured and Turner had been killed.

Turner and a few men were on a routine run between Kabul and Herat in Afghanistan. They were traveling by jeep at night, four US soldiers and two Afghanis. It was supposed to be a safe stretch of road. There had been no incidents on it for weeks. They were driving along an open stretch, nothing ahead of them or behind.

The attackers, dressed in the flowing white of Afghan insurgents and brandishing American-made machine guns using American-made ammunition, had come from the sharp hills rising up alongside the road.

The whole thing was over in a couple of minutes. Turner was dead, along with three of the other Americans and one of the Afghanis. The other Afghani was mostly unharmed. Ozgo, the only living American, was badly scarred and deaf in one ear. The Afghani gave what information he could, but Ozgo gave no information worth having. Along with his physical wounds, he had been psychologically devastated, so much so that it had been weeks before he could follow even a simple conversation for a few minutes.

He'd had nothing to say about the attack at all. It might as well have happened in another universe, except for the fact that it explained the mental state Ozgo was in now.

Kate sat back. She *had* heard that story, long ago, when Turner's body had first been flown back to the United States for burial in Arlington. In that telling, Ozgo had been a blank "he" rather than a star player and participant.

Kate found the URL for the official army historian's office and loaded up the page. The Department of Defense had taken its own sweet time figuring out how to operate on the Internet, but once it had, it had gone all out. There were interactive tutorials on the Revolutionary War and the Civil War. There was a slideshow with music telling the story of World War II.

Kate kept clicking through links until she found what she was looking for: the section devoted to ongoing projects and investigations. She found Afghanistan and scrolled carefully through 2013.

A couple of minutes later, she was through, and there was nothing. There was no mention of the attack in which Turner and four others had been killed. There was no mention at all of Turner, never mind Kevin Ozgo.

She went through again. Same result.

Kate minimized the window and brought up a new tab. This time, she went directly to the Department of Defense's main public website. She tried the casualty lists. Nothing. She tried the timeline of the war. Nothing that corresponded to the famous attack, and nothing that mentioned either Turner or Ozgo.

She tried to think of explanations that weren't entirely crazy, and she couldn't come up with any.

She went back through newspaper archives. She tried *Stars and Stripes*. She tried cable news archives.

In the end, all she could find were obituaries of Turner, including some showing the closed-casket burial at Arlington with Chan in attendance, looking destroyed.

The obituaries gave the story of the attack and Turner's heroic death just as Kate had heard for years, but the obituaries didn't link to anything. She'd been able to find no evidence that either Turner or Ozgo had been in Afghanistan at all.

★ ★ ★

Kate didn't see her father that night and didn't get to sleep until well after the time she should have. When her alarm clock jerked her awake at six o'clock in the morning, she nearly picked it up and threw it out her bedroom window.

She got up and threw on a robe. Out in the kitchen, Kate heard the frying pan on the stove burner, the clink of utensils on stoneware, and Jack and Frank talking.

The two of them looked up when she came in. Jack looked her up and down and shook his head. "That's nice," he said. "Get your picture taken just like that."

"You've got a tuft of hair sticking up right on the top of your head," Frank said. "It's like a—"

"Spout on a whale," Jack suggested innocently.

Kate gave him a significant look and took a place at the table. Jack put a coffee cup down in front her of and filled it.

"You don't really look ready for prime time," Jack said. "You want some of this stuff? Grandpa made waffles. In the waffle iron. I told him the freezer stuff would be just as good, but he wouldn't listen to me."

"The freezer stuff is not just as good," Frank said.

"There's also bacon and syrup," Jack said. "You have no idea how much syrup."

Jack started packing up to leave for school. "Did Grandpa tell you? He's going to substitute tomorrow. My grade but not my class, you know, because of the conflict of interest stuff or whatever that is. It's the stupidest thing I ever heard."

"They think I'll give you better grades than I give everybody else because you're my grandson," Frank said. "Or worse ones."

"Whatever."

Jack headed to the front door.

Kate was beginning to feel better. Coffee was medicinal. She turned to her father.

"Do you really think that's a good idea? I thought you'd decided to stop substituting."

"I'd decided to taper off, Kate. And I am tapering off. I haven't taken a class in two months. But I'm not gone yet. And I'm very bored. And there's no sign that I'm going to be the kind—well, you know what I mean."

"The kind of dementia patient that gets violent," Kate said.

Frank showed no reaction. "On the money. I'll be fine, Kate. If something happens, it will just be that I get vague or forget where I am. I won't hurt anybody. And if anybody notices, I won't get asked back. That's all."

"Eh," Kate said. She had finished her coffee. She got up and poured herself another cup.

"You're one to talk, anyway," Frank said when she came back to the table. "You must have been up all night. It was after two when I went to bed."

"I was trying to find some information," Kate said. "I know you think the sun rises and sets with the US Army, but it's impossible to get anything out of them. I know sometimes you don't want people to get intelligence. But you'd think they'd have some information up somewhere about battles and attacks and that kind of thing, if only so they could give some details to the families if a loved one's killed."

"You're still asleep," Frank said. "If you're saying they should have information on battles fought and attacks suffered publically available, they do."

"Really? Because I couldn't find a thing. I even went to this website called—I don't remember, something about military history."

"The Center for Military History."

"That's the one," Kate said.

"The website might have been your problem," Frank said. "What was it you were looking for?"

Kate explained about the attack that had killed Turner and four other people and left Ozgo physically wounded and psychologically shattered.

"I don't even know what I was looking for," Kate admitted. "I just wanted to get a feel for what kind of person he'd been before the attack. The attack has to have been the most significant event in his life. So I went looking for an account of it. And then—nothing. Nothing definite, maybe just nothing. Not that there weren't press accounts. Because there were. Sort of."

"What do you mean, 'sort of'?"

"Well," Kate said, "there weren't any press accounts from the time the thing actually happened. There weren't any of those stories that go, 'Today in Afghanistan, an IED killed . . .' The accounts I could find were all from the time of Turner's funeral. And they were all just sort of hashes. If you really paid attention, they didn't make any sense. It was like the reporters wrote them knowing that nobody would ever read them carefully. That's when I went to the Center for Military History website," Kate said. "It sounded like the right kind of place. I was a little afraid of the history thing. I thought maybe there wouldn't be anything as recent as Afghanistan and Iraq. But there was, lots of it. There just wasn't anything I could find on this particular event."

Frank picked up a piece of bacon and contemplated it. "I can think of a number of things that might be going wrong here. The first is that the press accounts, whenever they occurred, were so hashed that you don't have the information you need to find what you're looking for. Newspaper reporters being what they are, that's entirely likely. Especially since all these guys are lazy as hell. The first one reports the wrong town or area and the rest of them just take his stuff and stuff it into their own story. I know you think I'm being a fogey out of Fogey Central when I say the kids today don't have any sense of honor anymore, about themselves or their jobs or anything else, but this is the kind of thing I mean. And it happens all the time now."

"Maybe it happened all the time then, too," Kate said.

Frank ignored her. "The other possibility," he continued, "is that the people running this website are incompetent or lazy or both. Considering the kind of messed up crap that occurs on government websites, it's hard to remember that the army invented the Internet. The Center for Military History will have an account of that attack. Definitely. Every unit in every branch of the service is required to send reports of everything that happened on their watch to the CMH, and they have to do it every three months."

"Every three months? But that's crazy. There must be mountains of material—"

"—which take forever to sift through and process and file," Frank finished. "And although it should be done in a systematic way, there are lots of reasons it might not be. So the first thing is that the Center for Military History will definitely have accounts of that attack. The best thing you can do if you really want to know is to call them. Forget the website. Call them, tell them what you need, let them give you the information."

"You mean they'd tell me? Just like that?"

"Why not? It's not going to be classified information. And they exist to give people information. They've got a public relations officer or a press officer. Go through those. And then—"

"Yes?"

"There's something called a serious incident report. SIR. Officers have to file them every time anything happens that might be considered 'serious.' By anybody. It's a low bar for seriousness. And anytime anybody is killed, for any reason, it's a serious incident. Drown while you're swimming in the base pool. Have a heart attack at your desk that everybody's been expecting for years. It doesn't matter. Somebody dies, somebody has to file an SIR."

"That sounds classified," Kate said.

"It's not," Frank said. "It's so far from classified, I don't know where to begin. SIRs go up the chain of command. Everybody sees them. They even go out of military commands and end up in Congress. Especially if a congressperson has a kid in his district who's killed in the line of duty. They get the reports so they can talk to the families and give them more information than the service is going to give them."

"And I can ask for one of these SIRs myself?"

"You probably could, but since you might not know enough to identify the attack, beyond the fact that it was the one involving Turner, I've got a better idea. Turner lived in this congressional district. Your own congressman probably got that SIR at the time, and it's probably on file somewhere. Call his office and get them to make you a copy."

"And they'd do that?"

"They should," Frank said. "Senators are one thing, but congressmen live and die by constituent service. You call and you're a constituent, they're going to want to do everything they can to make you happy so that you'll go back and tell all your friends how good they were about making you happy. It's usually stuff like intervening in problems with Social Security or that kind of thing, but this will operate on the same principle."

"The things they don't teach you in civics class."

"Yeah," Frank said. "Although, I've got to admit, it's kind of a little odd."

"What is?"

"The fact that nobody seems to have done it already," Frank said. "It was a big story when Turner died. You'd think one of the reporters would have gotten hold of an SIR. You might want to be a little careful here."

"Because this really is classified and it was some kind of special secret operation and—?"

"You always did have an imagination," Frank said. "No, if people have been shying away from the story, it's possible that Turner wasn't as heroic as he's been made to appear."

"You mean a cover-up."

"No," Frank said. "Look, the army isn't heartless, not usually. It doesn't want to hurt people or their families. If some kid didn't quite make it up to grade, they don't want his parents feeling like crap. They just . . . let it go. And a lot of times the papers will let it go, too."

"Turner had no living parents," Kate pointed out. "And he was buried at Arlington. Don't they dig up people and move them when it turns out they didn't do the stuff that qualified them to be buried there?"

"You'd better go get ready if you're going to be on time to meet your new boyfriend and get that reserved seat. If I've got some time this afternoon, I'll go looking for that SIR myself."

★   ★   ★

Tom was waiting, as usual, in front of the parking lot, and her space was still empty.

"You know," Tom said, "it would make a lot more sense if you let me pick you up on the mornings you want to be here. I get to use reserve cop parking, if you get what I mean."

"We might not always want to leave at the same time," Kate said. "You've got a professional interest in the case. I might have to leave early."

"I might have to leave early myself," Tom said. "But it's beside the point."

She frowned at the traffic. "Maybe we ought to go over and take our seats. I know you said they were reserved, but—"

"Let's do something else. Let's skip this morning and go have some coffee."

Tom took her to a diner built into a shining, aluminum, retro dining car. Kate was sure it wasn't a holdover from the fifties, though. There was something about it that said . . . yuppie.

Tom noticed her face and smiled. Then he ushered her over to a booth near a window that looked out onto a busy street and said, "I didn't have time for breakfast, and I can get a decent omelet here if I insist on whole eggs instead of egg whites and declare my undying devotion to ham. I still can't get real bacon here—they've only got the turkey variety—but I'll make do. Someday I'd like to be involved in a case that takes place in a town full of truck drivers."

"I think you picked the wrong geographical area for that."

"Maybe."

The waitress came over, and Kate realized she hadn't had anything but coffee, either. She asked for decaf—no need to make an episode more likely if she didn't have to—and an English muffin with butter.

The coffee came immediately. The waitress assured them that both the decaf and the regular were fair trade. She walked away and came back with an English muffin the size of a Frisbee.

"At least they feed you," Kate said.

"This place serves breakfast all day," Tom said. "The first real diner is ten miles away, and I didn't want to go that far. Have you been following this case at all since you started coming to the trial?"

Kate settled in to tell him all about her investigation the night before and her talk with Frank this morning.

"I think I just wanted some sense of the relationship between Ozgo and Turner. I thought I'd start with the attack because I thought it would be the easiest thing to find material on, and it turned out to be no material at all."

"Your father was in the military and he doesn't think that was odd at all?"

"He does think it's sort of odd," Kate said, "but not odd-odd, if you get what I mean. Sometimes I think I'm making problems where they don't exist just to have something to do. I had no idea how hard it would be to stay home and do nothing."

"It would make me absolutely insane," Tom said. "But here's what I want to know. Ozgo is obviously so mentally impaired he belongs in an institution. Why is there a trial at all?"

"I used to wonder if Chan wasn't in love with Ozgo," Kate said, "but now that I've seen him, I don't think it would be possible."

"The official story is that Ozgo was a friend of Turner's in Afghanistan, a kind of mentor relationship. So, after Ozgo got out of the hospital, he showed up at Chan's door, and she took pity on him for Turner's sake and took him in."

"That actually is plausible," Kate said.

"To an extent," Tom said. "But it always has seemed to me to be a little extreme. Yes, give the guy some money. Maybe even let him live in one of the outbuildings. But the department looked into that relationship, and it was almost like they were married, minus the sex part. We don't think there was any sex. But they stuck together—or rather Chan stuck to Ozgo like they were Siamese twins."

"Huh," Kate said.

"I have a crazy idea of why you can't find any information, though," Tom said. "Maybe somebody hacked the military records."

Kate shook her head. "You can't just hack the military records," she said. "You could probably hack something like that military history website I told you about, but anything the military was doing for itself, anything that might in any way involve classified information—they don't even use the same Internet we do. They've got an entirely separate system just for themselves and the people they work with. That's how I got into so much trouble at work. I tried to access the regular Internet on a computer that was dedicated to military use only. I could have compromised the entire defense system."

"So why'd you do it?"

"It seemed like a good idea at the time?" Kate tried. Then she shook her head. "I got hit out of the blue with a firewall and a tripwire of a kind I'd never seen except on military files, and I got so carried away looking for answers that I didn't stop to think about the consequences. The next thing I knew . . ." Kate shrugged. "When I came across a military-grade tripwire, I thought that the Robotix files could actually be military files themselves, and I shouldn't have had them on my office computer. I think the reality is probably that Robotix is run by a flaming paranoid."

"That would work, too," Tom said. "What I'd like to know is why so much of the file on the Hamilton-Ozgo case is missing."

"Missing how?"

"Missing as in not available for the rest of us to look at. Usually, case files are all over the place: in the office of the presiding officer, at the DA's office, on every computer in the building. There's nothing secret about case files. We're not even legally allowed to keep things secret. We've got to hand over everything we know to the defense counsel in a process called 'discovery.' If we don't hand over everything we know and the guy's convicted, any judge worth her robes will throw the case out and make us start all over again. But there's a ton of stuff out there that has just gone missing, including all the stuff on the arson."

"Oh," Kate said. "That's—"

The sound of the opening chords of Beethoven's Symphony no. 5 cut through her thought, and Kate grabbed her bag off the seat beside her.

"That's my phone," she said.

She looked at the number. It wasn't familiar.

Kate opened the phone. "Hello?" she said.

"Oh," a mousy little voice said, as if she were surprised to find somebody speaking on the line. "Oh. Is this Ms. Ford? Kate?"

"This is Kate Ford," Kate said.

"Oh, I'm so glad. And I'm so glad I caught you. We've met a few times, but you probably don't remember me. This is Betsy Hare at the Rappahannock Pie Hole. You remember the Rappahannock Pie Hole? You come in every once in a while with your father and your son. Your son always has six hot dogs."

"Yes," Kate said. "I remember your shop."

"Yes, well," Betsy said. "I got your phone number off Mr. Ford's cell phone. Not that I usually take customers' cell phones, of course, but in this case, I didn't know what else to do. I didn't want to call the police. That wouldn't be nice for Mr. Ford or for you, and you're very good customers. And, anyway, I'm not sure the police would have been the right people to call. And an ambulance wouldn't make much sense either. I didn't know what to do. So I took his cell phone and found your number and tried it to see if you were in. And here you are, you see, so I guess I did the right thing."

Kate closed her eyes and counted to ten. "Is there something wrong with my father?"

"But that's the problem. It's hard to tell, isn't it?"

"All right," Kate said. "What exactly is it that's happening?"

"He's here, sitting in a booth. He's been here since at least eight thirty. I don't mind that, of course. We haven't been particularly busy, and he's been drinking coffee. And he's a very nice man, as a rule. But about forty-five minutes ago, he started to talk. Out loud. Not very loud, you understand, it's not that he's making a fuss or anything, but he keeps talking. I went over and asked him if there was anything I could do for him, but it's as if he couldn't really see me."

"Oh."

"Anyway," Betsy Hare said, "my father, before he died, you know, he had that Alzheimer's disease. I'm not saying your father has Alzheimer's disease, I'm just saying that it looks an awful lot like that and he doesn't seem to know where he is. And, you know, with things like that, especially in the beginning—"

"Yes," Kate said. She wanted this woman to stop talking.

"Well, I thought I'd call you. I don't know where you are or what you're doing, you're probably at work, but I think you might need to pick him up. And it's like I said, when they get spells like this, especially early on, well, there's no way to tell how long they'll last or what will happen. I did try to see if I could talk him into going home, but he keeps calling me Alice and wanting to know what I've done with his fishing rod."

"Right," Kate said.

"I know it's very difficult to take time off from work, and I know you have some kind of important job. But if you could just see your way to—"

"Yes," Kate said. She seemed to be saying the same things over and over again. "Thank you for calling. I'll be right down. I'm—it's going to take me about half an hour, I'm afraid. I'm quite a ways out."

"Well, you be careful. It won't do any of us much good if you have an accident getting here. But thank you very much. I don't think he's going to be much of a problem, you know, but then you never do know, do you? I think it would be so much better—"

"Yes," Kate said. "I'll be there. I'm going for my car right now."

"Well, good," Betsy Hare said.

Kate hung up.

It was only then that she realized that Tom had been sitting across the table all this time, staying silent, listening.

"Well," she said.

"I heard," he said. "Give me a couple of minutes to pay for this and I'll help. And I guarantee you it won't take half an hour to get you where you need to go."

Kate would have protested, but Tom had already left the table and was on his way to the cashier.

★ ★ ★

There were things police officers could do that no one else could, like drive a car very fast without fear of being pulled over. Tom didn't give Kate time to wonder if she wanted to be driven very fast. He just got out his cell phone and made a call.

"I was just thinking of a patrol car," he said as Kate gathered up her things and got ready to go. "An escort might be a little . . . yes . . . yes . . . I understand that, but it might— okay . . . yes . . . okay . . . all right. We'll do it your way. I'm parked in the . . . okay . . . We'll see you there in five minutes. Might be less."

Tom shoved his cell phone back into his jacket pocket. "Let's get moving. They'll be waiting when we get there."

"I don't understand what's going on."

"We're going in my car, and we're going to have a police escort. That way, we can drive very fast and get through traffic without getting stuck."

Kate tried to think. "But isn't that illegal? You can't use police escorts just like that without it being police business or something, and it's just my father, it's not—"

"There'll be nothing wrong with the police escort. The police can do that any time they think there's an emergency, which includes women about to give birth or matters of life and death. We may have to come up with a good story about life and death."

"It isn't life and death."

Tom was all ready to go. "There may be something illegal about using my car," he said, "so I'll have to make you a consultant or something like that. I'll think of something."

"What's illegal about your car?"

"It's my unmarked. It doesn't actually belong to me."

Kate wanted to ask questions, but she didn't have time. It wasn't only cars the police could make go very fast. She was out of that diner and on her way before she knew what had happened to her. Tom's unmarked car was in a small lot on a side street that contained almost nothing but black-and-whites.

Tom stuffed her into the passenger-side seat of a silver sedan, got in behind the wheel, and took the radio handset from under the dashboard.

"Ready to go," he said as he turned on the car.

The car pulled out of its space and headed for the street.

"You'd better not put the sirens on until we hit the highway," Tom said into the radio.

The radio said something back. It sounded to Kate like static squawking.

"This is where I say 'fasten your seat belts,'" Tom said, "but I'm not joking around. Make sure that belt is on tight. Once we get started, you're going to need it."

Kate tugged at the thing to show him it was on and functioning, and Tom got the car out onto the street.

For the first few minutes, Kate felt as if the whole thing had been just hyperbole and exaggeration. They were driving perfectly normally. They were going neither fast nor slow.

And then they pulled onto an on-ramp and headed for the highway.

Kate had been an observer of police escorts like this, but she was fairly sure she had never seen such an escort be this fast. Even the ones that accompanied ambulances had never seemed to be going so fast. This was absolutely crazy, and it was not fun. And the police sirens wailing continuously didn't help.

She tried closing her eyes and found that it was worse.

Were they going to drive with their sirens screaming and lights blaring right up to the Rappahannock Pie Hole? Right into the parking lot? They'd be a public spectacle from one end of town to the other.

But the off-ramp was coming up, and not only were they slowing down, but the sirens were petering out. The transition was very smooth. Tom didn't slam on the brakes. He just slowed the car effortlessly, as if it were a ball rolled across the carpet coming to rest.

The radio crackled. Tom got on. He said, "Gotcha," and turned right at the end of the ramp.

"I'm going to need your keys when we stop," he said.

"My keys?" Kate said.

"Your car keys," Tom said. "You'd better keep your house keys. You're going to need them when you get home. How long can you get by without your car?"

Kate could see the backlit plastic sign of the Rappahannock Pie Hole only a few yards away. There were no cars in the lot.

Tom pulled to a stop. Three patrol cars pulled in a line beside him.

"Car keys," he said. "How long can you be without your car?"

Kate got the keys out of her purse and tried to think. "I don't know," she said. "I think it depends on what's happening, if he has to go to the hospital, if he needs something I have to go out and get."

"If he needs something you have to go out and get, I'll get it for you," Tom said. "And if he needs to go to the hospital, I can drive you or you can call an ambulance. Never mind. I'll tell them it has to be sooner rather than later."

"*What* has to be sooner?"

"Getting your car back to you. Relax. I have this all planned. It's going to be fine."

"Right."

There seemed to be a million uniformed officers in the parking lot. They were all milling around aimlessly.

She started to open her door to get out, but Tom stopped her.

"There's one more thing. It's very important. If anybody asks, tell them you're giving me information on computer security for help in the Massalt case."

"The Massalt case? What's the Massalt case?"

"It's a cold case murder I work on when I have some downtime," Tom said. "You don't have to know what the Massalt case is. In fact, it's probably better if you don't. You just have to know that I asked you to give me expert testimony on computer security for the case."

"Are we doing something to break the law again?" Kate asked weakly.

"Not until tomorrow," Tom said. "Now I think we'd better go. I think that's probably the woman who called you."

★   ★   ★

The woman who had appeared at the front door of the Rappahannock Pie Hole was indeed Betsy Hare. Kate thought she looked exactly like her voice had sounded on the phone. She was short and round to the point of being squat, but she was also bouncy. She kept bopping up and down on the balls of her feet, making the violently pink apron she was wearing bop along with her. She had a violently pink bow in her hair, perched a little sideways on her violently red hair. She came rushing out to Kate as soon as she saw her.

"Oh, thank goodness," she said. "Suddenly there were all these cars, and I don't mind business, let me tell you, but we don't get much in the middle of a weekday, and now here are all these people, and I was hoping you'd get here before we got any more customers, just in case—"

"Is something wrong?" Kate cut in. "Has he caused any trouble or is he ill or—?"

"No, no, no," Betsey Hare said. "He's been a complete lamb. He's a lovely man, Ms. Ford, he really is. It's just what I told you on the phone. With Alzheimer's disease, you can never tell."

"Is he still in the restaurant?" Kate asked. "Is he alone?"

"He's still sitting at his same table," Betsy Hare said, "and my sister Julie is in there with him, talking about fishing. It's a marvel how . . ."

Kate wasn't listening any more.

She pushed past Betsy Hare and through the door that had been made up to look like a farmhouse door from some thirties movie. When she got inside, she had to go through a little foyer area with the cash register to one side and a long bench on the other before she could see the tables. When she could see the tables, the effect was almost as surreal as that ride she had just taken.

Her father was sitting at one of them, looking as calm and relaxed as if he were sitting in the living room at home. A short, squat, Betsy Hare–type woman was standing next to the table, her hands in the pockets of her apron, chatting away with a bright look on her face. Her apron and her bow were powder blue. Her hair was as black as tar. It was blacker than the multiple layers of mascara she wore.

Frank looked at her as she walked in, but he gave no sign that he recognized her.

The little powder-blue woman came rushing forward. "Oh, you must be Ms. Ford," she said. Her voice sounded exactly like her sister's. "I'm really very glad to meet you," she said. "I'm Julie Dumont. I've just been having a lovely talk with your father about fishing." She turned to Frank. "I was just telling your daughter that you know a lot about fishing."

"You must have me mixed up with somebody else," Frank said. "This isn't my daughter. I don't have a daughter. I don't have any children. I wanted to have children, but my wife wouldn't have it."

Kate sat down at the table across from Frank. He smiled at her, very politely, but said nothing.

Kate hadn't the faintest idea of what to do next.

"Daddy?" she tried. "Daddy, it's time to go home now. We've got things to do."

"I've always got things to do," Frank said. "It's like I've been telling Katie here. You're useless if you don't tie your own flies. The ones you can buy in the stores are all made by machines. Machines don't know anything. You just ask Katie. I told her."

"My name isn't Katie," Julie Dumont said. "It's Julie. Don't you remember?"

"If I had a daughter, I was going to name her Kate. I always thought Kate was the best name for a girl."

Tears streamed out of Kate's eyes and down her cheeks and neck. She could feel the wetness seeping into the collar of her shirt.

Then Tom sat down next to her and said, "I've got a lot of things to do, too, Mr. Ford. But Kate's right. It's time to get moving."

"I'm not Mr. Ford," Frank said. "Mr. Ford makes cars. I go fishing."

"If you're not Mr. Ford, who are you?" Kate asked him. It sounded like a demand.

Frank smiled.

If I got up and walked out of this room this very moment, he wouldn't know that I was gone. He wouldn't know that I had ever been here. He wouldn't know that I even existed.

The next thing she knew, Tom was holding her under the elbow. Frank was getting up, too.

"The kids coming in just don't have the dedication we had," Frank was saying. "They don't have the commitment. They don't have the sense of belonging to something greater than themselves. It's going to have an effect on the quality of the work. You just see if it doesn't."

"He thinks I'm a buddy of his from the army," Tom said calmly in a whisper in Kate's ear. "We're going to walk out of here right now, and I'll get you two home."

"He doesn't know I ever existed," Kate said. "It's not that he doesn't recognize me. He doesn't know that there was ever any me to recognize."

"And you're going to stop thinking like that," Tom said. "Immediately."

NINE

Frank was better in the morning. He was so much better that it was as if the incident had never happened. In fact, it was almost better than that. After Kate had gotten him home, he'd announced that he needed a nap and gone off and taken one. It was only while he was asleep that Kate let herself acknowledge what had happened.

Two uniformed officers drove up to the townhouse just as Jack was getting home from school. One of them was driving Kate's car. That one got out and came to the door to give Kate her keys. He mumbled something about how he hoped Kate's father was doing better, then turned around and got in the passenger side of the patrol car that had the other uniformed officer in it. Kate couldn't stop herself from thinking that she'd just cost the county untold thousands of dollars that she would have to pay back.

Jack waited until the two uniformed officers pulled out of their driveway and said, "Did you have another episode?"

"No," Kate said. She let him go without saying anything, waiting for Frank to wake up.

"Can't remember a thing about it," Frank told Kate sheepishly when dinner was done and Jack had gone silently up to his room. "I don't like the way this is going."

Kate waited until she was sure Jack must be asleep before she told Frank what had happened. She couldn't bring herself to tell him all of it.

Frank took it all much more calmly than Kate had expected him to.

"I think the first thing," he said, "is that I should withdraw from the substitute list. What if this had happened tomorrow, when Jack was there to see it?"

"We haven't talked about it," Kate said.

"It would have been a lot worse if I had shown up tomorrow and been as out of it as you say I was," Frank said. "We can't just pretend this isn't happening."

"I don't know what that means—'We can't pretend it isn't happening,'" Kate said. "Do I quit work to stay home with you? Do you go to live in one of those assisted facilities, or a nursing home, or—?"

"I don't think I could handle a nursing home," Frank said. "Not yet. Not while I'm still spending most of my time in my right mind."

"Exactly," Kate said.

But nothing had been decided.

They all went to bed and woke up the next morning as if nothing had changed for any of them.

So she reverted to normal. She made breakfast for Jack and Frank and had coffee herself. She got Jack out the door without an argument, mostly because he was as reluctant to discuss the problem as she was.

Then she sat down at the kitchen table and waited for an idea to come to her. None did. Frank went off to use the computer. Kate made more coffee.

She was sitting over a cold cup of the stuff when she heard a car pull into her driveway. She got up to look out the window in the foyer to see who it was. She wasn't surprised when she saw Tom emerge from the silver unmarked he had been driving the day before.

Kate opened the front door and walked out. Tom waved. Then Frank followed and stood beside Kate.

Tom stepped forward and held out his hand. "How do you do, Mr. Ford? We met yesterday."

Frank looked Tom over. He had that expression on his face that said he was not about to cut anybody any slack.

Frank sighed. "As I understand it, there's a lot I don't remember about yesterday. And that's not a good sign."

"I want to take Kate out to look at something this morning," Tom said. "I hope she can help me think."

"She's always been pretty good at thinking," Frank said dryly.

"It's just the Ozgo trial," Kate said.

"I'm not taking you to the courthouse today," Tom said.

Frank gave Tom another appraising look and said, "You been in the military?"

"Four years, US Army," Tom said.

"Officer or enlisted?"

"ROTC to first lieutenant."

"ROTC," Frank said. "College boy."

★ ★ ★

Sitting out in Tom's car less than three minutes later, Kate felt as if her head was going to explode.

"I should stay," she was still protesting. "He's my father. He's my responsibility."

"Listen," Tom said. "Alzheimer's is a heavy-duty disease. Family can't handle it, especially once the disease becomes advanced. I take it you have consulted an actual doctor and gotten an actual diagnosis?"

"Yes," Kate said. "About a year ago. And, of course, he goes back every month or so to get checked out. And we tried some pills, but they gave him side effects. I think we've tried everything. But it doesn't seem right that so many people have this thing and there isn't anything anybody can do about it."

"Medicine isn't magic, Kate," Tom said.

"You're a very cynical person," Kate said.

"I could say that I'm not cynical, just realistic, but that's what you'd expect me to say. Let's just say that I have a touch of cop's disease: I tend to think that all of humanity is scum. That's because most of the humanity I run into is scum."

She had her cheek pressed to the window glass when she became aware of her surroundings. She sat up and looked around. They were surrounded by rolling hills. There were white rail fences lining the roadside. She had no idea where she was.

"What are we doing exactly?" she asked him.

"Wondered when you were going to get around to that," Tom said. "Thought I'd let you talk yourself out before I brought it up. See all the land around here, on both sides of the road? That's the Hamilton estate."

"Richard Hamilton's estate?"

"That's the one. And about half a mile in the direction we're heading, there's a fork in the road. Take the right branch, and you end up at the cottage."

"How can we be going to Chan's cottage? It's private property, isn't it? And it burned to the ground. I saw the pictures."

"It is private property and it burned to the ground," Tom said, "but at the moment, it's also in the hands of Richard Hamilton's insurance company. We're going to meet a man named Ignazio Arnoldi. He's the company's prime arson investigator."

"I don't understand. Don't insurance companies refuse to pay off when there's any suspicion? And this isn't even suspicion. Everybody knows it was arson."

"Well," Tom said, "in the first place, you probably don't want to try to pull anything on Richard Hamilton. He represents a lot of businesses and a lot of power. And in the second place, insurance companies do pay off in cases of arson as long as the arson wasn't committed by the person holding the policy or at his or her instigation. It's Ozgo who's supposed to have torched the house. And then there is the possible third person."

"Oh," Kate said. "Yes, of course. The third conspirator or whatever he was."

"Whatever he was is the question," Tom said. "That's what Iggy is trying to find out. That's what I'm trying to find out. Because I think Jed Paterson is a psychopath."

"Who?"

"There's the gate," Tom said. "I can see Iggy's car from here."

Tom parked their car well down the long drive, and as soon as Kate got out, she could see why. There was nothing left where the house had been. The massive residence had been cleared away. There was nothing left but dead and uncultivated ground.

The cottage had been a cottage only by comparison with Richard Hamilton's house. Kate could see the outlines on the ground where the cottage had been, and it was six times the size of her townhouse.

The man standing near the top of the hill was tall, gaunt, and didn't look anything like somebody who would be called "Iggy." If Kate had been asked what she thought his profession was, she'd have gone with the sinister second-in-command or a mad scientist from an old B horror movie. But he also had shirt cuffs that were just a little frayed, as if he was sliding down the income ladder, or else too preoccupied to pay attention to his clothes. Kate noticed he had no wedding ring.

The man looked up as they came closer. He didn't bother to hail them until they were only a few steps away.

"Tom," Iggy said in a flat accent that sounded nothing like Virginia. "And this will be Miss Ford. Ms. Ford. However she wants me to put it."

"Kate," Kate said.

Iggy nodded, then turned back to look at the empty space where the cottage had been. "They're going to start putting up the new one any day now. And then I won't even be able to come here and commune with the spirit of the arson."

"Will it matter?" Tom asked him.

Iggy shrugged.

There was a set of old-fashioned lawn furniture across the yard from where the cottage had been. Tom strode over to the picnic table and sat down on one of the benches.

"Iggy here agrees with me," he said. "It was Jed Paterson who masterminded the kidnapping. When Richard Hamilton refused to pay up, Paterson torched the house to show Hamilton what could happen to Chan."

"Who's Jed Paterson?"

"The guy Chan was dating at the time."

"But Chan was in the house," Kate protested.

"She was, and Iggy can't ignore it," Tom said. "Because if she started the fire, his company isn't going to have to pay out."

Kate sat down on the other side of the picnic table from Tom. "I don't know," she said. "It sounds so complicated. Either way."

"My point exactly," Iggy said.

"It seems elaborate. Burning down a big house like this just to try to scare Hamilton," Kate said. "It doesn't sound like what a real person would do."

"Also my point exactly," Iggy said. "There's too much in all of this that feels as if it isn't real. Of course, Tom has his own theory."

"It's not a theory. It's Occam's razor. Ozgo almost didn't make it out of the fire. You've got to consider the possibility that Ozgo wasn't *supposed* to make it out of the fire."

"The business implications of that one are beyond me," Iggy said.

Tom shrugged. "You guys would still have to pay out. My idea is a lot more in line with the kind of people they are. And were. Ozgo couldn't plan his way out of a paper bag in the shape he's in. And from what I've managed to dig up about him before the events in question, he couldn't ever."

"I've never disagreed with you about Paterson," Iggy said.

"Then you've got to admit," Tom said, "he's the best candidate we have for devising a kidnapping and extortion scheme and carrying it out. And nobody who's ever dealt with the man would want to go on dealing with him if they didn't have to."

"Wait." Kate looked across the lawn. "So this Jed Paterson was the one people saw coming out of the house before the firefighters got to the scene?"

"There was a footprint on the ground that definitely belonged to him," Iggy said. "He was here sometime around the fire."

"Of course he was here," Tom said. "He was dating Chan. He's a good match for what I'm looking for, too. Former Navy SEAL. Spent some time in Afghanistan and Iraq. And a world-class whack job, the scary kind."

"I think I've seen him," Kate said suddenly.

"What? How?"

"The day I got into all that trouble at work, first thing in the morning when I came in. There was a man walking by the side of the road. And then in one of the pictures of the fire I found, there was a man in it who I was sure was the same guy."

"There was all kinds of evidence he'd been at the cottage," Tom said, "but it didn't matter, because he'd been at the cottage before. There was nothing to say he'd been there that night."

"There's a story about Paterson that's been going around for years," Iggy said. "They say he was in charge of intel on an operation in Afghanistan, and he deliberately faked his reports. He underreported the resistance they were going to face, reduced it to half of what it was, just so he could go ramming his people in there to make a big splash about how he could conquer anything. Like he was setting himself up for a Medal of Honor."

"They were onto him," Tom said. "He didn't get away with it. Assuming it happened at all. Since he's been out of the service, he's been arrested half a dozen times on domestic abuse charges. Never convicted, of course, but arrested. And very strange things happen to anybody who gets him angry. Some guy tried to pick up a girl Paterson had his eye on one night in a bar. Guy comes out of the bar to find his Porsche ripped apart like a dinosaur had gone after it. Pieces of the thing on the ground and mangled up like something had chewed them. Leather upholstery torn to shreds. The thing was in a parking lot full of security cameras. The cameras were all disabled. The cops did the usual. No fingerprints, no DNA, nothing."

"What's worse than a psychopath? A *trained* psychopath," Iggy said. "And the navy knows how to train them."

"The clincher, for me," Tom said, "is that Paterson needed money. Paterson always needed money. Most people would say he had a gambling addiction, but I don't think that's what it was. It was the risk-taking thing. Most people who take risks do it for the thrill of it. I think Paterson did it to prove something. That he was in control of the universe."

"Now he sounds like the wacko you were talking about in the beginning," Kate said.

"Yeah," Iggy said, "but he was wrong, and he ended up half a million dollars in the hole to some very bad guys. And the only reason they didn't collect immediately is that they were almost as afraid of him as everybody else was."

"But here's the thing," Kate said. "I listen to all this and it doesn't matter either way. I mean, okay, maybe this Jed Paterson kidnapped Chan Hamilton and Kevin Ozgo— he'd have to kidnap them both, wouldn't he?"

"Not necessarily," Tom said. "He could have kidnapped Chan but worked on Ozgo from the military angle. The kid's obviously messed up beyond hope. Maybe he accepted Paterson as a military commander and trusted him."

"All right," Kate said, "but it's still all messed up. Why would somebody like Paterson bother to kidnap Chan? If he was in hock, why didn't he just offer his services to someone or get out of the country? He sounds like he could make a pile of money as a mercenary and would get the thrills he has been missing."

"I told you," Tom said. "She sees right into the middle of things. That's why I wanted her to take a look at it."

"Take a look at what?" Kate asked.

"You really can't look at it anymore," Iggy said. "The house is gone."

There was a part of this that Kate really didn't like. "I think you should get your real partner," she told Tom. "You've got a partner, right? That's whose seat I've been taking. He's got to be a trained detective. He'd know more about this stuff than I do. I don't know anything about how to investigate a crime."

"My partner," Tom said, "is a very good man who thinks I'm nuts. He isn't even interested enough to come to the trial. And I've already twisted my captain into a pretzel getting permission to keep looking into this. I need someone with a good mind and a first-rate ability to pay attention to detail. I've been listening to you for days now, and you pick up on more than anyone I've ever encountered."

Kate didn't know if she believed this or not, but she allowed herself to be helped to her feet.

Then Iggy began marching his way around the side of what used to be the house, forcing them to catch up.

"It's odd what happens with fires," Iggy said. "I've seen it a thousand times. You'd think, with the firefighters tramping in and out and the hoses with the power nozzles and what have you, you'd think everything would be smashed about and upended. But it doesn't work that way. There are always a few things that are left the way they were." Then Iggy stopped moving and pointed to what looked to Kate like plain dirt.

"Right here," he said, "was where the front door was. And if you walk just four steps this way," Iggy headed four steps toward the back, "you can imagine a hall table in the foyer. And on that hall table was a small stack of magazines that had come in the mail. And on that stack of magazines and the wood just underneath it, there was a cigarette burn."

"So?"

"So that's all he found," Tom said. "There's supposed to have been an arson. The state of Virginia has charged Ozgo with arson and the attempted murder of Chan Hamilton because he tried to burn down the cottage while she was tied up inside it."

"But all I've ever found that could be the cause of the fire," Iggy said, "was a cigarette burn on that stack of magazines. Nothing else. No accelerant. Nothing." Iggy paused, and then added, "Just one more thing." Iggy took her wrist in one hand and tugged her in a direction.

"Look at this," Iggy said, stopping. "Look right here. What do you see?"

Kate opened her eyes. What she saw wasn't much: an indentation in the ground. It wasn't what Iggy was pointing to.

"You'd be amazed at what we can do in a lab these days," Iggy said. "I'm not saying it's like *CSI*, you get that, right? That's fiction. But we can do a lot in a lab, and we did it with this."

"Mmm," Kate said. She let herself overfocus. She had a feeling there was something here she should have caught. She went from left to right: the grass was unevenly cut near one of the two large trees; the tiled patio with the gas grill also had pet bowls and the pet bowls were bright red with paw prints painted on them; the second of the large trees had a broken branch down toward the lawn—

And then there he was.

A man. Dressed in black. Looking at them.

And that man had distended earlobes.

Kate didn't think twice. She turned toward the figure and took off. But she was too late. The man slipped off the lawn and into the tree cover beyond and disappeared.

TEN

Kate sat silently in the passenger's seat, completely seething; they were pulling into the driveway of her townhouse before either of them spoke.

"Do you want to tell me what's bugging you?"

Kate looked away from him, out the side window. "I really did see him. I didn't imagine it."

"No," Tom said dryly. "I don't think you imagined it."

"You know what I mean."

"We took it seriously, Kate. We went out and looked. We just couldn't find him or find a trace of him. And if you'd stop and think for a minute, you'd realize that that wouldn't make us believe you less."

"Really?"

"He's a former Navy SEAL, Kate. He's trained to get in and out of places by stealth, and he's also trained to plan. So if he decided to go out there, he would have scoped the place first, and he'd have had an escape route handy."

"And you think it makes sense he would go out there?"

Tom looked thoughtful. "You saw Ozgo. Do you think he's capable of planning and executing a kidnapping?"

"No," Kate said.

"Neither do I. And I said so when I was still on the case. And I've been saying so ever since. But Jed Paterson—there's a man who could plan and execute a kidnapping."

"Why would he?" Kate asked. "I thought you said he was dating Chan Hamilton. I suppose they could have broken up and he kidnapped her for the money, but then Chan would have said so. She said Ozgo did it."

"I know," Tom said. "But I don't know what it's all about."

★ ★ ★

For just a moment, Kate thought Frank was going to start grilling Tom the way he'd grilled Kate's dates when she was sixteen. What he did instead was pick up a stack of papers and announce, "I've been doing your work for you. I figured that if you were going to be out and about instead of getting down to business, I could at least make a few phone calls. I called the Center for Military History."

"Oh," Kate said.

"Don't sound so pleased," Frank said. "It didn't help."

"You didn't find out anything about the attack?"

"Honey, I don't think there was an attack," Frank said. "At least, there wasn't one at that place and time and involving those people. The best explanation I can come up with is that the press reports got the story so badly mangled that I'm looking for the wrong things in the wrong period. But even that doesn't completely cover it, because I asked them to cross-reference it with the names of Rafael Turner and Kevin Ozgo, and I still came up with nothing. The Office of Military History has no report of any incident involving either of them. They do have half a dozen involving Turner, but none of those include a report of his being killed. They have nothing at all on Ozgo."

Tom straightened up. "What do you mean, nothing at all?"

"Nothing at all," Frank said. "They ran his name and it came up nowhere. He is not mentioned in any report of any incident anywhere. Not just in Afghanistan or Iraq. Anywhere."

Kate tried to make this fit. "You told me that every unit everywhere has to send reports to the Office of Military History at least once every three months."

"That's right," Frank said.

"And they were in a war zone, so something must have happened to him sometime," Kate said. "He couldn't have spent all his time typing or in the medical tent, could he?"

"He could have," Frank said, "but even then he almost certainly would have been written up somewhere. Medical tents and clerks' offices get bombed, too."

"So what happened?" Kate asked. "Was he never in Afghanistan at all? Did he just lie to Chan about being under the command of Turner? It doesn't sound plausible, does it, that Chan didn't check out his story when he showed up or that Richard Hamilton didn't once he found out Ozgo was living in that outbuilding?"

"I think it's worse than that," Tom said. "Your father said he had them run the names, and he didn't turn up a report where Turner died."

"I thought that was because the press reports were badly mangled," Kate said.

"No." Frank was positive. "The press reports wouldn't matter. I asked the CMH for what they had on Turner. They had no report of his death. None. They had no report on his death in combat, or in an accident, or in a bar fight, or anything. They had no report of his dying *while he was still in the army*."

"But he's dead," Kate said. "There was a funeral. There was a body. And he's buried at Arlington. Most people have to die in combat if they're going to be buried in Arlington."

"There was a closed casket," Tom said. "There was a body, but that doesn't mean it was a recognizable body."

"But the army had the body," Kate said. "It came back on one of those planes. There were reporters there and pictures."

"They don't let people take pictures of the coffins coming back," Tom said.

"They do publish the names of the soldiers coming back in caskets," Frank said. "And those lists are not classified."

"And?" Kate said.

"And Turner's name is definitely on one of those lists at the right time," Frank said. "His body was returned and released to Chan per his own instructions. She seems to have been the closest thing he had to family."

"Okay," Kate said, "then Chan must have seen the body when it was at the funeral home or whatever."

"Not necessarily," Tom said. "He was supposed to have been killed in an armed attack. His body may have been too badly mutilated to show to anybody and too badly mutilated to be recognizable."

"But they would have checked," Kate protested. "The army would have. They'd have looked at dental records or DNA or something."

"They would have," Frank agreed.

"Then that will prove that he's dead," Kate said.

"It will if we can find that material," Frank said, "but that was beyond my scope for the day. What was within my scope was the SIRs, and for that I made a few private phone calls. I talked to Hollis Reed."

"General Hollis Reed?" Tom asked.

Frank cleared his throat. "Hollis had his secretary pull the SIRs for me. I couldn't get as good a scan as I did with the CMH. Nobody is required to cross-reference and index SIRs. There are hundreds of them every month. He did get her to pull everything they had for a year before that incident was supposed to have happened and for a year after. Not just SIRs from Afghanistan, but all of them. Then she uploaded them and sent them to me as PDF files."

"And I take it the incident wasn't there," Kate said.

"I only gave them a quick look," Frank said. "I didn't see anything that could even vaguely correspond to the stories of that attack. I fooled around on the Internet for a while, but I kept running into the same roadblock again and again.

When I Google the names, I definitely get hits, but the hits are always press stories from when Turner's body was returned to the United States. If I hadn't actually laid eyes on Ozgo on television, I'd start to wonder if any of these people existed."

Kate was thinking furiously. "There have to be other records," she said. "Turner would have a military personnel file. There's no question he was actually in the army. He went to West Point. If Ozgo was ever in the army—"

"We do know that," Tom said. "That was part of the background investigation after the arson. He enlisted right after high school. He did his basic training in South Carolina."

"There should be some information on how and why he left the army," Frank said. "But I asked about that, too, and you know what I got? Every single person in Ozgo's unit is listed as having been honorably discharged. Ozgo isn't listed at all."

Later, when Jack was home and Tom had left, Kate went to her bedroom to lie down.

She lay flat on her back in bed and put the CIA teddy bear on her chest. No matter what Frank and Tom had been hinting at, she didn't believe for a moment that Turner wasn't dead. For things to be as they were—for Turner to have been buried at Arlington—he had to have died in combat, which meant that somebody had to be covering up the particulars of how he'd died. There had to be something about the attack that was . . . wrong. There had to be a reason important people—important enough to be able to pull off this high level of a cover-up—did not want to let anyone know how he had died.

The problem was how to find out who and what that was.

What she was thinking was crazy. Doing something like that wasn't just an invitation to get fired. That was an invitation to end up in Leavenworth.

She turned on her side and held the teddy bear the way she had held teddy bears when she was small.

It was a really crazy idea, but it might actually get her somewhere.

And she would feel much better if she could get somewhere.

★   ★   ★

The next morning, Kate was surprised to find Tom waiting for her at the usual place. The impression she'd gotten was that he'd expected her to stay with Frank. But he was there, and Kate was glad to see him.

They were almost to the courthouse steps when Tom pulled out a photograph and said, "Who's that?"

"That's the man," Kate said.

"Is it?"

"The one in the photograph and the one I saw yesterday," Kate said. "He's got something wrong with his earlobes. Haven't you noticed? They hang. But they don't have holes in them."

"Jed Paterson," Tom said, taking the photograph back just as the light turned green.

Kate stopped dead. They had come to the steps of the courthouse. "Jed Paterson. The guy you think was in the house when it burned and got away. The guy you think set up Ozgo."

"Then let's assume you saw Paterson," Tom said, "which leaves us with the question of what he was doing near Almador."

"Not what he was doing near the cottage?"

"That might be because he was following me," Tom said. "Now, think for a minute about Ozgo's lawyer."

"He's jumpy," Kate said.

"He's Dalton Brayde," Tom said. "He's not usually a criminal defense attorney, and he's not an attorney you'd want to hire unless you want to lose a case. And he doesn't usually do pro bono work. And Richard Hamilton is paying for him."

"What?" Kate said.

"That's another part of the police investigation Flanagan didn't bother pursuing," Tom said.

★   ★   ★

It was one of the realities of a real trial in real time that it was, as Tom had promised, almost mind-numbingly boring. Courtroom dramas were always full of dramatic revelations, shocking reversals, and significant testimony. This trial always seemed to be eating up time with procedural questions. Today, as soon as the judge came in and the crowd was seated again, Evans asked if he could approach the bench and was granted permission. He got up there and stayed.

The crowd did not take this well, and in no time at all, they had begun to rustle and murmur.

"The jury isn't even in court yet," Kate said. "I wonder what they're talking about up there."

"Order of witnesses," Tom said. "Or maybe stipulating something. There's no way to tell."

"I like *Perry Mason* better. Everything happens fast, it always means something, and at the end, you get a big explosion."

"If you got a big explosion in a real courtroom, you'd end up with a mistrial. Do what I told you to do. Look at Ozgo's lawyer."

Kate looked. Brayde was very young, and he had had tilted his chair back so that its front two legs were off the ground. He looked exasperated.

"What's Brayde doing with the chair?" Kate asked.

"Now that's a very interesting question. That's why I say that the defense isn't really interested in defending this case."

"He's on the side of the prosecution?"

"He might as well be," Tom said. "Dalton Brayde. Brayde Pharmaceuticals. Dalton Brayde is everything a tabloid newspaper is asking for in a rich kid. And I do mean everything. Spent all four of his years at Brown crashing cars into buildings. Dormitories. Local stores and restaurants. Private houses. He'd get himself stoked to the gills on alcohol and dope and total another Ferrari. And the troubles with girls? You wouldn't believe it. He got himself accused of sexual assault four times, including once by the local police. And there are rumors of a dozen more. None of it stuck, but none of it stopped, either. He had the same reputation at Harvard Law, and he's had the same reputation ever since. If I was a shrink, I'd be wondering if he was trying to get himself jailed."

"Maybe he is."

"If he is, he's going to fail. His connections are just too good."

Kate considered Brayde. He was tall, slender, angular, and arrogant. He would have made a wonderful illustration for the cover of a romance novel. He reminded her, in many ways, of her ex-husband.

And just as she had been attracted to her ex-husband, she found herself attracted to Brayde.

"You wouldn't think he would have to go in for sexual assault," she said. "He's very good looking."

Tom gave her an incredulous look. "He's also certifiable. And dangerous."

Up at the judge's bench, the little conference concluded. The lawyers went back to their tables. The jury was brought into the jury box. The judge pounded his gavel even more forcefully this time, and the crowd quieted down.

Kate sat back in her chair, her mind going a mile a minute.

This session of the trial turned out to be a long and convoluted journey through the evidence for arson. She was paying enough attention to notice that the police arson investigator's story was not the same as the things Iggy had told her, but she didn't know enough to tell if they were just differences of opinion.

One of them had to do with the source of the fire, which Iggy had said was a cigarette but the police arson investigator said must have been a fuse, with the "must have been" sticking awkwardly and unreasonably to the testimony.

She filed the discrepancy in the back of her mind, thinking she would ask Tom about it later. Then the judge called the lunch recess, and everybody headed for the doors.

"I'll buy you a tuna fish sandwich," Tom said. "I don't think you eat enough tuna fish."

"I've just got to stop for a minute and send some e-mail," Kate said.

There was a line at the security table. It was moving as slowly as lines like that ever moved. Kate thought she was going to scream, it was taking so long.

Then she was right in front of the same young woman court officer who had checked her bag when she came in. Kate took out her driver's license. She accepted the manila envelope with her phone and her tablet. She shoved both those things into her bag and raced outside.

She got over to the side where she could rest next to the marble steps, started up the tablet, and typed Dalton Brayde's name into Google.

★ ★ ★

The ten minutes away from Tom hadn't been nearly enough time, but it was better than nothing. The plan that was formulating in her mind was completely insane, but she was convinced it was a way forward. She was also convinced that Tom would try to talk her out of it.

She did let Tom buy her a sandwich. She even let it be an actual tuna fish sandwich. She didn't want to eat. She wasn't hungry. She could barely sit still.

Tom noticed it, of course. "If you're about to faint again or whatever that was the other day," he said, "I'm taking you to an emergency room right this minute. You're not looking so good."

"No," Kate said. "It's nothing like that. I'm just a little distracted. The last time I left home for any amount of time, my dad—"

"Why don't you call him?"

"I tried, when I was in the ladies' room," Kate lied. She was a very bad liar.

"I can take you out there right now," Tom said.

"But that's the thing," Kate said desperately. This time she was not lying. "He turns the ringer off on the cell phone because he hates it going off in public places. I always have trouble getting in touch with him if he's away from home. I'm sure there isn't anything wrong. There almost never is. It's just that after the other day, I'm a little jumpy."

"All the more reason we should go out and check," Tom said.

Kate shook her head. "That would just embarrass him. He's embarrassed enough already." Kate started to gather up her things. "I'm just going to run home by myself and check," she said. "That way he won't know I was upset or anything. Thank you for the sandwich. And for yesterday, of course. I can't thank you enough."

I'm babbling, Kate thought.

"Tomorrow's Saturday," Tom said. "How about I pick you up around ten and we can look through some of the things I've collected about the case?"

"Saturday," she said. "Jack's got a track meet." Another lie. "So," she said, "I'll just—"

"Sunday, then," Tom said. "Ten o'clock. Twelve if you go to church."

"Twelve will be fine," Kate said, even though she didn't know if it would. Her words were coming out in gasps.

Then she started for the door, but it didn't work.

"There was one more thing I wanted to do today," Tom said "And I want you to come with me."

He grabbed her arm. It didn't take long for Kate to realize that where she was being propelled was Tom's unmarked car or to pick up on Tom's increasing change of mood.

"Are you really sure this couldn't wait until tomorrow?" she asked him as she got into the passenger seat. "You've got to have things to do today. I've got things to do today."

Kate was about to say more, but Tom suddenly put the car in reverse, did a violent but entirely accurate K-turn, and shot out down the intersection.

"Are you going to tell me where we're going?" she asked. "What's so important that we've got to race to get there?"

Tom didn't take his eyes off the road.

"We're going to go settle one thing," he said. "The one thing that really bothers me."

★　★　★

They made their way through a leafy-green area of compact, single-family houses. It was not dark, but some of the houses had their lights on, and Kate could see through the windows to scenes of family life: children setting dinner tables, women opening pizza boxes, men changing channels on television sets.

All the details were sharp and clear and impossible to avoid, and that *was* one of the things she associated with the start of an episode. Suddenly, her mouth began to feel very dry, and she put her hands down on her seat and held on tight.

Tom made his way down one residential street after another, then suddenly flung them into the driveway of a medium-sized cottage with faux-Bavarian trimmings. The car came to an abrupt halt, and Kate looked through the large front window to see a man she recognized drinking straight out of a bottle of Glenlivit whiskey.

"Isn't that—isn't that Detective Flanagan?" she asked. "We came out to talk to Detective Flanagan?"

"Stay in the car," Tom said. "I'll be right back."

"I thought you wanted me to come."

"I want you the hell out of trouble while I get something done."

Tom got out of the car and slammed the door behind him. Then he strode right up over the grass to the front porch and knocked. A moment later, he began to pound. A moment after that, the door opened and Flanagan stood framed in the light behind him, still holding his bottle of Glenlivit.

Then the door closed, and Kate turned her attention to the other thing she'd noticed. The houses here were fairly close together, and in the house on her right, there was a woman peering out a window, holding a pair of binoculars.

Binoculars.

Kate could hardly believe it.

She didn't get out of the car and go over to the other house right away, since Tom might be back almost immediately, but it didn't take long before she got angry. What was it about the people in her life—*all* the people in her life, even Jack—that made them think they could jerk her around like a puppet any time they wanted? Do this. Do that. Do the other thing. Go here. Sit there. It was as if she had no say in her own life.

The woman at the other house was still standing at the window, looking through her binoculars. Either she was a very patient woman, or she had reason to think that keeping vigilance would pay off. What was it that could go on at Flanagan's house that would repay lots of surveillance in the middle of a weekday afternoon—or any other time, for that matter?

She took her phone out of her jeans and checked the time. Tom must have been in the house for a good five minutes. What if he was in there for half an hour more? Was she just supposed to sit here and do nothing?

Kate popped open her car door and got out. She closed it gently, in case anybody inside might be able to hear. Tom and Flanagan weren't anywhere near the living room window, though, so they couldn't see her. And that was all for the better.

She headed across the lawn to the neighbor's house, looking up as she crossed from one property to the next.

The neighbor had her binoculars trained on Kate now. Kate had expected it.

She went up the steps to the neighbor's front door and rang the bell. Part of her thought the neighbor would pretend not to be home. She was elderly. She probably lived alone. On the other hand, she was also curious and probably lonely, and—

It took no time at all for Kate to hear shuffling behind the front door. Then the door opened and she was faced with a *very* elderly woman, thin, frail, and rickety. But there was nothing frail or rickety about the light in that woman's eyes. She would notice everything, and remember it, too.

Kate had to think fast. She hadn't come prepared with a story if the woman opened up.

"Excuse me," she said. "I'm Kaitlyn Plymouth." *There* was a pseudonym. Maybe she should have called herself Buick. "I'm a reporter for the *Washington Post*. We're working on a story about the Kevin Ozgo trial. The trial is set to go to the jury in a few days, and we're trying to get all angles in the case cleared up and—"

"You don't look like a reporter," the woman said. "You're a mess."

"I *am* a mess," Kate said. "It's been a long day. Mrs.—"

"Leeds," the woman said. "Lucy Leeds. Is your friend over there a reporter, too?"

"Yes," Kate said. "Yes, he is. He's the head reporter on this, to tell you the truth. We're trying to find out something about Mr. Flanagan, you know, as human interest and that kind of thing."

This story sounded so incredibly lame, Kate almost winced visibly.

Mrs. Leeds was standing in the door in such a way that Kate couldn't enter. "I was just wondering if you had any thoughts on Mr. Flanagan," she said. "We'd like to know what kind of a person he is when he's not on the job. That kind of thing."

"Seems like everybody wants to know about Bill Flanagan," Leeds said. "That other one said she was a reporter, too."

"That other one?"

"That Chan Hamilton woman," Leeds said. "Thought I wouldn't recognize her. Idiot. My mind is as good as it ever was. Maybe better."

"Yes, I see, that's interesting," Kate said. "Why would Chan Hamilton want to talk to you?"

"How am I supposed to know what idiots like that want to do? She lied to me. I kicked her out of here and slammed the door in her face. If she'd stayed one more minute in the driveway, I'd have called the police. But I wouldn't have called Flanagan. He wouldn't have been any help at all."

"Well, no," Kate said. "He's not the right kind of police, is he? He's a detective. You'd need a patrol car."

Leeds snorted. "He could have been Superman with a cape for all it would matter. If you ask him for help with something, he just tells you to call nine-one-one. Like I didn't know enough to call nine-one-one. And then there's the goings-on at night."

"At night?"

"He's only home at night, isn't he?" Leeds said. "Until the last couple of days. I don't know what that's about. Before that he went off in the morning and he came back in the evening and then at night people started showing up. Maybe I should say *still show up*. Maybe I should say *person*. It's always the same one, isn't it?"

"The same man?"

"The same man. Has a black SUV like the ones they use for the president. Monster of a thing."

"Do you know who he is?"

"Of course I don't know who he is. Do you think Flanagan is going to tell me who he is?"

"Would you recognize him in a picture?" She could bring the pictures of Jed Paterson and have Leeds identify them.

But Leeds wasn't going to be that much help. "Of course I couldn't recognize him in a picture," she snorted. "He never gets out of the car, does he? He just sits out there in the driveway until Flanagan comes out, and then they drive off. And when Flanagan comes out, he's always blind drunk, and he's always got a bottle."

"Blind drunk," Kate repeated.

"Staggering like he can't stand up straight," Leeds said. "The man drinks like a fish. Even when he doesn't get picked up. Goes and drinks in his backyard when the weather is amenable. She went over there too, you know, Chan Hamilton. He threw her out on her ear."

"Chan Hamilton went to see Flanagan?" Kate was trying to get it all nailed down.

"There's a lot of funny stuff going on over at that house," Leeds said. "And now they say he's going to go build himself a big house in one of those subdivisions. A McMansion, they call it. Where'd he get the money? And why is it so many people are asking questions about him and pretending to be reporters when they do it?"

"Oh," Kate said. "I—"

"Look, girlie," Leeds said. "You want people to believe you're a reporter, you'd better bring a notebook or a little tape recorder or something so you can get it all down. Reporters don't go jabbering with people without taking it down."

"But I'm just doing background," Kate said desperately. "I would have taken it down if I was going to quote you—"

"Give it up," Leeds said, more than a little triumphantly.

Kate was expecting her to step back into her house and shut the door, but just then the door to Flanagan's house opened and both Flanagan and Tom came out.

"I know what you're doing, you goddamned prick," Flanagan shouted.

★   ★   ★

Kate's mad dash back to Tom's car in Flanagan's driveway was half to get away from Leeds and half from fear of Tom's reaction when he found out she'd left the car.

At the moment, though, he wasn't noticing her.

"You *framed* Ozgo," he shouted. "You framed him, and I can prove it. You got me taken off that case because you knew I wouldn't put up with it."

Flanagan still had his bottle of Glenlivit. He was waving it around in the air and liquid was dropping out of it in arcs.

"You got taken off that case because you weren't to be trusted, and you damned well know it."

"Ozgo is a vet, for God's sake. He's a vet with PTSD. I don't care what else is going on here, but I want him off the hook and off the hook for good."

"You're the one who's on the hook, Tommy boy," Flanagan said. "You're so on the hook, you look like fish bait. Stop acting like a first-class asshole or you're going to end up deader than Turner."

Then one minute Flanagan was standing in his own front door, waving the Glenlivit around with no particular purpose. The next he was out in the yard and heading for Tom.

Flanagan was a big man, but nowhere near as big as Tom, and he was the worse for alcohol. He was also older and out of shape. He still managed to cross the yard to Tom's car in record time. The punch he threw was wild, but Flanagan's fist managed to connect to Tom's jaw with a hard *crack*. Tom fell backward onto the lawn.

Tom was up in a moment, but he wasn't heading for Flanagan. He was heading for the car. He saw Kate standing near the passenger-side door and roared, "Get in! Right now!"

Kate did what he told her, and a second later, Tom was in the car, too, locking the door at his side and pulling on his seat belt.

Flanagan reached the car and started pounding on the hood, hitting hard enough so that little dents appeared where his fist landed.

"Son of a bitch," he screamed. "Son of a goddamned bitch! I'm going to puree your intestines and feed them to the goddamned trout!"

Tom started the car and put it in reverse. Flanagan seemed not to have noticed. He was still pounding, moving along the car, smashing more and more dents and heading for the driver's side window. Flanagan hit the windshield but to no effect. Tom hit the gas and careened out of the driveway and back onto the street, leaving Flanagan lying flat on his stomach on the driveway's asphalt.

"For God's sake," Kate said as they sped back the way they came.

Tom didn't look at her. Kate was convinced he didn't know that she had been talking to Leeds or even that she'd been out of the car before he came out of the house with Flanagan on his heels. He was staring straight ahead and concentrating on the road.

"If that asshole thinks he's getting away with this," he said.

"Getting away with framing Ozgo?"

"Well, I told you that was what I thought from the beginning."

★　★　★

Close to an hour later, Kate pulled into her driveway, got out of the car, threw her tote bag over her shoulder, and entered through the side door of the townhouse. Jack was home. She could see his backpack on the kitchen table. Frank was home, too. She could hear him talking, a little too loudly, in the living room. She put her bag on the kitchen table and headed through the house toward her bedroom.

"Kate?" Frank asked tentatively.

"Hi," Kate said.

"We were talking about getting Chinese," Jack said. "You want some Chinese?"

Kate was still in that place where she couldn't have eaten if she'd wanted to, and she didn't want to because it would take up too much time.

"You two get Chinese," she said. "I've—ah—I'm going out."

"Going out?" Jack said.

"It's just like I said," Frank told him. "It's that Tom from yesterday. They're going out."

"It's not Tom," Kate said quickly, "and it's not a date. I'm just going out to the Barnes and Noble to hear Alice Hoffman speak. I meant to mention it before, but things have been crazy the last couple of days."

"Alice Hoffman?" Jack said. "She wrote *Practical Magic*. Can I come?"

"You hated *Practical Magic*," Frank said.

"You need tickets," Kate said. "She's a big draw. You had to reserve in advance. It never occurred to me you wanted to go."

"Yeah," Jack said. "I've never been to hear a writer, that's all. I thought it might be interesting. You know . . ."

"Right," Kate said. "I'm sorry."

She rushed to her bedroom, closed the door behind her, and then locked it. She stripped out of her clothes and started opening drawers right and left. She didn't wear a lot of dark things. Dark clothes made her depressed.

She found a black sweatshirt. Completely black. No writing on it. No symbols. She put on dark jeans to go with it. Then she hit a snag. She had black shoes, but they were all dress shoes. Her running shoes were a gleaming, glistening white. She had no black socks of any kind. All her socks were also white.

That could be a very big problem.

She put on the socks and running shoes anyway. Then she headed on out again. She'd been so intent on making sure that everything was dark enough, she hadn't considered how odd she must look, but she considered it as soon as she saw Jack and Frank, who couldn't seem to help staring at her.

She tried to ignore it.

"I'm off," she said, as brightly as she could.

"In that?" Jack demanded.

"I shouldn't be too late," Kate said.

She reached the kitchen at close to a run. She stopped long enough to get her wallet, her keys, and her cell phone out of her tote bag. She stuffed it all in the jeans' two shallow pockets and headed for the car.

She took off in the car, not slowing down until she was three blocks past the townhouse. She made a left turn. Then she made two more rights, another left, and another right, and pulled into the lot of the Target.

Kate had about three hours to wait until full dark. In the meantime, she'd get herself black socks and black running shoes.

After the shoes problem was the parking, because if there was one thing Kate knew she couldn't do, it was drive into that parking garage and pull into a convenient space. She couldn't park on the street in front of Almador's headquarters, either. In all the time she'd been working for the company, Kate had never once seen a vehicle parked at the curb.

Unfortunately, the nobody-parks-at-the-curb thing wasn't specific to Almador's street. All the streets in the vicinity were the same. You didn't just drive up and park willy-nilly in suburban Virginia.

What she needed was a convenience store, a gas station with a side lot, or someplace cars might park for long intervals. Looking for a spot ate up a chunk of time. In the end, she found a gas station with just three small spaces to the side of its concrete, one-story building, all of them unoccupied. Unluckily, there was a sign on the building just above the middle space: "Parking for Shell Customers Only. Others Will Be Towed."

There was nothing she could do. She would just have to risk it. She got out and locked up. Then she had to pull out her phone to find the GPS to figure out where she was.

She was as far out of the way as she could be and still be considered walking distance: 1.2 miles. It was going to take forever to get back to Almador. She was going to be caught on every security camera in the several neighborhoods she was going to have to pass through.

And in the end, it wasn't going to matter, because she'd get to the door and her security code wouldn't work. Or she'd get in and get to a secure computer station and her security code wouldn't work with that.

Even Harvey Ballard couldn't be stupid enough not to block her access when he'd thrown her out of the building.

★ ★ ★

As it turned out, Harvey Ballard could be that stupid. A competent manager would have closed down all her clearances as soon as he'd thrown her out of the building. Harvey, being Harvey, would more probably have spent that time running around hyperventilating and forgotten all about it.

Kate got to the Almador building right about the time she thought her knees were going to crack in half. The trip had been not only long but accomplished on road shoulders that were uneven and sporadically filled with debris she couldn't see in the dark and kept stumbling over. Kate was in good shape, but the walk was still murder. When it was over, she found herself looking up at the building she knew so well and thinking that if she had to make the walk all the way back with nothing gained, she was going to start screaming.

There were two security cameras above the front door, one on either side. There was nothing she was going to be able to do about them.

She got out her card, went up to the front door, and slid it into the slot. She entered her code and held her breath.

The door popped open.

Just like that.

Kate hurried through the door and closed it behind her. Inside, the main lobby was expansive, constructed to impress visitors. Kate moved quickly through to the elevators. The elevators were not security-code protected, at least on this floor. It was getting off them that was going to pose the next problem.

She got on, pushed the button for the sixth floor, and made herself breathe normally as the elevator ascended. There had been security cameras in the lobby and above each of the elevator doors. There were more security cameras in the elevator car with her. This place had better coverage than a reality show.

The car stopped on six, and a red light began flashing next to the door, demanding her card. Kate put in her card, waited for the flash that demanded her code, and then put that in. It all went without a hitch. The elevator car doors opened. She stepped out onto her own floor.

Kate passed the door to the secure computer room she'd been using at the time Harvey jumped in on her. The next secure computer room was on the other side of the building. She closed it behind her without turning on the overhead lights and sat down at one of the computers.

Kate brought up the authorization screen and went through the routine: name, authorization number, PIN, clearance code, security code.

The authorization screen disappeared, and she was on the secured Internet. Two more authorization screens and she was into the Pentagon.

Kate was pretty sure that this thing would not let her launch a nuclear weapon. At least, she told herself she was sure, because she didn't want to contemplate the possibilities if it would. But short of that, she could find out anything she wanted.

She could find out what happened to Rafael Turner and Kevin Ozgo and what Jed Paterson had to do with all of it.

Two hours went by without Kate noticing it, and in those two hours, she found out everything and nothing. Once she'd gotten into the personnel records, it was easy enough to establish that both Turner and Ozgo had been in the army and that Ozgo had been honorably discharged nearly two years before the attack was supposed to have happened for reasons that were vague but telling. She'd found that there had been an attack, that Turner had been in the attack, but that the attack was more than a year and a half earlier than had been reported by the press.

She started opening more and more windows, trying to get the information in a form she could use to straighten out the time line, but she didn't write anything down. Being here without authorization got you sent to prison; being here and writing it all down probably got you executed. It was a good thing she had a decent memory.

The screen was clogged with open pages, so many that the system was severely slowed down.

She'd found an incident that involved Ozgo and Turner, but it was a month earlier than the one that was supposed to have resulted in Turner's death, and it was all the way over in Herat, Afghanistan. And there were no Afghan insurgents.

There was a truck with members of Turner and Ozgo's unit. There was a drone that had bombed the hell out of a complex of buildings where Turner's unit was working. Then there was a group of people who seemed to be General Solutions contractors led by Jed Paterson. Kate knew General Solutions. They were a huge military contracting firm.

Kate looked at it again and again and again. What *seemed* to have happened was that the drone strike hit, and then the contractors showed up, and then, and only then, did people start dying.

Could that be right? The way it should have worked was that the drone killed the people, and then Paterson's group had come in and tried to help. But no matter how many times she looked at these sequences, she couldn't make it come out that way.

She took another tack and looked up the contracts the military had with General Solutions. They were all for reconstructions. When facilities were destroyed, General Solutions rebuilt them.

She went at it one more time.

She'd just started moving windows around to put them in roughly chronological order when she suddenly became convinced that she was not alone. She hadn't heard the door open, but she might not have been paying attention. There couldn't be anybody but the security staff here this late at night. Even the cleaning staff wasn't allowed in any of these rooms alone.

She closed her eyes. She would count to ten and then turn around to see if there was somebody there.

She got to four before the sounds of motion in the room became unmistakable.

Then a voice said, "I believe it's Miss Ford, isn't it? I suppose I should have suspected."

Kate nearly sank through the floor right there.

There was no mistaking that voice: it belonged to Richard Hamilton.

Kate swiveled her chair in his direction and opened her eyes. Hamilton was there alone. He was completely calm. The man had a legendary temper, a coldhearted boil that ripped adversaries to shreds and reduced errant employees to dust, but he was displaying none of it.

He wore chinos and a bright-red cotton sweater that looked expensive enough to use for currency. He had his hands in his pockets and was leaning back against the door.

No escape that way, Kate told herself.

She croaked, "Mr. Hamilton." She couldn't think of anything else *to* say.

Hamilton looked up at the ceiling and then down again.

"You do realize you are on a Department of Defense secure computer," he said.

"Yes," Kate said. "Yes, I do realize that."

"And you do realize that you are in this building without authorization of any kind to be here. In fact, in contradiction to a direct order from this company not to be here."

"Yes," Kate said. This was definitely going where she thought it was going.

Hamilton closed his eyes and shook his head. When he looked at her again, he seemed almost sad. "It's unbelievable, really," he told her. "The defense of this nation and of a dozen or more nations across the world depends on our ability to keep secret what would aid our enemies if it were revealed. First there was Snowden. Now there's you."

"I'm not pulling a Snowden," Kate protested. "I'm not looking for classified documents to send out to the newspapers—"

"Virtually every piece of information you could access on that computer is classified," Hamilton pointed out. "And I know you don't want to embarrass the United States government. You want to embarrass Almador and you want to embarrass me. In retaliation for your suspension."

"No," Kate said. "No, I don't care about the suspension—"

"I'm going to hand Ballard his ass on a platter," Hamilton said. "The man is a train wreck of unbelievable proportions."

"Well, that's something we can agree on," Kate said.

"You do realize you are never going to work at Almador again."

"I thought that had already been decided," Kate said, "even if Harvey didn't come right out and say so."

"And you're never going to work anywhere you need a clearance again. I'm not Ballard. I'll have your clearances pulled two minutes after you're out of here. All of them. And I can probably arrange to make sure you never work anywhere again, if I feel like it."

"I sort of thought you were going to arrange to have me put in jail," Kate said.

"Ah," Hamilton said.

Kate didn't know what he was waiting for. If she'd been him, she'd have walked out the door, secured it one way or another, and called security. But Richard Hamilton wasn't moving.

He looked her up and down. He looked over the computer station and then at the floor beneath her feet.

"You don't have a purse with you."

"Oh," Kate said. "No, no, I didn't bring one with me."

"But you brought a phone," Hamilton said. "You brought a cell phone."

"Yes," Kate said. "Yes, of course I did. I have it in one of my pockets. I have people with medical problems at home. I need it in case of an emergency."

"You're on a Department of Defense secure computer without authorization, you are looking at classified documents you are not allowed to see, and you have a camera with you."

"Oh," Kate said.

"Exactly," Hamilton said. "I think we're looking at fifteen to twenty. It might be twenty to twenty-five."

"Right," Kate said. Now she *really* couldn't breathe.

"And you won't be able to deny it," Hamilton said. "I don't know how you got in here, but there isn't a door or an elevator car in this building without security cameras. And that includes the door to this room. We'll have footage to show that you got into this building and into this room. And if we get a security guard in here, he'll make you turn out your pockets, and he'll find the phone."

Kate's brain did a turn around and screeched to a halt.

"If?" she asked him.

Kate didn't think she'd ever seen anybody who could be this calm or go for this long without blinking. She felt as if the man was staring right through her.

Hamilton suddenly moved away from the door and walked to the computer. He looked at the screen, then moved the mouse to look at a few of the others. Then he stepped back.

"Interesting," he said. He took out his cell phone and took a picture of her holding her own opened cell phone in her hand. "You're going to walk out of this room by yourself. You're going to walk out of this building by yourself. And while you're doing it, I'm going to be having you watched. When you're well away from here, I'll come out myself. But not until you're very well away."

"Great," Kate said.

"You should get moving," Hamilton said.

Kate started to back out of the room, but she must have been more panicked than she thought. She bumped against the doorframe as she went, and when she did, she heard a double thump: herself against the door and something heavy hitting the ground.

Hamilton walked forward, leaned over, and straightened up, holding Kate's healing stone in his hand.

She reached for it, but Hamilton was pushing her farther out into the corridor.

"I think I'll keep it," he said.

And then he smiled at her in a deep and vicious way that made Kate want to run.

⋆ ⋆ ⋆

Kate got moving. Going down and going out, she did nothing to hide her presence in the building. She double-checked her pockets for her keys, her cell phone, and her wallet and headed out into the night.

It had been bad enough walking in. Now it was even darker—or it seemed even darker—and the ground felt rockier and even more uneven. At one point, she stumbled so badly, she almost turned her ankle. But it was only almost, and she had to keep going, so she did.

About halfway out, her cell phone began going off, and she stopped for a moment to check it. She had six voice mail messages, all of them from Frank and Jack and all of them saying the same thing: Where are you? Are you all right? Should we call the police?

This was not good. If they had called the police, there was going to be a fuss. She checked the time on the phone's clock: 1:35 p.m.

She made the call. It was answered before the first ring ended.

"Mom?" Jack said.

He hadn't waited to hear her voice.

"It's okay," Kate said. "I'm fine. I'm sorry. I went out for drinks with some friends and we went to this place in the country and I guess there wasn't service. I didn't mean to worry you—"

"Of course I was going to be worried," Jack said. "You weren't at the bookstore. We called. The Alice Hoffmann talk doesn't happen for two weeks. We didn't know where you were."

"Let me have that," Frank's voice said from the background.

While Jack had been talking, Kate had been moving, and she'd been making much better time than she had in the beginning. Worrying about Jack and what to say to him took her mind off the throbbing in her ankle, which was getting worse by the second. It also took her mind off the ruts and rocks.

"Kate?"

There were lights just ahead. Street lamps. Small stores. That damned gas station.

"Daddy," Kate said. "It's all right. I'm okay. I'm coming right home. It won't take me more than half an hour."

"You should've let us know you were going to be out this late," Frank said. "You had us both frantic. Are you sure you're all right now?"

"I'm just fine," Kate said. "There's nothing wrong. I'll be home any minute now, and I'll tell you everything when I get there. Just let me get off the phone so I can get there."

"All right," Frank said.

"Make her stay on that phone until she pulls into the driveway," Jack said. "I don't care if she gets a ticket."

"Daddy," she said.

"That's all right," Frank said. "I'm going to hang up now. Come straight home. Call us if anything holds you up."

"Yes," Kate said. "Yes, I promise. Tell Jack I love him. And I'll be right there."

She turned the phone off and shoved it back into her pocket. She forced herself into an aggressive power walk. She was close to completely out of breath. Her throbbing ankle was numb. Her back and shoulders felt like they'd been wrung out like a wet towel.

She got to the gas station. It was closed and dark except for the brand sign above the price list. She pushed as fast as she could around to the side and found . . .

. . . three parking spaces.

All of them empty.

ELEVEN

It was dangerous being out there in the dark, with every store and gas station in sight deserted for the night, but Kate still took a good five minutes making up her mind what to do next. She didn't want to make an idiot of herself, and she didn't know what she was going to say when she made the only phone call she could make.

But it couldn't be helped. She called Tom.

When Tom showed up nearly half an hour later, he was driving a green Subaru instead of his usual silver unmarked police car. Kate didn't recognize it when he first pulled into the station, and for a panicked moment, she wondered if she ought to hide.

Tom parked the car next to where she was standing, braking so hard the squeal hurt Kate's eardrums, and jumped out onto the pavement like Superman emerging from a phone booth.

"What the *hell* do you think you're doing?" he demanded.

Kate ran over to the passenger-side door and tugged at the handle. Locked.

"Could you please let me in the car?" she asked. "I'm freezing."

Tom got in behind the wheel and shut his own door. Kate got in and fussed with her seat belt so that she didn't have to look him.

"Let me try this again," he said. "What the hell do you think you're doing?"

Kate's seat belt was fastened. Tom was not starting the car.

"I went in to work," she said. "I mean, I went in to Almador. I figured I had a good shot at being able to get in because my old manager was really disorganized. He should have shut down all my codes and passwords and had my security clearances yanked, but I was pretty sure he wouldn't have remembered to do all that because he never does. He gets distracted. So I thought I'd go in and use the secure computers."

"Let me make a guess," Tom said. "Secure computers and you need a security clearance to get into them . . . a *government* security clearance."

"Yes," Kate said.

"And people who don't have those clearances aren't allowed to work on those computers."

"Yes," Kate said again. She really didn't like where this was going.

"And," Tom said, "the only reason you have those clearances at the moment is that some idiot manager forgot to rescind them when you were put on leave."

"Okay," Kate said. "All right. I see where you're going with this—"

"See where I'm going? *See where I'm going?* Are you out of your mind? You just broke into a building you had no right to enter, used codes and clearances you knew you had no right to have—for God's sake, you must have broken fifty laws. Or worse. I should probably be arresting you right now."

"No," Kate said, "I don't think so. It's not your jurisdiction."

Tom sent her a withering glance, and she sank a little deeper in her seat. She really wished he'd make the car move, but he gave no indication of leaving.

"Then," he said, staring out at the wall now, "you park your car all the way out here."

"There's no street parking near Almador," Kate said. "And I didn't want to park in the parking garage because there are all these cameras."

"Oh, wonderful. Proof that you knew what you were doing was wrong. And you'll have been caught on camera. I'll bet the Almador building has thousands of cameras."

"Yes," Kate said.

"And then you end up down here, in the dark, by yourself. It's not the worst neighborhood in the world, Kate, but a woman on her own and unarmed is always a target. Oh, Christ. You *are* unarmed? You didn't bring a gun with you?"

"Of course not," Kate said.

"What about something sensible? Pepper spray? Mace?"

"Do all the people you know go around with that sort of stuff on them all the time?" Kate asked. "Why would I have anything like that? What would be the point?"

"Not being raped, robbed, and left for dead in the Virginia suburbs would be the point," Tom said. "Great God almighty. You really are out of your mind."

Tom put the key in the ignition and the engine roared back to life. He put his own seat belt on and began backing up.

He was out onto the road before he spoke again.

"Was there some point in doing what you did here?" he asked. "Was there really something so important that you had to break I don't know how many federal laws and a few local ones and risk your life wandering around on your own with no protection? Really?"

Kate hunkered down. They were out in the neighborhoods now. Most of the houses were dead dark, just like the gas station a few blocks away.

"I just needed to know what happened in that raid. And to double-check that Turner was dead."

Tom actually looked interested. "And?"

"He's dead," Kate admitted, "but not when and how the papers said he was. As far as I could tell, your Jed Paterson person murdered him."

"What?"

Kate outlined the whole thing for him—the raid with Jed Paterson in charge, the attack in Herat and its aftermath, Jed Paterson's connection to General Solutions.

Tom's driving had slowed considerably, and he no longer seemed to be angry at her.

"So," he said slowly, "Turner died because he knew about the corruption? Is this a case of corruption?"

"I think so," Kate said. "General Solutions reconstructs things. The facility was destroyed by a General Solutions drone. Except—my head is starting to hurt."

"There was some kind of 'bilking the government' thing going on, and Turner got wise to it. Paterson staged a raid to shut him up, and then General Solutions' cronies at the Pentagon got the whole thing hushed up. Think about it. It's the only thing that makes sense. Why else would Paterson kill Turner?"

"But, Tom, if you look at the records, it doesn't look like that. It doesn't look like Paterson knew Turner was there. It looks like there was a drone strike and Paterson brought a team in to finish up, and Turner just happened to be there. But then I can't figure out why Paterson would kill them all instead of helping them."

"I don't like coincidences," Tom said. "I especially don't like double and triple coincidences, and that's what this would have to be. Paterson is responsible for Turner's death in a friendly fire incident, and then he comes back to the states and is still working for General Solutions. And the friendly fire incident is covered up six ways to Sunday and that means Paterson's name is out of it? You couldn't sell that one to Hollywood."

"I'm not trying to sell it to Hollywood," Kate said. "I'm just trying to figure out what this is. And if it's connected to Ozgo and the kidnapping and the trial."

"Of course it's connected," Tom said. "It's all about Richard Hamilton."

Twenty minutes later, Kate was sitting in her own driveway. Tom's car was still running and the headlights were still
on, and the townhouse's front door was open, too, spilling
light onto the front walk. Frank and Jack were there, right
behind it. Kate had the impression that Frank was forcibly
restraining Jack from bursting through the door to see for
himself how she was.

"All right," Tom said, "I suppose I—"

"Would you like to come in for some coffee? I'm sure
we could—"

"Not right now," Tom said. "They're going to want you
to explain it all to them, and I'm going to want to go back to
sleep. You've got that track meet thing tomorrow?"

Kate had to switch gears, fast. She caught herself just in
time. "Yes. Yes I do. Jack—"

But Tom wasn't listening, and Kate was glad he wasn't
listening. She got herself out of her seat belt and then out of
the car, muttering frantic apologies all the way.

Then Jack *did* burst through the front door and came
running.

★   ★   ★

It was the car that saved her, the car that had been towed
and needed to be retrieved from whatever impound it had
been hauled off to while Kate was trapped at Almador with
Richard Hamilton. If she hadn't needed to do something
about that and do it right away, she would have been trapped
in her own kitchen that morning listening to all of Jack and
Frank's scolding.

In the end, she told them another pack of lies—no, Tom couldn't help today, Tom had things he had to do—and spent some time on the computer finding the gas station where she'd parked and talking to the attendant to find out where her car was likely to be.

The impound yard turned out to be all the way on the other side of Almador, near the county line, and the cab fare looked like the budget for a Hollywood blockbuster. Frank dropped her off, threatening to wait for her, but the line was long. She convinced him instead to run by the grocery store to pick up food for the week.

The impound yard had exactly one employee on duty and approximately fifty people waiting to retrieve their cars. Most of those people were in even worse moods than she was, and the attendant was a dedicated passive-aggressive. The more infuriated a customer became, the slower and more inarticulate he got. At one point, he seemed to be pretending not to speak English.

It was eleven thirty before she finally reached the attendant's counter and described her car for him. The attendant gave no indication that he cared or that he'd ever seen it, but he took her keys and went off into the back, where there was a door to the fenced yard. Kate didn't think she had ever been in such a hurry to get out of a place in her life.

The attendant came back with a clipboard and pushed it across to her—she had to sign at the bottom, put her driver's license number in the little box, agree that her car had not been damaged by the people who towed it, and pay $845.02 in fines and towing charges.

She hauled out a credit card and handed it over. Then she took her keys back and went outside to pick up her car.

Kate drove around for a while along roads that were neither really urban nor really rural. She and Tom needed help, and she had an idea where they could get it. She made a call and began to head back into town and ended up in her parking space outside of the courthouse. She wandered down the street and looked into the windows of a few of the small restaurants. Most of them were full with the brunch crowd. In the fourth one on the block, she found the man she was looking for. Kate noted the rumpled suit and the hair that looked as if it had been applied to his bald scalp with Elmer's glue—and then she had it. This might be lucky if she played it right. She went into the restaurant, ignored the hostess, and headed straight for him.

"Excuse me," she said when she reached him. "It's Mike Alexander from the *Washington Post?*"

Mike shot her a look of exasperation that changed quickly to one of interest. "You're the woman who fainted in court the first day," he said.

Kate sat down. "That's right," she said.

"You work for Almador."

"Right again. I've been thinking about you. You don't usually do local crime stories, do you? I thought you specialized in government corruption."

"This is the biggest game in town at the moment," Mike said. "What about you? You come in every day with that cop."

"No," Kate said. "I'm just interested in the trial. And I've been looking at some things I'd think you'd be more interested in."

"Like?"

"Like government corruption," Kate said. "Like General Solutions."

"There isn't a whole lot of difference between General Solutions and Almador. They're pretty much the same company."

"I know that," Kate said. "And I know for a fact that Turner wasn't killed when and how the papers reported he was, including your paper. And I think it's connected with some kind of scam General Solutions is running on the government."

"So what happened?"

"Jed Paterson."

Alexander sat back. "Is that so?"

Kate sighed. "You could look into it. It's right up your alley."

Mike shrugged. "I'm on a story. And you work for Almador."

"Think of me as a disgruntled employee."

It was the right thing to say. Now Mike was interested.

He asked for her number and handed Kate his card. "I'll think about it," he said. "That's where you reach me if your disgruntlement gets a little more expansive."

★ ★ ★

She had no idea if she'd really convinced Mike to look into the death of Turner, but she'd given it a try. She couldn't do this all herself.

The problem was what to do next. She threaded through the streets on her way back to the small side lot and her car. When she got there, she opened it up and got in. She sat behind the wheel and got her phone out of her bag. She opened her search history and found the Facebook page for Dalton Brayde. That's where she had left things at the courthouse, when she'd decided she'd taken too much time searching while Tom was waiting for her. Then she ran through the pros and cons of this idea.

Brayde was only a backup plan, a secondary resource in case her investigation this evening came to nothing. Unfortunately, even as a secondary source, he had to be approached carefully. She couldn't just march up to him somewhere and present herself. Her first quick search for Brayde had come up with the kind of details she'd expected from what Tom had already said about the man. There were dozens of images of Brayde with one woman after another, with whole little clutches of women in various bars around the Washington, DC, area. The pictures led to captions. The captions led to stories. The stories were all accounts of wild nights, but the wild nights didn't always happen in the same places. That was how she had ended up on Facebook.

She had her own Facebook account, but she didn't want to use that one for this. Brayde almost certainly wouldn't be able to recognize her from a picture, but if she used her own name, he could Google it, and it might result in a story about her episode on the first day of the trial. Kate couldn't risk the possibility that any connection would look suspicious.

She opened her picture file and went through it frame by frame. Almost all her pictures were of Jack, Frank, or her either together or in individual shots. The picture she wanted was the very last one. It showed a Kate a good five years younger than she was now dressed in a black silk cocktail dress so sheer it almost didn't look like material.

She went back to Facebook and began the process of creating a new account. She called herself Kaitlyn Plymouth. Why not? She allowed herself to put in the details of her own life, leaving out the marriage and Jack.

She uploaded her picture, finished creating her account, and then looked through the friend suggestions the site threw up. On a whim, she sent requests to all twenty of them and then to another thirty that those requests generated.

The gambit worked almost immediately. She'd barely finished the next round of requests when six of her requests were accepted.

She stopped at a hundred because she had to stop somewhere.

Then she brought up Brayde and sent a friend request to him.

She was still looking at the page, wondering what she expected to get out of what she'd just done, when Frank's ringtone chimed.

"Katie?" he said, sounding strained. "Katie, something's happened. I've called the police. Everyone is all right, but you have to get back here right away."

"Jack?"

"No, Jack's all right. I'm all right. Get back here now. Will you do that? Wherever you are."

"Yes," Kate said. "Yes, of course. I'm in the car right now."

"Don't talk on the phone when you drive," Frank said. "Just get back here."

He hung up.

TWELVE

Kate was almost all the way home before she stopped thinking the worst. Even though her father had told her that Jack was all right and that whatever the crisis was had nothing to do with him, she didn't entirely believe it until she turned onto her own road and saw, from just ten houses away, what the immediate problem had to be.

It was impossible to miss. She was on the long end of the T, and her townhouse was right at the end of it. Her townhouse's big front window was . . . gone. Kate could see jagged shards of glass along the edges of the frame. She switched her attention to the police car in her driveway and the policewoman talking to Frank.

Jack was there, too, sitting on the front steps. He was not hurt, though he did look royally annoyed.

Kate didn't see Tom until she was pulling into her driveway next to the police car. She cut her engine, leaped out of the car, and headed straight for the policewoman. As she did, the woman's partner leaned out the broken front window and said, "We should at least take fingerprints, even if it's going to be useless."

Kate came to a stop next to Frank. "I'm Kate Ford. I own this townhouse. What—?"

"I'll tell you what," Frank said. "A rock came right through our front window."

The policewoman turned to her and smiled a little grimly. "It was almost certainly a deliberate case of vandalism," she said. "The rock in question is still sitting in the living room, if you want to look at it. It's much too large to have landed there accidentally. It couldn't have been thrown up by a passing car, for instance. We've been trying to discover if there is anyone who may be holding a grudge, maybe a neighbor you might be having a dispute with."

"I don't even know the neighbors," Kate said. "I say hello to them if I see them, but I haven't had a whole conversation with any of them since I moved here. I'm not even sure I know their names."

"Possibly somebody at your place of work?" the policewoman asked.

Kate shook her head. "I don't think so. I'm on pretty good terms with the people I see there on a daily basis. My manager is a bit of a jerk, but I don't think he hates me. And besides, why would he do something like throw a huge rock through my window? I'm going to go in and look at the mess for a minute."

She turned her back on Tom and practically ran to her front door, passing Jack on the way up the steps.

"There's glass everywhere in there," he told her. "We're going to be picking glass out of our asses for months."

Kate didn't stop long enough to tell him to watch his language. She went on through and into the foyer and then into the living room.

The policeman in the living room was standing in front of the window frame and talking into a cell phone. The living room was beyond being a mess. The rock was—

It was her healing stone. Her own healing stone. The one Richard Hamilton had taken from her only last night. Her throat began to constrict.

There was glass everywhere. It crunched under Kate's feet as she walked. Kate could see shards and glass powder on the couch, on the two side chairs, and on the small table that held the television set. The television set was intact, but a lamp had fallen over. Kate went to it automatically to make sure the bulb hadn't broken, because these new light bulbs had to be disposed of immediately if they cracked.

"Please don't touch that," the policeman said as Kate leaned over to check.

Kate straightened up. "You've got to check them," she said, feeling stupid. "They've got mercury in them, and if they crack, they could make someone sick."

"Just a minute," the policeman said. He took a pair of latex gloves out of his pocket and put them on. Then he leaned over and picked up the lamp, turning it around and around until he could see every part of the light bulb. Then he put the lamp down on the floor again. "Okay. It doesn't seem to be broken."

"Are you expecting to get fingerprints off the lamp?" Kate demanded. "I thought you said the rock was thrown from the outside. Why would there be fingerprints on the lamp?"

"You can never be too careful," the policeman said stiffly.

Kate gave up and went back outside. A police van had just driven up, and the policewoman had approached it to talk to the technicians. Jack was still on the stairs, and Frank was talking to Tom, who was watching her.

Kate paused next to Jack. Jack looked up at her and shrugged.

"I told you before," he said, "if you're going to lie to people and use me as an alibi, you have to tell me about it first. Second time you lied to him. He's a little pissed."

Frank and Tom had both turned and were looking at her. Kate sighed.

She walked over to the two men, barely noticing the march of the crime technicians into her house.

"I don't see why they're going through all this," she said. "A rock through a window. They aren't going to be able to collect much evidence."

"Tom and I have been having a conversation about you," Frank said. "For instance, about where you've been today."

"You saw the line at the impound lot."

"And that was it?" Tom demanded. "You spent all this time getting your car out of impound? Five or six hours?"

"What do you think I've been doing?" Kate demanded, turning to face him for the first time. "You think I've got a secret life? You think I've got something going on I don't tell my own family about?"

"I think you've been freelancing, that's what I think," Tom said. "I think you've been playing private investigator—I think that's what you were doing last night, I think that's what you were doing today, and I think that's why there's a rock sitting in the middle of your living room."

Another van pulled up and parked at the curb. It belonged to Ace's Windows, the same company Kate had used to get all the back windows in the townhouse changed to vinyl only two years ago.

"I called the glass people," Frank said mildly. "They can't get a new window in until Monday, but they'll board the thing up to last 'til then."

"They won't be able to do that until the forensic people are gone," Tom said.

"Were the forensic people your idea?" Kate asked.

"Why don't I go over and talk to the glass people?" Frank said. "They're going to want some money."

"Somebody has to knock some sense into your head," Tom said.

"I've *got* sense in my head," Kate said furiously. "You're the one who told me you thought Ozgo was being set up. I believe that, too. And there's so much strange stuff going on and nobody is paying attention to it."

"I'm paying attention to it," Tom said. "And I've seen the rock, Kate. It's your rock. You had it in your bag that first day when you felt faint or whatever it was in court."

"All right," Kate said.

"Somebody took the trouble to get hold of something that belonged to you," Tom said. "And that means that this rock through this window is not random. Somebody was targeting you."

"Maybe I dropped it on the road," Kate said. "Maybe somebody came by and picked it up."

"'What were you really doing last night?" Tom demanded.

"I was doing what I said I was doing," Kate insisted. And it was true, too, as far as it went. Kate couldn't see how it would be possible to tell him about Richard Hamilton without taking the whole situation to a level that she didn't want to think about.

"So what are you not telling me?"

Before she could answer, Frank walked up and the mood broke.

"The glass people want to talk to you," he told Kate, "and the policewoman, too. Jack and I have already given statements."

"You were here," Kate said. "Did you see anything? Were you in any danger—?"

"We were both in the back. Jack was on the computer, and I was in the kitchen."

"Oh," Kate said. "Okay, I'll go talk to them."

"I don't like you freelancing, Kate. I don't like you looking into this thing when I'm not around. You can get yourself into serious trouble. That rock is the beginning of serious trouble."

"I know," she said, backing up. "I've got to go talk to these people."

★   ★   ★

If Kate had been the kind of person who drank alcohol in quantity, she would have done it that night. It was the longest night of her life—except for one year when Jack was a baby and had been running a high fever; she had been convinced he was going to die that night. Jack and Frank weren't interested in cutting her any slack.

"I said I thought you should take an interest in it," Frank said, "not that you should go running all over the place acting like Nancy Drew. And I don't think Tom is going to enjoy being Ned Nickerson."

"Ned Nickerson was hopeless," Kate said flippantly, desperate to escape to her bedroom. "He'd haul off to save Nancy from the villains and get caught himself, and then Nancy would have to save him."

"Beside the point," Frank said.

Kate managed to get into her room without too much more talk, but that didn't help either, because as soon as she did, she realized she was never going to sleep. The past two days had been insanely informative, and she couldn't stop the various elements from whirling through her mind.

And at the middle of it all was Kevin Ozgo, who either had or had not caused the death of Rafael Turner, who either had or had not kidnapped Chan Hamilton, who either was or was not being railroaded on the charges for which he had been brought to trial.

Kevin Ozgo. In some ways, he seemed like the least significant character in the whole mess. He wasn't a high-level operative in the military contracting trade. He wasn't a rich kid with a family full of entitled jerks to help him along. He hadn't even been an officer in the United States Army.

All the things Ozgo was accused of doing would have been done much more plausibly by Jed Paterson. Kate never got more than a sideways look at Paterson and the way he operated, but he scared the hell out of her. And both of the times she had actually set eyes on him, he'd looked menacing and dangerous.

The other thing that drove her crazy was the incident with Richard Hamilton. He'd been absolutely right. It was a breach of half a dozen laws and a hundred regulations for her to have been in that room with that computer without clearance. The fact that Ballard hadn't bothered to pull her clearances didn't change that. And the fact that she had been there with a camera phone was a breach of even more laws and regulations.

At three o'clock in the morning, she gave up on sleep. The house was quiet. She went out into the computer room and got printer paper and pencils.

She wrote down whatever she remembered from the attack on Turner's men. If something sinister was going on with the trial of Ozgo, certainly the friendly fire incident would be at the center of it. The most important of those things was that Turner, although killed in a raid, had not been killed in a raid led by Afghan insurgents. Instead, he'd been brought down by a General Solutions operation that had then been covered up at a level usually reserved for the secret assassinations of heads of state. The question was, why? Friendly fire incidents were not uncommon, even ones carried out by contractors. War wasn't a board game. Things went wrong.

Of course, the military would not like to admit that there had been such a huge screw-up and that they'd ended up killing people on their own side. The thing was, though, that the military usually documented these incidents. This time, somebody had given out false details not only of the nature of the incident but also of the date, time, and place where it had happened.

Maybe that was the key. Maybe the date, time, and place had been changed because it wasn't possible to completely cover up what had gone on. Maybe if you knew those things, you could look through open and public sources and piece the whole thing together.

That would have to mean that there was something about this friendly fire incident that was different and far worse than other friendly fire incidents.

But by then, Kate was beyond exhausted. All she could think of was Paterson, Turner, and the shriveled, terrified figure of Ozgo in the courtroom.

Somehow, Ozgo had to be the key to it all.

Look at it this way, she told herself. *Maybe the raid wasn't an accident or a matter of somebody's incompetence. Maybe Tom was right. Maybe the raid was on purpose. Maybe Paterson or the people he was hooked up with had a reason to want to be rid of Turner.*

It was one hell of an idea, and it only made sense if the cover-up went through the highest levels of the Pentagon.

★　★　★

Frank was in the kitchen when Kate walked in. He had eggs and bacon out and cooking, which smelled wonderful but also felt like an assault on her senses. She looked up at the wall clock and saw that it was almost exactly noon.

"Jack went out to the park with the Kramer kid," Frank said as Kate sat down. "I gave him a ten in case he wanted to get something to eat."

"You sound like you were trying to get rid of him."

"I wanted to talk to you for a bit."

Frank put a plate of eggs, bacon, and buttered toast in front of Kate. Kate stared at it as if food were a novel concept she was never going to get used to.

Frank sat down across the table. "Tom was worried about you," he said. "And I think maybe he had reason."

"I really wasn't doing anything all that crazy," Kate said. "I was just asking some questions. And, you know, checking the computer at work."

"Checking the Department of Defense computer?" Frank said.

"I was thinking we maybe shouldn't talk about that," Kate said. "I could get you into a lot of trouble."

"And it would be a terrible thing for a man of my age to spend the rest of his days under investigation on felony security charges."

Kate coughed and kept her eyes on her toast.

Frank sat there for a while, drinking coffee. Kate didn't look at him.

"You know," he said finally, "I meant what I said last night. I really didn't mean for you to run around acting like Nancy Drew. Or that other character . . . the Agatha Christie woman . . ."

"Miss Marple," Kate said. "I'm not old enough to be Miss Marple."

"You're old enough to get yourself killed if you act like an idiot."

"I'm less worried about getting killed than I am about ending up in jail," Kate said.

Frank harrumphed. "We've got plywood where the glass used to be in the living room," he pointed out.

"You were the one who thought I should look into this."

"I thought you should look into this the way reporters do," Frank said. "I thought you'd look into the obvious things and write an op-ed or something. Not get yourself into classified files."

"You know," Kate said innocently, "I never actually told you I did that. If anybody asks you what I said, the best you could do was tell them I went in to use the computers at work, and most of the computers at work aren't linked to the United States government."

"I don't really think that's the most sensible response to my concerns, Kate."

Kate took an enormous swallow of coffee and shrugged. "It probably doesn't make any difference anymore," she said. "Tom wants me to back off and shut up, and my guess is that's going to mean no more free rides into the courtroom on his reserved passes. And without a pass, I'm not getting into that courtroom at all. Especially with final arguments and the case going to the jury. They've got people who camp out on the courthouse steps overnight to get one of those open seats."

"Ah," Frank said. "Why is it you never think of the obvious things?"

"I am thinking of the obvious things," Kate said.

"Well, I'm more obvious than you are. Grab your coffee and come look at the computer for a second." Frank pulled out the chair and made Kate sit down. Then he tapped the space key to bring up the computer's monitor.

Kate found herself staring at a color picture of a whole slew of men and women in basic camo arranged in three rows and smiling broadly. Next to them was an older man in camo not smiling at all.

"That's their sergeant," Frank said. "Ignore him. Look here." He tapped the screen, indicating a young man almost exactly in the middle of the group.

Kate leaned forward and frowned. "He looks familiar."

"He ought to look familiar," Frank said. "That's Ozgo."

Kate tapped a couple of keys and made the image larger.

"My God," she said. "It is Ozgo. He looks twelve years old."

"He's nineteen in that picture," Frank said. "Remember how I told you there are always records out there of anything that happens in the armed forces? This is Ozgo's class at basic, taken on the day they graduated. Fort Bragg."

"Okay," Kate said. "But they wouldn't all have been sent to Afghanistan together, would they?"

"Actually, they almost certainly were," Frank said. "But at the moment, I want you to notice something. The first thing is this." Frank stepped forward and tapped a few keys. What came up was a long list of people and places.

"That," Frank said, "is the caption. Every soldier there and their hometowns. I tried to see if the unit had a Facebook page, but I couldn't find one, which is interesting in and of itself."

"Why?"

"Because Facebook is full of unit pages. Almost every unit in the army seems to have one. Except this unit. It fits in with the whole idea of making it seem as if Ozgo didn't exist in the military."

"Except there's this, and it shows he did."

"It's one of the first rules of covert operations. Once something is public, you can never get entirely rid of it. That's why, when you're running an op, you try to put the lid on from before the beginning. Even that doesn't work most of the time anymore. Everybody has too much of a web presence, as the people at Jack's school like to put it to me."

"You can't put a lid on something you don't know about yet," Kate said.

"Exactly," Frank agreed. "So whatever went on hadn't been thought of when this picture was taken. Nobody covered this up because nobody had any reason to cover it up."

"I'm surprised they didn't go back and get it later."

Frank tapped a few more keys. "This picture," he said, "I found on the website of a woman named Hannah Arles.

She's the sister-in-law of this woman here," Frank tapped the photograph, "and the website has no other mention of Ozgo's name or the name of the unit. The name of the woman in the photograph is Linda Blenham. Even if you were actively searching for every reference anywhere to Ozgo, there's a good chance you wouldn't have found this. I almost found it entirely by accident. I made a guess at Ozgo's term of service and then I went looking through the classes at Bragg. I couldn't find Ozgo, but I tried Googling the members of each of the classes in turn, and I finally came up with this."

"You must have been working all morning," Kate said.

"I have been," Frank said. "At least some of the people that Ozgo graduated basic training with would have had to be deployed with him in his same unit to Afghanistan. And some of those people would have had to be on hand when that attack happened. The times are just too short for Ozgo to have been completely separated from his original unit. For that to have happened, either Ozgo was something special, and I can't see that he was, or Ozgo would have to have screwed up in a major way, which I can't find any evidence of. I'll tell you what I did find, though. I found no evidence of the other American soldiers the papers said were also killed in that attack. They weren't in Ozgo's original unit, and they don't seem to have been in anybody else's original unit, either. Hell, most of them don't seem to exist."

"Wait," Kate said, feeling a chill run up her spine. "If the ones the papers said were there didn't exist, then that means that the ones who were there had to be . . . some of them could have been—"

"In Ozgo's training unit," Frank said. "Exactly. Once I knew that that had to be the case, I Googled the rest of the people in that photograph. I came up with three names. Sarah Bray. Eveta Elwin. Martin Edelman."

"Who are they?"

"They're people who should be here but aren't," Frank said. "They're listed as honorably discharged. The whole unit except for Ozgo himself is listed as honorably discharged. But here on Facebook, their relatives have put up information that says they're posted to places like Rio and Germany."

"You think they're undercover or something like that?" Kate asked.

"I think they're dead," Frank said. "I think they died in that attack. But before you go looking into that, you should look into something else."

"What?"

"This Sarah Bray? She's got a mother in Baltimore."

THIRTEEN

The name and address her father had found her were just a name and address: they could mean anything. For all Kate knew, she was about to drive into a maelstrom.

Drive, though, she definitely was going to do. Frank looked nonplussed.

"I didn't mean for you to go haring out there in person right this minute," he said.

"It's the weekend," Kate said. "It's relatively quiet. There won't be any rush hour traffic. And people are likely to be home."

"People are likely to be out doing errands. Or they might have activities at church."

"They'd have been in church this morning. They'll be home now."

"Some churches have Bible study and children's activities on the weekends."

"I'll be as fast as I can," Kate said.

Then she headed straight out the door.

At the best of times, Baltimore was a good two hours away, and to get there, she had to use the Beltway, the worst piece of road design in the history of creation. When she got through the Beltway and out the other side, she pulled into the compact little neighborhood where Marianna Bray was supposed to live.

It was a beautiful neighborhood, lined with small brick houses on neat, eight-acre plots. All the lawns were mowed. All the window boxes were full of flowers. All the front windows had white lace curtains pulled back to let in the sun.

Kate found number 486 Maldives Street right away. The mailbox on the wall next to the front door was painted red and blue and had a tiny figure of a bluebird on the front flap. There was a driveway next to the house, but no garage, and a monster SUV parked toward the back. It looked brand new and very expensive, both to buy and to run. Kate pulled in behind it and cut her engine.

It always seemed a lot easier in books when amateur detectives went around questioning people. The people they questioned always seemed very amenable to *being* questioned.

She got out of the car and headed for the front door. There were people in their front yards up and down the street, and she could tell that they were looking at her. This was the kind of neighborhood where people watched. And she probably made a very interesting figure on a boring afternoon.

When she got to the front door, she rang the doorbell. There was an instant response from somewhere inside—"I'm coming! I'm coming!"—and the sound of something hard hitting wood.

That something turned out to be a cane. It was a beautiful thing, made of polished dark wood and topped with a shined silver nob that reflected images better than a mirror.

A man's voice came from somewhere back in the house. "Mama, what did I tell you? I'll get the door. I said I'll get the door."

The tiny African American woman with the cane, frail and rickety and looking far from well, looked at Kate and shrugged. "That's Noah. That's my son. I named all my children from the Bible, and that worked out. Noah's a pastor at our church now. He went to seminary and got ordained and everything."

The man who came out from the back was neither tiny nor frail. He was a good six foot three and massively built, and his head was bald.

The man frowned when he saw Kate. "Is it my mother you're looking for or me?"

Kate hadn't really thought out this part. "My name's Kate Ford," she said, not even thinking about giving the Plymouth pseudonym. "I'm a freelance reporter. I'm working on a story about what happens to recruits when they finish basic, where they go, if they stay in the service, that kind of thing. I'm going to follow the lives of everybody in one unit, and I think from the information I have that one of those recruits may have been your . . . sister? Maybe. Her name is Sarah Bray."

"That's my daughter," the old lady piped up. "I told you, didn't I? I named all my children from the Bible. They all turned out fine. They all did. Sarah and Noah here and Judith and Ezekiel. Ezekiel never liked his name, though."

"Maybe you ought to come inside," Noah said. "Mama likes talking about Sarah. She likes talking about all of us."

"I'll get you some sweet tea," the old woman said.

Noah practically dragged Kate through the door and propelled her into the tiny living room.

"*I'll* get the sweet tea, Mama. You go sit down. You're not supposed to be tiring yourself out."

"It's not going to tire me out to get some sweet tea and put it on a tray."

"You can't carry a tray with that cane," Noah said.

The old lady allowed herself to be manhandled into a big armchair.

"Proud of all of them, that's what I am," she said. "And I've got every reason to be."

The sweet tea turned out to be very sweet, even by the standards of the South. Kate had to force herself not to blanch. Learning from her mistake the last time she lied about being a journalist, she took a notebook out of her bag and started to pretend to write things down in her own personal shorthand.

"We've been very fortunate," Noah was saying. "When Sarah was deployed to Afghanistan, we were worried as hell."

"People die there," the old lady pronounced solemnly.

"But it worked out all right," Noah said. "She was there for six months, and then she was routed out of there. They tell you they send soldiers back to the states after a combat deployment, but you know how it is. It doesn't always work out."

"So where is she now?" Kate asked. "I'm hoping to talk to her as part of the piece."

"She's in Rio de Janeiro, Brazil," the old lady said. "She sends us pictures from there all the time. Every month. Just like clockwork."

Noah nodded. "She's good about writing. And she seems like she's having a good time. I just wish she'd do one of those video chats where you can sit at the computer and see the person while you're talking to them."

"Noah bought me a computer," the old lady said. "And Judith taught me how to use it. She does things with computers where she works—"

"Software engineering, Mama," Noah said. "She's a software engineer."

"Sounds like she's making pillows," the old lady said. "And I know she isn't doing that. Graduated from Johns Hopkins right here in Baltimore. That's a good place to graduate from. You have to be real smart or they won't even talk to you."

"I graduated from Howard," Noah said.

"Nothin' wrong with Howard," the old lady said. "Ezekiel went to Howard, too. He's a lawyer, Ezekiel. Noah here thinks Ezekiel sold his soul to the devil because he works for some big corporation."

"He's a partner in a law firm, Mama. He has big corporations for clients."

"Sarah's going to make a career of the military," the old lady said. "She went to American University, and then she went into the service. I thought that was a fine thing, but I worried when she was in Afghanistan. She's a real women's libber, my girl, always wants the army to let women into combat because if you go into combat, you get promoted faster. I say it's a good thing they don't, even if it means it's going to take her a while to get where she wants to go."

"She does write every month," Noah said, "and she sends money, a lot of money. More than she should. The four of us, we always wanted to make sure Mama could rest easy in her old age."

"Well, I can do *that*," the old woman said.

"We all decided we'd all contribute," Noah said. "We decided that when we were still kids. I just worry about it sometimes with Sarah, because she must be sending us her whole paycheck. And she does it every month."

"She does other things," the old lady said. "Don't make it sound like it's just about money. She picked out this living room set."

"She did do that," Noah said. He frowned. Kate could see the lines of tension in his face. "She had it sent, just like that. Mama wrote her that the living room couch was getting threadbare and that she was going to try mending it, and the next thing we know, all these things showed up. Just like that. No warning or anything."

"They took away the old furniture, too," the old lady said. "That's the part I really liked about it. Usually, you get new furniture in, you've got to spend a couple of days finding something to do with the old things if you can't give them away, and I never was able to give anything away. Then you've got to haul them down to the curb and pay the garbage extra to pick them up."

By now, Noah was so tense, his face looked paralyzed. "I don't like to think of Sarah sending all her money or spending it all to buy things for Mama," he said. "It's not right and it's not necessary. Mama doesn't want Sarah to practically starve just to send new furniture. She knows she doesn't have to do anything on her own. There's the rest of us. We all get things done around here."

"I told you," the old lady said. "She thinks the army isn't good enough. Not next to what the rest of you got done. She's trying to make it up to me."

"She doesn't have to make it up to you," Noah said sharply.

"I know that," the old lady said. "And I told her that. But you know Sarah."

Noah looked as if he didn't believe any of it.

Kate put her pad and pen back in her bag. She had managed to finish the sweet tea, but she didn't intend to have any more.

"She bought that car out there, too," the old lady said. "I had to get a step stool just to get into it. It's that high off the ground."

"Well, I think it's an inspiring story," Kate said bravely. "And I thank you both for talking to me. I won't take up any more of your time."

Noah stood up from where he had been sitting near his mother's recliner. "You parked around here somewhere? I'll walk you to your car."

★   ★   ★

When they exited the house, Noah carefully closed both the main door and the screen. Kate's car was still safely in the driveway, not all that far away, but he started walking her toward it anyway.

"There's something wrong, and I know it," he said when they were halfway there. "She doesn't get it. She's not that good about money. We never had any when we were all growing up. She just hammered on ahead and got it all done. But there isn't any way Sarah's sending entire living room sets on what she makes."

"Maybe she's paying for them over time?" Kate suggested. "Maybe she's just making the monthly payments out of her salary."

Noah shook his head vigorously. "See that SUV? We've got the pink slip for it. Paid in full. And I looked it up. Costs nearly sixty thousand dollars."

"What do you think is going on?"

"I don't know that I think anything is going on," Noah said. "I know what the usual thing would be. Drugs. Especially the places she's been. Afghanistan. Southeast Asia for a while. South America. Lots of drugs. And where there's lots of drugs, there's usually lots of money. But I also know Sarah. And that doesn't sound like Sarah."

"Maybe she's got some kind of job on the side."

"I don't think the military lets you do that. You said you were going to try to talk to her?"

"Yes," Kate said, feeling a little miserable about lying. "To all the members of the unit who are still alive."

"They can do those video chats right from combat zones. It shouldn't be all that hard to do one of them from Brazil."

"I suppose not," Kate said.

"I want to have one of those video chats with Sarah," Noah said. "If you get a chance to talk to her, tell her that. She's an open book, that girl. She always has been. If I can see her face to face, I'll know if anything's wrong."

"I'll be sure to make a point of it."

"I've sent a dozen letters asking her, and it's like I never sent anything at all. She writes once a month but ignores anything I've said, and the letters are always for Mama, anyway. And it would kill Mama if there's anything like drugs. It would kill her."

"I can see that it would."

"Yeah," Noah said, his face looking suddenly bleak. "This is a nice neighborhood, you know, but it wasn't where we grew up. That was a couple of miles that way, and it was bad. Judith and I bought this house for Mama. It was all working out all right. And now there's this."

"You don't know anything's wrong yet," Kate said.

Noah looked grim. "I know there's something wrong, all right," he said. "And so do you."

★   ★   ★

The story Noah had told had to be bad news. Kate was sure of it. She didn't believe Sarah could be making the kind of money that would buy the kinds of gifts she was sending home, at least not as an ordinary soldier. And the lack of direct contact—that wasn't just bad, it was ominous. Obviously, somebody somewhere wanted Sarah out of the way. Whether they'd left her alive was the question. Kate wondered if the same sort of thing was happening to all the soldiers in Ozgo's old unit.

Kate was working out a plan to investigate each of the soldiers in that unit that she could find when the eighties rock station she had been not quite listening to broke for the news, and a name caught her attention.

Flanagan.

Bill Flanagan.

She turned the sound up: "Police are treating the death as suspicious. Fairholt Bridge has been closed for repairs for three months. Police have erected a new barrier farther along the access road and designated the area a crime scene."

Crime scene, Kate thought.

Like everybody else in the area, Kate was familiar with the Fairholt Bridge. It was a shorter and more efficient route to a lot of things than the regular highway, and she had used it dozens of times. But the Fairholt Bridge was closed for repairs and had been for months. All the traffic that normally would use it had been detoured in a big loop that took them out to Virginia 7.

When Kate got to the detour signs, she ignored them. At first, that didn't make any difference. Then she began to see cars, all of them stopped, and, ahead, a pair of police officers with their patrol cars parked crosswise to keep both cars and people from getting any closer. Behind the patrol cars was a mass of yellow crime scene tape.

Kate pulled off to the side well back from the last parked car. She got out without bothering to lock up and headed for the knot of people. The police were bound to look at her as just another rubbernecker, unless Tom himself was here, and she doubted it.

Most of the people had moved as close to the crime scene as they could. As far as Kate could tell, it wasn't doing them any good. The barrier had been placed far back enough so that there was little chance of seeing what was going on.

A few people were hanging back, just milling around. Kate chose one—middle aged and looking vaguely like Frank—and sidled up to him.

"Hello?" she said. "Do you know what's going on?"

The man turned to her. He looked less like Frank when she saw him close up. "It's Bill Flanagan," he said. "The head homicide guy who was testifying in that big case. There was an accident."

"There was a lot of commotion on the road," Kate said. "I—he's dead?"

"Went off the bridge," the man said. "Word is he went right over the side of the Fairholt Bridge down there. Supposed to be an accident. Accident my ass."

"They've got crime scene tape up," Kate said. "They can't really think it's an accident."

"Yeah, well, they've got crime scene tape up because they know nobody would believe it. Got drunk and went off the side of the bridge. That's what they were telling people when I first got here."

"And that's not possible?"

The man gave her the kind of look he'd visit on a complete idiot. "This is a construction site. If you accidentally got onto the roads that lead up to the bridge on a weekday in the daytime, it wouldn't matter because there would be equipment everywhere. At night, they've got barriers up."

"I don't understand," Kate said. "If it's all blocked off like that, how did Flanagan get onto the bridge?"

"That's a good question, isn't it?" the man said. He sounded triumphant. "They said Flanagan got into a car dead drunk and then drove out here and went off the bridge. But the roads were all blocked up. If he got into his car and forgot the bridge was closed, seriously, he'd have come to a barrier; he'd have had to stop. Then he'd have to get out of his car and move those barriers, and they're fucking concrete."

"Oh," Kate said. She looked up at the crowd at the barrier. The man had stopped paying attention to her and gone back to milling around.

There was, she decided, no harm in trying. She made her way through the little crowd of people and all the way to the barrier. The two patrolmen were steadfast, and they determinedly would not make eye contact with her.

Another middle-aged man was crammed up almost next to one of the patrol cars, and Kate tried him.

"Hey," she said.

This man was younger and had a beard, but he was just as contemptuous. "Don't bother," he said. "They're not giving anything out."

Kate could see that. "They haven't made any public statements?"

The man rolled his eyes. "They're not going to make any public statements," he said. "The whole thing's a mess. But I've got a police band."

"Do you?" All Kate wanted to do was keep him talking.

"Yeah, and they were doing a lot of talking on it," the younger man said. "There was an anonymous call that came in at two thirty-five this morning saying a car had driven over the side of Fairholt Bridge, and it was submerged entirely in the water. They were all annoyed at it. They thought it was a hoax, but you can't let that kind of thing go, so they sent a couple of patrolmen out."

"You were listening to the police band at two thirty in the morning?" Kate said.

"It was Saturday night, wasn't it? Still, I didn't pay it no mind until the stuff started coming over about it being Bill Flanagan."

"And they found the car?" Kate said.

"They did."

"What about the barriers?"

"The northbound road had one of the barriers pulled aside."

"I still don't understand," Kate said. "Bill Flanagan is supposed to have driven out there for some reason unknown, stopped, pulled aside a barrier, and then driven over the bridge and over the side because he was . . . drunk? He did all this because he was drunk? Or because he wanted to commit suicide? I thought the barriers were heavy. If they're that heavy, how did he move them around when he was drunk and, well, out of shape?"

"Exactly," the younger man said.

Kate looked at the two patrol cars and past them, but although she could see a little more from here, she couldn't see much. There was a large piece of equipment. That was probably what they were using to pull the car out of the river. Since they knew Flanagan was dead, they must already have the body.

Kate thought of Lucy Leeds and her story about the man who came to Flanagan's house and sat in the driveway.

"Okay," she said.

It was just a placeholder response so she didn't seem rude. She wanted to get back to her car and back home. She wanted to talk to Tom. Tom would know the particulars of this.

She was halfway back to the spot she'd parked her car when a man stepped out of the crowd barely a foot in front of her. He was very tall and dressed in black, and Kate recognized him instantly.

It was Jed Paterson. Kate had never been close to him before. His eyes were so cold, they felt like death.

Paterson was running those eyes up and down Kate's body, and Kate backed away instinctively. Then he looked directly into her eyes and smiled.

Kate maneuvered around him and headed to her car. It took all the control she had not to run.

FOURTEEN

Part of Kate wanted to closet herself in the computer room and find out as much about Jed Paterson as she could. Instead, she confined herself to checking the news websites and the television news for information about what had happened to Flanagan. It took the police until nearly six o'clock to finally admit that what they had on their hands was probably murder. Other than that, they weren't admitting much.

It was a good evening on the home front, though. Jack and Frank were both in good moods, and Kate made a point of taking the cooking seriously. They actually had dinner together for the first time in forever. Then they sat around for four hours playing Monopoly. Kate found herself forced to admit that she'd been missing "normal" for quite a while.

"You'd don't have to miss it if you don't want to," Frank said when she brought the subject up. "You've just got to decide you want to."

Kate didn't know what that meant, but she let it go. Jack was already "in bed," meaning in his room reading something. She went to bed herself.

When she got up on Sunday morning, Jack was in the computer room working on a school assignment and Frank was doing the Sunday crossword in the paper. Kate didn't want to interrupt either of them, so she got herself a cup of coffee and went back to her bedroom. She even made the bed before she sat down on it. Then she got out her laptop and went to work.

She checked the news sites for more information on the Flanagan murder and got not much more than she'd had the night before. She started to look up Jed Paterson but then stopped. Paterson made her scared. It was more doom and gloom than she wanted for a Sunday morning.

Instead, she got the Facebook account for Kaitlyn Plymouth up and looked to see what was coming through her newsfeed. Most of it was cats. There were dozens of cats. Maybe hundreds of cats. One of the people "Kaitlyn Plymouth" had friended appeared to think of nothing but cats. Even her profile picture was a cat.

She had six notifications. The first one was the confirmation that Brayde had accepted her friend request.

Kate wasn't really surprised. She'd learned enough about Brayde from Tom and Google to figure that he wasn't going to turn down a friend request from nearly anyone in a short dress.

When Kate looked around some more, she found a message: *That night at the Gresham was unfuckingbelievable. We should do it again.*

Kate had no idea what the Gresham was. Probably a bar. Probably an expensive bar with a bad reputation. Did

Brayde just think he recognized her from a night when he couldn't recognize anything? Knowing Brayde, the woman he thought she was had been an expert in abandoned and acrobatic sex. *Enthusiastic* abandoned and acrobatic sex.

She clicked on Brayde's name. The profile was as to be expected: St. Alban's, of course, and then Dartmouth, with membership in Sigma Chi. Then there was law school. Dalton Brayde might be an unmitigated ass, but he wasn't stupid.

Kate checked out a couple of other things, none of which were really interesting. There was a picture of him at the age of eight or nine at somebody's dance class. He was wearing a tuxedo and looked cherubic. There was a picture of an enormous sailboat called the *Easy Virtue*. There was no mention of the firm he worked for or even of the fact that he was a lawyer.

Kate checked out a few pictures, saw nothing interesting, and navigated back to her (fake) page. Now that she thought about it, she had no firm idea of what she had expected to get out of friending Brayde on Facebook.

But a notification had appeared that Brayde had also invited Kaitlyn to an event.

Come to the Bonfire and Burn Up Your Weekend.

She checked the date. It was today. She checked the time on her watch.

The bonfire had started half an hour ago.

She got up and headed for her closet. She had to have something suitable for a picnic thrown by a satyr. And although she didn't know what she could get out of Brayde, it wouldn't hurt to find out.

Brayde had invited his entire friend list to this bonfire thing, and Kate had seen by looking through his profile that almost all of his "friends" were women whose profile pictures were suitable for placement in a Victoria's Secret catalog.

The clothes she'd found weren't quite right for the kind of party Brayde was probably throwing, but she couldn't see herself buying another outfit just to fit the profile. She compromised by tying her T-shirt in the back so it hugged her chest. Then she pulled her hair into a ponytail and put on enough makeup to constitute a disguise for a bank robbery. Then she got into her car and looked at herself in the rearview mirror. The sight made her wince. She was making a hash of this.

Hash or not, she was determined.

It turned out the bonfire was being held in a broad field in the Burning Tree Country Club. The field was all the way at the back and not marked for golf. The clubhouse was out of sight.

Kate parked in a small lot just to the side of the opening in the stone wall. As soon as she got out of the car, she realized that she'd had no reason to worry about the way she was dressed. She'd underestimated how drunk everybody would already be.

The bonfire itself was huge, a massive circular thing well off the road. Most of the people at the party were staying well away from it. At the edge of the broad field, near the trees and a good four hundred yards from the fire, there was a table set up with bottles of alcohol arranged on it. Behind the table stood a small man in a tuxedo making drinks. He looked like he'd just swallowed vinegar.

The people attending the party were, as Kate had prophesied, almost all women, and they were dressed any which way. Most of them looked expensive. There was nobody checking invitations or checking guests off a clipboard list. Attila the Hun could have walked in here and nobody would have noticed.

Right then, Kate spotted Brayde himself. He was standing between two women. He had his arms around both of them. They appeared to be holding him up. He also had a tall, metal mug in one hand with a top on it so that none of the liquid could spill.

Kate went straight across the lawn to Brayde. He was obviously hammered, so there was no reason to be subtle.

She'd just about got to him when she recognized one of the two women. It was Chan Hamilton, and Kate could tell right away that Chan was not even a little bit drunk. She wasn't even a little bit happy, either. In fact, she looked murderous.

Brayde was weaving back and forth. Every once in a while, he seemed to half-lose his balance so that he fell forward on the two women and looked as if he was about to drop to the ground. Then he righted himself again, and Kate realized that every single item of his clothing had a tiny embroidered whale on it: Vineyard Vines, the choice of people who thought Izod and L.L. Bean were too cheap.

Kate was close when Brayde finally noticed she was there. He immediately took his arm from around Chan's neck and staggered in Kate's direction.

"A new one!" he shouted. "I've got a new one!"

Chan stayed standing right where she was, staring daggers at Brayde's back.

Brayde pulled his right arm from around the other woman so that he could stagger faster. He was in front of Kate before she was ready for him.

"Well, *hello*, whoever you are. Did you just walk in off the street? I don't know you. Or maybe I do know you. If you're from Vegas, I'm not admitting to anything."

"I'm not from Vegas," Kate said. "I'm from Facebook."

"Facebook!" Brayde cried. "I love Facebook. You can meet a dozen screws a day on Facebook." He threw his right arm around Kate's neck.

She pushed him off her. "Get away from me!" she demanded. "What's wrong with you?"

"There's nothing wrong with me," Brayde said. "I'm ready and willing to go. You know how you hear all that stuff about alcohol getting a man down? Not this man. Nothing gets this man down."

"Nothing gets you down because you eat Viagra like candy," Chan said.

"Don't believe her," Brayde said. "Channie and I grew up together. Yes we did. I even asked her to marry me once. Only woman I ever asked to marry me. She turned me down. She likes men in uniform. Do you like men in uniform? I've got camo boxers, if you want to see them."

At just that moment, a man emerged out of the crowd. Kate hadn't noticed this man when she first came in; if she had, she would have known immediately who he was. There were those elongated ear lobes. And there were the clothes, still all black, even on this bright, sunny, early afternoon.

Brayde threw his arms around Kate's shoulders one more time and began to stagger toward the drink table.

"We've got to get you caught up," he said. "You should've primed yourself before coming over. Put a little something in a coffee mug." He waved his coffee mug. Kate caught the little whale on one side of it.

They reached the drinks table. The tuxedoed bartender stared at both of them without expression.

"Give the lady a white lightning," Brayde said.

The bartender started to work.

"What's a white lightning?" Kate asked.

Dalton Brayde laughed. "It's a secret recipe. Looks just like water."

The bartender had finished pouring what looked like an ocean of vodka into the mug and started on the gin.

"Is there anything in that besides alcohol?" Kate asked.

"Why'd you need anything in it besides alcohol?" Dalton demanded. "Christ, I don't know what's wrong with people these days."

The bartender had started on the rum.

"Couldn't I just have a martini?" Kate asked. She didn't want a martini, but it was the only cocktail she could think of. She just didn't want that—thing.

The bartender had the top on the mug and shook it vigorously. When he was done, he handed the mug to Kate.

"Drink up!" Brayde said cheerfully.

Kate had no idea what to do next.

Then help came from an unexpected quarter. The unknown woman had disappeared into the crowd, but Chan hadn't. Chan walked directly up to Brayde and shoved him. She shoved him hard enough that he let go of Kate and stumbled backward. He fell flat on his ass.

"What the fuck," he said.

"Leave the woman alone. You invited her to a party. You invited half the universe to a party. Let people have a party."

Brayde got to his feet slowly and awkwardly. "Fucking bitch," he said. He turned to Kate. "Channie's here to find out what's up with her boyfriend."

"He's not my boyfriend, Dalton," Chan said.

"I'm her boyfriend," a deep voice said.

Kate had been so engrossed in Brayde's behavior and Chan's anger that she hadn't noticed Paterson coming up behind them. Now that she did notice, she was more and more sure she would never want to be anywhere alone with him.

Except—Kate tried to get him straight in her mind. Paterson was a terrifying man. Just standing in the middle of a field holding a drink, he looked poised to kill. His eyes were both cold and laser-focused. They were also a bright, brilliant green.

"He's a fucking basket case is what he is," Brayde said.

"There's only one reason to put you on a criminal case, Dalton," Chan said, "and that's if you want to lose it. And that's fine with me. I want to see him in jail. But I also want to know what I'm in for."

"How the hell am I supposed to know what you're in for?" Dalton said. "I haven't gotten my marching orders from St. Reggie."

Paterson took a long swig of his St. Pauli Girl. "I think the issue at hand, Brayde, is that this is beginning to look like a setup. It looks like so much of a setup, we've decided we want to know what kind of defense you're going to put on."

"You mean *you* want to know," Brayde said to Paterson. "You're jerking Channie around like she's a rag doll."

"Nobody jerks me around," Chan said.

"You can screw up a defense so badly, the verdict gets set aside," Paterson said. He was very patient. Kate didn't think he'd blinked the entire time he was staring at Dalton Brayde.

Brayde shrugged. "He's going to throw himself on the mercy of the court."

"Is this my father's idea?" Chan demanded. "Is this one more of his twisty little games?"

Paterson put a hand on Chan's elbow. Chan stopped talking immediately.

Paterson turned his attention to Kate. "It's an interesting question—as is what you're doing here." he said.

Kate started to repeat her story about Facebook, but Paterson was staring at her so steadily, she found herself losing all sense of reality.

"I think you're right," Chan said, turning to Paterson. "I think there is something going on here."

"I've got a call coming in from Washington," Paterson said. "I have to take it on the landline."

"That's fine. I can take care of this," Chan said.

Then she grabbed Kate by the wrist and started pulling her away.

It was only at the last moment that Kate was able to figure out what was going on between Chan and Paterson: sex and hatred. They were so sexually attracted to each other, the air between them was explosive, but they also couldn't stand each other.

Kate was thinking frantically, trying to figure out what she was supposed to do next, how to talk to Chan, when Chan said, "Where is your car?"

"It's in this little parking lot on the edge over there," Kate said.

"Good," Chan told her. "Mine is out in front of the clubhouse. It's not convenient, and besides, everybody on the planet can recognize it. We'll use yours."

"Use mine for what?"

Chan stopped. They were well away from the drinks table now, and Brayde had lost interest in them. He was staggering around through the little crowd of female guests.

"I know who you are," she said. "I don't know your name, but I know who you are. You were in court with that police detective, the one who was the first person running the case. I asked my father. You work for Almador."

"Kate Ford," Kate said.

"Let's go."

★ ★ ★

Seeing Chan up close was not like seeing her in pictures or even in person from afar. Her body language was stiff and cold and more than a little angry. Her posture was straight and unyielding. Her clothes were so expensive, they almost smelled like money. Then there was the tennis bracelet, a thin circlet of diamonds set in platinum with a little ruby heart at the clasp. Kate was willing to bet the stones were all real, just as she was willing to bet that the thin, red hairband holding back Chan's short, black hair hadn't been picked up at Target for $2.95.

But it wasn't the money that held Kate's attention. It was the thin bead of bruises just along the underside of Chan's right jaw. The dots were so tiny, it was almost impossible to see them, but Kate knew exactly what they were. She'd seen dozens of photographs of women with those marks in every domestic violence report to hit the local news.

"Somebody hit you," she said.

She hadn't noticed how fast they were walking. Chan stopped dead, and Kate realized they had already made it all the way out to the little parking lot.

Chan looked out over the cars and sighed.

"Crap," she said. "You're going to be a pain in the ass."

"There are bruises on your jaw," Kate said. "Little bruises. You couldn't get bruises like that in that place by falling down. Someone had to—"

"Which one is your car?"

Kate gestured to her spot along the edge near the road, and Chan marched her along.

"It's incredible the things people try to get away with," Chan said. "It really is. Get your keys and open up."

They were right next to the car. Kate got out her keys and opened the front passenger door.

"Go ahead," Chan said. "Go get in behind the wheel. I'm not going to drive this thing."

"Why are we driving?" Kate demanded.

"I told you. My own car is in the front lot. You're going to drive me to the front lot. So get in and drive," Chan said. "I don't have time for this."

Kate got behind the wheel. The entire situation seemed surreal. First Chan had saved her from the clutches of Brayde, who'd turned out to be even more of a jerk than he was rumored to be. Then Paterson had shown up. Now Chan sat in the passenger seat of Kate's car, quietly furious and loaded for bear.

Hostile, Kate thought. That was the word. And it fit. Chan was widely reputed to be a hostile witness for the prosecution in the kidnapping trial, which was one of the things that had fed the media frenzy about the trial. Why would a kidnap victim be hostile to the idea of trying her kidnapper? Especially when she so obviously wanted the man convicted.

Kate put the keys in the car and started it up.

"You've got to give me directions," she said.

Chan did not say anything. She stared out the windshield at the line of trees that made the barrier between the parking lot and the road.

Kate had read once that people find it very hard to sit in silence when another person is present. She now found that she couldn't stop talking.

"I was really surprised to see you there," she babbled, feeling like an idiot. "I should have realized you'd know Brayde. I mean, he works for the law firm that handles some work for Almador, doesn't he? And—"

"We grew up together," Chan said.

"Pretty amazing coincidence. I mean—"

"For God's sake," Chan said. "Stop saying 'I mean.' You sound like you're in junior high. Of course it isn't a coincidence. Everybody knows everybody out here. Don't you know that? We all go to the same schools. We all belong to the same clubs. We all go to each other's deb parties. And yes, we all get hired by each other's fathers. Which is a damned good thing for Dalton, because he couldn't get hired by anybody else."

Kate felt miserably embarrassed. "He did seem—I mean—"

There was an exasperated snort from Chan.

"I mean," Kate said again, "well, he didn't seem to me to be your type."

"Dalton Brayde isn't anybody's type," Chan said. "Except maybe for cheap girls who think they'll be able to get hold of some of his money, which they can't, because Dalton's father is not an idiot. You don't look like one of those kinds of girls to me."

"Oh," Kate said, "no, of course not. I just got the invitation and I thought I'd—"

"You thought you'd what? Come see how the other half lives? Never mind. You don't care how the other half lives. I can tell. You thought you'd come out and see if you could pump Dalton about the trial."

"I was just curious," Kate said. "It's a big deal, and it's got connections with my boss, and—"

"Oh, stop it," Chan said. "You didn't just get curious. You were with that cop, the one who kept saying there was something wrong. I'm rescued from a kidnapping and the man is telling me there's something wrong. Like I made it all up. My father said you were in a reserved seat. That means you must have some kind of connection. I just don't know what that connection is."

Kate hardly knew where to start. "I was just curious," she insisted. "I only met Tom there at the courthouse on the first day. And then, I don't know, everything just seemed odd. Ozgo had these expensive attorneys, pro bono, but only the second string—"

"Brayde isn't second string," Chan said. "Brayde is bottom of the barrel. You only send Dalton to court if you want to lose."

"I thought I could find out about the trial," Kate said. "I just thought he'd be easy to talk to."

"That he'd be so drunk, he wouldn't notice he was telling you things he shouldn't tell anybody?"

"Something like that," Kate said.

"Well, you're shit out of luck," Chan said. "I thought the same thing. And he's drunk enough today to give away the nuclear launch codes if he had them. Except he doesn't have them."

"You were pumping him, too," Kate said.

"For an hour before you showed up," Chan said. "So was Jed, and nobody holds out on Jed, no matter how much they want to. Dalton is a void. And a jackass. And worse."

"I'm beginning to get that impression," Kate admitted.

"I bet. Get the car in gear. Turn right when you come out of the parking lot and follow the road."

Kate bumped carefully through the parking lot, which was only sort of graveled. When she got to the road, she turned right as Chan had directed her, then picked up speed until she was going forty. The road was clear of traffic. The surrounding land was free of people.

"It's a bit of a drive," Chan said. "But all you have to do is follow this road and always veer right. You came out here to pump Dalton, and that means you're up to something. I want to know what you're up to. I want to know who you're working for," Chan said. "It has to be my father or that cop. How much do you know about that cop?"

"You mean Tom? I don't know him much at all. He took pity on me and let me use his spare reserved seat. He gave me a ride when I needed to help my father. There really hasn't been anything else."

"How well do you know Bill Flanagan?"

Kate was astonished. "The police detective? The one who just died?"

"Did you know he was building a house? Brand new, great big house, out over on the other side of Montgomery

County. Fifty-five hundred square feet. An octagonal deck. A hot tub that seats fourteen. He bought the land just two weeks after he was put in charge of Kevin's case. Don't you think that's interesting?"

"I don't know."

"Want to know the name of the architects?" Chan said. "Holloway and Maine. Funnily enough, they're the same architects who are going to rebuild my house. They're not a low-rent operation. In fact, I think they're the most expensive architects in the entire DC region."

"You think Flanagan was taking bribes?" Kate said. "Or blackmailing someone? Your father? But if Ozgo is actually guilty, your father wouldn't have to bribe Flanagan to arrest him."

Chan leaned forward. "The entrance is going to be on your right, and it's hard to see. No gates until you come up the drive a little. When you get to the gates, stop."

There was a curve within a curve. She turned right as directed and found herself on a broad gravel drive, broad enough for three lanes of traffic, except that there were no lanes. There were trees on either side, though, tall ones that bent in toward each other over the road and made a leafy tunnel.

The gates came soon enough, but they also seemed to come out of nowhere. Kate pulled the car up to them and stopped.

Chan opened her window and stuck her head out and waved. "Jackson? It's me with a friend. If you could just—"

Jackson made no sound. He did not come out of the booth Kate assumed he was occupying. She could see the booth but not the man. The gates opened as if by themselves. She put the car back in gear and rolled through.

"When you get to the end of this, there will be a roundabout. My car's in the big lot to the left. Just drop me at the front entrance and leave." Chan paused. "I don't know whose side you're on."

"I don't know whose side you want me to be on," Kate said.

"Jed told me all about it," Chan said. "Maybe Kevin has PTSD now, but he didn't then. He should have known what he was doing. Instead, he was out there, screwing off and not following orders, and Raf got killed because of it."

"Jed told you Ozgo wasn't following orders and that was why Rafael was killed?" Kate asked, a little confused. "You mean you know that Jed was there the night Rafael died?"

"Don't be ridiculous," Chan said. "Jed was in the military. They all hear these things."

"Okay," Kate slowed as she approached Chan's parking lot, and Chan spent no more time waiting. She was out of the car and striding away before Kate had time to stop.

FIFTEEN

The first surprise of that Monday morning was Tom pulling into the driveway just as Jack was headed out the door. By then, Kate had been up for an hour puttering around, unsure what to do next.

The good news was that she had not been awakened by one of Evans's campaign vans. Granted, she'd gotten up at four thirty, which was far too early for all but the most insane campaign vehicle, but no van had shown up in the hours since. That had been an unalloyed blessing.

No one else was up when she first came out of her bedroom. She stopped for a moment to look at the plywood still covering the living room window. It looked just as ugly as before. Thankfully, the glass people were coming to install a new window today.

She walked by it and went into the computer room. Then she changed her mind, went into the kitchen, and made coffee. Only after she had a full cup of absolutely black coffee did she go to the computer. She put the coffee cup down on the little side table and brought up the home screen. Frank had left her several bookmarked pages concerning the members of Ozgo's class at basic, but Kate bypassed those for a moment to give herself a chance to poke around and wake up while she was doing it.

The news sites were largely uninteresting, both nationally and locally, except for more of the usual nothing-in-particular about Flanagan's death.

There was news about the Ozgo trial, but it amounted to announcing that the case was supposed to go to the jury today or tomorrow, depending on how long summations took.

Kate gave just a moment's thought to whether she ought to go out to the courthouse right that minute and see if she could get one of the public seats. Then she remembered the crush of people on the first day and dismissed the idea as lunacy.

Feeling at a loss for something to do, she began to look at the material her father had left her. Most of it was second or third hand, blogs, websites, and Facebook pages posted by parents, siblings, wives, or lovers. Kate had seen most of it yesterday, both before she went to that wretched bonfire and after.

Kate couldn't stop being amazed at how similar all these websites and blogs were: lots of pictures, lots of promises of love and support, practically no specifics on the soldiers themselves. It was possible there were no specifics to post, since a lot of things about deployment to a war zone would be classified. But *were* these people deployed to a war zone?

She hit a Facebook page for a man named Robert Edward Lawrence Jr., known to all his friends as Flip. The page had been put up by Flip's girlfriend, who called herself Sil. Flip and Sil. It made Kate's head ache.

There were dozens of pictures on the page: Flip and Sil at junior prom at Hillsboro Consolidated High School in Hillsboro, Oklahoma; Flip and Sil at senior prom; Flip and Sil on the beach; Flip and Sil in a convertible with the top down. Beneath those, there were pictures of Flip in uniform, sometimes by himself and sometimes with other people. There was that picture of the whole basic class on the day of their graduation that Frank had also found somewhere else. There was a formal photographic portrait in dress uniform.

She scrolled a little more and stopped: here was a photograph labeled "Flip and Kev," and the "Kev" was very definitely Ozgo. Kate stared at the picture as if it could tell her something, but all it did was confirm what she already knew. Before the attack, Ozgo had been young and fresh faced and probably a little naïve. He'd certainly not been the kind of person you'd expect to end up being on trial for kidnapping and arson.

Outside the computer room's small window, the sun was coming up, and Kate could hear sounds in the rest of the townhouse: water running and people moving around. She went back to flipping through the pages Frank had bookmarked for her. There was a feature on CNN about how soldiers' families tried to help protect them by buying them extra body armor.

She was listlessly scanning through the piece when she saw a picture that looked familiar but wasn't exactly. There were no people in it, just what looked at first sight like a fighter jet. Kate looked at the caption.

The X980 Barrier Drone is implicated in six separate friendly fire incidents and is believed by soldiers to be dangerous whenever it is used.

Kate stared at the picture for a little longer, then maximized the image.

She stared at the tip of the drone's nose.

Painted there was the legend "X980," but above it read, "Robotix."

★   ★   ★

Breakfast was not a happy meal. Frank was calm enough, but Jack was furious. He was furious about the window. He was furious about her trip to Baltimore, even though he hadn't been at the time. He was furious about everything.

Usually, Jack's anger took the form of lengthy, oddly adult-sounding lectures. This morning, it took the form of stubborn silence. Kate couldn't get him to tell her what he was working on, what he was doing with the track team, what he was reading, or even what video game he was playing in his spare time. Questions were met with monosyllables, when they were met with anything at all. All of Jack's longer sentences were directed at Frank. Frank looked increasingly bemused.

Jack had marched out of the kitchen without a good-bye to anybody when the doorbell rang. Jack got it on his way out.

"Oh, you," he said.

Kate got up to find out who the "you" was, but by then, Tom had come all the way back and was standing in the kitchen door.

"Not a good morning, I take it?" Tom said as he came in and sat down.

"Jack's just being thirteen this morning," Frank said mildly. "Tomorrow he'll take another whack at being fifty-three. You want some coffee?"

"No," Tom said, surprising Frank. "We're in something of a hurry. I just came to pick up Kate."

"You never pick me up," Kate said.

"I've decided it's more sensible than letting you wander around on your own," Tom said. "And I've got news, which you may or may not have heard."

"What news?" Kate asked. She was still standing. It made her feel a little silly. She sat down. She wanted more coffee, even if Tom didn't.

She poured herself a cup.

"I thought you'd stopped talking to me," she said.

Tom brushed this statement away.

"Have you been listening to the news?" Tom asked.

"If you mean the news about Flanagan dying," Kate said, "yes, I did. It would have been hard to avoid it."

"Did the news report that the body had been in the water more than twenty-four hours?"

That hit home. "Wait," Kate said. "That would mean that it had to have happened on the night that we went over there."

"Exactly."

"My God," Kate said. She went back over their meeting with Flanagan in her head. Then she bit the bullet and decided to tell Tom what she hadn't told him, because she was afraid he'd be furious with her. "You know when you were in talking to Flanagan?" she asked.

"I do," Tom said ruefully. "We had a bar brawl without the bar."

"I got out of the car and went next door," Kate said. "To the house on the right. There's an old lady over there named Lucy Leeds."

"You think she might have seen something? Later that night, maybe, after we left?"

"She's got binoculars and not a whole lot else to do."

★　★　★

It was a good thing Tom had decided to let Kate use his partner's reserved seat, because the courthouse and everything near it had exploded into madness. Kate remembered the very first day of the trial. She'd thought that was insane, but this was much, much worse. For one thing, there were many more people. As eager as the public had been to see the opening of the trial, they had been nowhere near as interested as they now were at the close. There was so much pushing and shoving, the police had had to put up a cordon around the courthouse steps. Two police officers stood right in front of the ascent to the court's front door and stopped every person trying to get through, asking for identification and destination.

The crowd was packed in so closely, Tom didn't even try to navigate it. He parked his standard unmarked police car in one of the police spaces and took Kate around the back to where the professionals went in.

"Technically, I shouldn't be doing this," he said, "but it's this or wait for an hour and maybe not get in even then."

Kate didn't argue. The crowd made her feel claustrophobic.

She let Tom guide her through the back entrance and then through the series of halls that came out, surprisingly, right in the front lobby. There was a security guard there, too, but as soon as she saw Tom, she smiled.

"Wouldn't brave the howling mob?" she said. "You always were a wuss, Tom."

"I didn't have the time," Tom said. "You heard about Flanagan?"

"Everybody's heard about it. And everybody's been talking about it, you can bet on that. The news is full of it. And the gossip is full of it."

"What I want to know is whether we're even going to have court today," Tom said. "I know he wasn't the prosecutor, and we've got everybody we need to close up, but he was the lead detective, and this has to throw a wrench into the proceedings somehow."

"Maybe they'll ask for a postponement," the guard said. "I'll tell you one thing, the judge is not happy, because we were told to be strict about collecting cell phones and things today. Which brings me to—"

Tom took out his cell phone, then turned to Kate. Kate took out hers and handed it over. The policewoman put both cell phones in a single manila envelope and put Tom's name on it. Then she dropped it into a box of similar envelopes.

"I guess we ought to go in there and see what's happening," he said. "Have as good a day as this one will let you, Sharon."

"Don't worry about it. No matter what else this day is, it's going to be a great excuse for a little extra wine after dinner."

Tom steered Kate in through the doors of the courtroom that had played host for two weeks to the trial of Kevin Ozgo.

"This is going to get really awful," Kate said. "Media armageddon."

"Don't worry about it," Tom said. "These days, media armageddon is standard operating procedure."

Kate looked around her. Richard Hamilton was in his usual seat, and so was Chan. Closing arguments were about to begin, which meant all the witnesses had already been called and heard. Chan sat ramrod straight, her back not touching the back of the bench in any way. She looked like she'd been turned to stone.

In front of Chan, just past the wooden barrier, Ozgo was not sitting but half collapsed, a puddle of sheer terror. His body was shaking, just as it had been on that first day, but now the shaking was subdued, more like pond ripples than full tremors. His face, on the other hand, was immobile. His eyes were blank and dead.

"I wish there was a way to talk to him," Kate said. "If anybody knows something about all this, it should be him. But nobody except his lawyers can get to him."

Tom looked bemused. "Of course other people can get to him," he said. "He can talk to anybody he wants to. There's the presumption of innocence."

Kate frowned. "But the police take him back to jail. He didn't get bail, so—"

"He got bail," Tom said patiently. "He just couldn't make it. He didn't have the money and he didn't have the collateral to put up for a bondsman. But he doesn't go back to jail every time the court breaks for lunch or calls a recess. There's a couple of rooms in the back where defendants without bail are held when they're not in court."

"And he can talk to anybody he wants to?" Kate looked back at Ozgo.

"Well, his lawyer might have something to say about it," Tom said, "if Ozgo wanted to listen to him. And if I was Ozgo's lawyer, I'd try to make sure he was kept out of contact at all times. There have to be three dozen reporters all trying to find a way in, and talking to reporters is one thing Ozgo shouldn't do."

Kate frowned. "But if you went to him and asked him to see you and he said yes, you could talk to him?"

Tom gave her a quizzical look. "I don't know what's on your mind, but Ozgo is not going to talk to you. From what I've heard, he barely talks to his own lawyer, and I know he's refused to see Chan at least three times now."

"Where is the room where they take him? Can you just walk to it from here?"

"It's in the building, if that's what you mean."

"I meant do you have to have official permission or that kind of thing?"

"You have to send in a request with the officer. The officer will probably ask the lawyers if they're around to be asked. I'm serious, Kate. What is it you're trying to do?"

"It has to make sense," Kate said. "If Ozgo kidnapped Chan, then it makes sense because all Richard Hamilton is doing is trying to make sure that the person who hurt his daughter is punished. But if Ozgo didn't kidnap Chan, then there has to be some reason somebody would want to frame him for it. To frame *him*, in particular. And today could be the last day of the trial."

"It probably will be the last day of the trial."

"If it's the last day of the trial," Kate said, "this might be the last chance we'll have to talk to him face to face, if that's possible at all. And it has to be me who talks to him, because you know he won't trust you. So if you have a way to get me in there, I think you should do it first chance you get."

★   ★   ★

First they all rose. Then the judge came in. Then the judge sat down. Then they all sat down. Finally, there were what sounded like a thousand cries of, "Your honor, may I approach the bench?"

"Evans looks like he's about to croak," Tom said.

"But why?" Kate said. "You said it yourself. Flanagan wasn't the prosecutor. He's a policeman. And he's already given his testimony. So why should his dying make any difference?"

"If I was Brayde, I'd ask for a mistrial," Tom said. "The most important witness suddenly dead? And not able to testify at any subsequent trial? I don't think he'd get it, but if I were him, I'd ask."

The lawyers—a whole passel of them now, with the prosecution's associate counsel crammed in together—were arguing furiously, but the words came through only as fuzzy mumbles. Kate looked over at Ozgo and the Hamiltons. Ozgo had no expression on his face. Richard Hamilton looked bored. Chan was honestly interested, training her eyes on the lawyers at the bench and frowning.

Finally, the judge sat back, looking exasperated.

"Ladies and gentlemen, I don't disagree that this is a serious matter. I do disagree that this is a serious matter for this court at this time. We're at the end of a complicated trial. We're ready to hear closing arguments. It's in the best interests of the defendant and of the rest of us if we get this done."

"I completely agree," Evans said. He sounded triumphant.

Brayde was scowling. "Your honor—"

"Mr. Brayde," the judge said, "I'm willing to go this far. We'll take half an hour of recess. You can regroup as much as you feel you need to. You'll all be back here at twenty minutes to ten. And then we'll go on. Is that understood?"

"Your honor!" Brayde said.

The judge gave him a look, and Brayde receded.

Then they all rose again, and Ozgo was led out.

Kate watched him go.

"Are they taking him to that place you told me about?"

"I want to know what you think you're doing."

"We only have half an hour," Kate pleaded.

Tom hesitated, but only for a moment. Then he stood up abruptly and started making his way out of the courtroom.

Kate had to hurry to keep up. She had no idea where she was, although she had noticed that every one of the wall sconces were topped with molded plaster fleurs-de-lis.

When they got to the table with the police officer sitting at it, Kate was out of breath. The officer smiled at Tom and said, "You know better, Tom. Defense counsel left explicit instructions that no police personnel were to be allowed in to see the defendant during trial."

"I don't want to be let in to see the defendant," Tom said. "She does." He cocked his head at Kate.

The officer raised an eyebrow.

"I think he might be willing to see me," Kate said. "I'm worried about him, and I thought I'd check it out."

"And you're somebody he knows?"

Kate skirted that one. "He may not remember me, but I'm sure he'll remember Flip. Flip was his best friend in basic."

"Flip," the officer said.

Kate felt as if she could hardly manage to suck in air. "Just tell him that Sil is here. Flip's girlfriend Sil is here and she just wants . . . I just want to know how he's holding up and if he needs anything. Just that."

"Your name is Sil?" the officer said.

"Short for Silvia."

"I got that part," the officer said.

"And Flip's a nickname, too. His real name is Robert. Robert Edward Jr. But everybody always calls him Flip."

"Just a minute," the officer said.

She got up, left the table, and went through the door at the back of it. The door closed behind her with an audible click.

Tom gave Kate a long, distrustful stare and a disbelieving eyebrow raise.

The door opened and the police officer came out, looking more than a little surprised.

"I'll admit, I didn't expect that," she said. "He perked right up. You do understand, if you're a reporter, we can arrest you for—"

Kate didn't want to know what she could be arrested for, although she was sure it included a long list of things that would sound terrifying if she heard it.

"I'm not a reporter," she promised, hurrying around the table to the door and going through as the police officer held it open to her.

"Five minutes," the officer said. "Then I'll give you a warning."

Kate rushed into the room and let the door shut behind her. Ozgo stood by the window, staring out. He looked even frailer and more vulnerable up close than he had in the courtroom. The room was tiny and boxy and not very comfortable. There was another table with three chairs, all with arms. There were four bare white walls. There was a single bottle of water on the table, open, with its cap nowhere to be seen.

Kate stood where she was. Nothing happened. She gave a little cough.

Ozgo heaved an enormous sigh and turned around to face her. Kate hadn't thought beyond getting into the room, but she had thought she'd be able to work something up when she finally got there.

She didn't have a chance.

At first, Ozgo only frowned at her, seeming confused, but almost immediately after, he stepped back, as far as he could go, all the way to the window. The window had mesh in it, so he couldn't fall out or escape. But he pressed back against it anyway.

"You're not Sil," he whispered. Then he opened his mouth and began to scream. "You're going to kill me! You're going to kill me!"

He repeated that over and over, as loud as he could make it, until four uniformed police officers burst through the door.

★ ★ ★

To say that all hell broke loose was putting it mildly, but to Kate, as it happened, it seemed to be a long string of unrelated explosions, none of them connected to any other.

Ozgo went on screaming for what felt like forever. "You think I killed Rafael!" he said. The words came out in a high-pitched shriek. Kate had heard him speak once or twice on the news, and this was nothing like that. "You're going to kill me! You came here to kill me!"

If Kate had been thinking straight, she would have responded differently. Instead, she plunged her hand into her bag and came up with her soothing rock, the same one that had been thrown through the living room window, and tossed it to him.

Kate had no idea what she was doing. Ozgo didn't catch the rock or reach out to it like to a lifeline. He just screamed louder and jumped away. The rock hit the windowpane and the glass cracked. The sound was like a bullet going off in the tiny room, and Ozgo was out of control.

The police, who had burst in when Ozgo first started screaming, must have thought she was trying to kill him, too. One of them tackled her and brought her crashing down to the floor. Kate hit the wood with the entire right half of her body. She only managed to avoid hitting her head on that same floor by a hair.

At first, her shoulder and side were numb, but the pain came on quickly, and it was made worse by the fact that the police officer who had tackled her was now rolling her over on her stomach and pulling her arms back.

"Watch out," somebody said. It took Kate a couple of beats to realize it was Tom's voice shouting over the rest of the din. "She wasn't trying to kill the man. She's got a condition—"

"She had a weapon," somebody else said.

"What in hell was she doing in here?" a third voice said. Kate recognized that one, too: Reggie Evans.

She was finding it very hard to breathe and impossible to think.

Her hands were cuffed behind her back now, and the cuffs were so tight, they hurt her wrists. She couldn't believe how badly they hurt.

"You're trying to kill me," Ozgo kept saying over and over.

Kate realized he was no longer talking about her. He was talking about everybody. Everybody was trying to kill him.

Kate felt the throbbing start at the back of her head. Throb. Pulse. Throb. Pulse. Throb. Pulse. The floor underneath her was only inches from her face. It was throbbing, too, pulsing and throbbing. The damned thing looked like it was *breathing*. Kate could see the diaphragm that wasn't there expand and contract.

She felt sick. She felt incredibly sick. She was going to throw up right where she was.

"What the flying fuck do you think you're doing?" Evans shouted. "What the fuck is she doing here? I'm going to have your ass for this, Abbott. I'm going to have you off this police force before you can get back to your car. And if I ever see this woman anywhere near this case again, I'm going to—"

Kate never found out what Evans was going to do. The throbbing was getting bigger and bigger, more and more intense. She wasn't going to throw up. Whatever she was about to throw up was being pushed down into her throat, making her gag.

And the lights were getting brighter. The sounds were getting sharper. Every sight and sound had a sharp edge to it. Every detail she could see from the position she was in looked like it had been cut out of its background with a very sharp knife.

The police officer standing right next to her nose had a frayed edge on the outside of his left shoe. The shoe had a rubber sole but looked like an Oxford.

There was an old-fashioned steam element on the wall next to the window. It was painted white, but it had once been painted green. Kate could see the chipped white paint at the very bottom and the light-green paint underneath.

Ozgo was wearing sneakers. Not running shoes. Not trainers. Sneakers, the canvas kind. The canvas of his sneakers was red, and the laces were white. The canvas was completely clean. The sneakers looked brand new. All his clothes looked brand new. Could they have bought him new clothes? Why? Were his old ones gone in the fire? Were they too much of a mess for court?

She got a sudden flash of Ozgo in the picture outside the house the night of the fire. He was wearing sneakers then, too, but they were high tops and there were deep gullies in the ankles.

As if something had been tied there, around his ankles, very tightly.

She tried to think it through and couldn't.

Everything was too bright now. Every sound was too sharp.

Kate closed her eyes to try to make it go away. Ozgo was still screaming. Tom was still bellowing. The police should be doing something to stop all this noise. How long had she been on the floor? How long could she possibly have been on the floor?

"Will you please let the goddamned woman up?" Tom was saying.

All of a sudden, the thing she dreaded most was there, coursing through her body like an electrical charge.

Kate tried to stop it by force of will, but it was too late, and she knew it.

Her body started to shudder and arch and spasm.

SIXTEEN

Sometimes, when the episodes were over, Kate was calm and almost refreshed. Sometimes she was drained. Sometimes it was worse, and this was one of those times.

She knew where she was before she opened her eyes. The smell was unmistakable: that wet tang of rubbing alcohol that permeated all hospitals everywhere.

A hospital meant it had gone terribly wrong, as terribly wrong as it could go. She was lying in a bed. She moved a little in it and felt someone come up close to her.

"Kate?" Frank said. She couldn't hide from Frank.

By the time Kate let her eyes drift open, Frank was standing by the curtains that opened, as far as Kate could tell, on a corridor. The lights were not too bright now and the sounds were not too sharp—everything was normal again.

Kate had always worried that there would come a time when the episodes ceased to be episodes and became the default mode instead, that she would have to live in a world where everything had too much of an edge to it, a world she couldn't live in at all.

But it was all right now. It was over.

Frank must have noticed that her eyes were open. He came to the side of her bed immediately.

"Kate?"

"I'm very tired," Kate said. Her throat felt raw, as if she'd swallowed glass.

"Just a minute," Frank said.

He left the little curtained cubicle and went into the corridor. Kate closed her eyes again. Having her eyes closed made her feel better. She just wanted to let herself drift here, drift and float.

Frank came back with a woman in a white coat.

The woman leaned close. "Ms. Ford? Can you hear me?"

"I could hear you better if you didn't shout," Kate said.

The woman lowered her voice. "Do you think you can sit up?"

Kate didn't want to sit up. But it turned out to be relatively easy. She dragged herself forward and then rested on her elbows.

"My throat is killing me," she said. "Can't I have some water?"

"In just a moment," the woman said.

Kate decided the woman was a doctor, not a nurse. A nurse would have pumped up the bed so Kate didn't have to go on resting on her elbows. This woman took out her stethoscope and checked Kate's chest and then her back. *Heart and lungs*, Kate thought, feeling thoroughly miserable.

The woman dragged the stethoscope back around her neck and frowned. "You seem to be all right," she said. "Your father says you've had these seizures before?"

"I've had them since I was ten," Kate said. "Can we put the bed up so I can sit back? And can I please have some water? Or even some ice cream? Something for my throat."

The woman frowned. It was Frank who came around to crank the bed up.

"And you've consulted a physician about this problem?" the woman said.

"I've consulted a dozen of them," Kate said. "And no, none of them has come up with any explanation. And no, it's not epilepsy. I've been tested for that over and over again. And no, it doesn't happen often, not with episodes big enough to land me in a hospital."

"You also have smaller seizures?"

"I mostly have smaller whatever-they-ares," Kate said.

"Do you drive?"

"Yes."

"You probably shouldn't drive."

"They don't come on all of a sudden. I'd always have time to pull over if I had to."

"Can you tell me what happens right before these attacks begin?"

"*Nothing* happens," Kate said. "Not in the way you mean. Lights get brighter and sounds get sharper, but that's the start of an episode, not what causes it. And nothing in particular happens to set it all off. I've been in bars with strobe lights and haven't felt a thing. I've been sitting by myself in a quiet room and found myself in the middle of a bad one. They just happen. Nothing sets them off."

"Did anything happen before this one today?"

"Well," Kate said, "I was thrown to the floor by a cop and handcuffed, but other than that there wasn't anything."

The woman in the white coat frowned again. Frank coughed loudly. Frank had heard the sarcasm in Kate's voice.

"Can't I have some water?" Kate asked. "My throat feels like hell."

"Do you usually want water after one of these . . . episodes?"

"I usually want water, yes, but I don't usually have a sore throat as bad as the one I have now. But I would really like some water now. Please."

The woman stepped away from the bed. "I'll see if I can send a nurse in with some ice water," she said.

Then she turned away and walked out into the corridor.

Kate watched her as long as she was visible. "Is Jack here?"

Frank pulled up the cubicle's single chair and sat down. "She was only doing her job," he said mildly.

"I just get so tired of it," Kate said. "It's been *decades* now, for God's sake. I think I've resigned myself to the fact that there isn't any answer to this. I just don't want to do another round of tests and another round of consultations that amount to using a lot of fancy words to say they have no idea what it is. Is Jack here?"

"It's only a little after noon," Frank said. "Jack's at school."

"Does he know about this?"

"Not yet," Frank said. "But you're going to have to tell him."

"I wouldn't not tell him," Kate said.

A chipper young woman in bright-pink scrubs came in carrying a pitcher of water and a glass. It was a plastic pitcher, and Kate could hear the ice clinking against its sides.

"Dr. Arroyan said I should bring you this," the chipper young woman said. She poured the glass full of water and ice and handed it to Kate. Then she put the pitcher down on the side table Kate hadn't noticed before then.

"There's a buzzer right here," she said. "If you need anything, just press that."

Kate hadn't noticed the buzzer, either. She really was off her game.

Frank and Kate watched the young woman walk out. Kate drank half the glass of water in a single gulp. It was very cold.

"So," Frank said, "I've been thinking."

"Thinking about what?" Kate finished the glass of water in one more gulp. Then she reached across the table for the pitcher.

"I've been thinking that I was wrong," Frank said. "I was worried about you. You'd been . . . listless, I guess the word is. For weeks. And then there was the suspension from your job. I thought getting you interested in the trial might help pull you out of it. I didn't expect you to get this involved."

"You mean you didn't expect for me to go talk to people on my own, check the computer stuff out on my own, and—?"

"It isn't that. I could handle your doing a little on-site investigating, within reason. It's this thing I can't handle. You don't usually have episodes bad enough to pass out."

"And you think getting interested in the trial set off this episode?"

"It's not that, exactly. But something set it off."

"So you want me to do what?" Kate asked him.

Frank got out of the chair and started to pace. "I was thinking I'd take you and Jack up to the cabin for a couple of weeks. We could arrange things with his school. It would be nice and quiet up there. You wouldn't have to hear about the trial, never mind look into it. You could relax."

"Because I had an episode."

"You had a really bad episode. But also because of the rock through the window. Your rock. Somebody thinks you're a problem."

"Listen to yourself," Kate said. "I'm supposed to, what? Withdraw from the world? Because I had an episode? What happens to me if I start doing that? What happens to all of us? How do I hold a job? How do I have a life? You were the one who told me I should never give into this, that I should work around it however I could so that I didn't just *become* the episodes."

"Kate—"

"And now you want me to give in," Kate said. "Is that it?"

SEVENTEEN

Back at home and after nearly eighteen hours in bed, Kate decided to take a shower. As she finished up and walked out of the bathroom, she heard the sounds of someone in the kitchen. She wondered if it was Jack or Frank who was making the noise. It was just about the time Jack got home. She went through the living room and saw that the glass had been replaced sometime yesterday. She couldn't remember if it had been replaced when she got home from the hospital yesterday evening. She didn't remember much about yesterday evening. By the time she'd managed to get back home, she was exhausted both from the episode and from the ER doctor's hammering insistence that she stay in the hospital for "observation."

Kate had spent time in hospitals for "observation" before. It never did any good, and it was always uncomfortable.

She went into the kitchen and stopped. There, sitting at the kitchen table, was Tom, drinking one of Frank's Budweisers straight from the bottle.

He looked up when she came in.

"There you are," he said. "I thought you were going to sleep all day. Frank's gone to the store to get something. Not dinner."

Kate sat down at the table. "He wants us to go up to the cabin today," she said. "How we're going to do that with Jack in school, I don't know. And besides—"

"He told me all about the cabin," Tom said. He got up and started a pot of coffee. Kate let him. "I think it's a good idea. I didn't like the look of that thing yesterday."

"That thing?"

"I didn't realize your spells could get that severe. I didn't even realize what they were until Frank and Jack explained them to me," Tom said. He put a cup of coffee down in front of Kate. "You want something else? You've got cold cuts. I could make you a sandwich."

"Thank you," Kate said. "Not right now. What are you doing here? Why aren't you at the trial, or doing police work, or something?"

Tom sat down again. "I am well and truly suspended."

Kate blanched. "Was that my fault? Was it because you helped me to get in to see Ozgo yesterday?"

"I think getting you in to see Ozgo was the last straw in a long parade of straws," Tom said. "Don't worry about it. The verdict was announced half an hour ago."

"What?"

"Jury came back. Didn't take them five hours today. Ozgo is guilty on all counts."

Kate took the longest drink of coffee she ever had in her life. "Well," she said, after what sounded like forever. "That's that."

"Is it?"

Kate glanced at the wall clock. It was almost quarter to four. She got up and went to the wall calendar Jack was so careful to keep current, but there was no notice on today's little square of a track meet or club meeting. She looked around a little helplessly.

"Have you seen my bag?" she asked Tom.

"If you're thinking of going somewhere, forget it," he said. "Frank took your keys."

"I don't need my keys. I need my cell phone to call Jack."

Tom sighed, reached into his jacket pocket, and handed over the cell phone. "I retrieved it from Sharon along with mine."

She dialed Jack and the phone rang and rang. Then it rang some more. By the time she was back to her coffee, she'd been routed to voice mail.

Kate put the phone down on the table. "He's not picking up," she said.

"Is that unusual?"

Kate shrugged. "I don't know. It's unusual for him to be late if he doesn't have anything after school." She sat down again and tried Jack one more time. This time, her call went directly to voice mail.

"The thing that interests me," Tom said, going back to the case, "is who set this all up. And yes, I do still think somebody set this all up. I don't think Ozgo is guilty of anything. For God's sake, Kate. You've seen him. The kid's a mess. He couldn't have planned a picnic, never mind a kidnapping. I think he was just the handiest person around to pin it all on."

"To pin what all on?" Kate asked. "Didn't you ever wonder what it was that happened? Chan Hamilton says she was kidnapped, and maybe she was. But when I think about all this, I get this big, shadowy conspiracy."

"I agree," Tom said. "But maybe we're making too much of it. Maybe it's just about the kidnapping. Maybe somebody tried the kidnapping, and then when he saw it wasn't going to work, he tried putting the blame on Ozgo."

"Are we thinking about Jed Paterson again?"

"Could be," Tom said.

"But you think Ozgo was framed," Kate said, "and Paterson couldn't make that happen. That would have to be someone with the right kinds of connections."

"Richard Hamilton," Tom said.

"Why?" Kate asked. "Why would Richard Hamilton want to kidnap his own daughter? And if he did, why would Flanagan and Evans go along with an attempt to frame Ozgo instead?"

"Flanagan would do just about anything if money was involved," Tom said. "And as for Evans, maybe Richard Hamilton has been shoving a ton of cash in Reggie's direction under the guise of campaign funds to make sure that all of this gets pinned on Ozgo."

"It's harder to conceal campaign contributions than you think," she said. "And Richard Hamilton didn't conceal some of it. Individual donor lists are public information. I've seen newspaper reports about Hamilton's contributions to Evans's campaign, and everybody in the office knew Hamilton was endorsing him. I'd think that if there really was some big conspiracy, Hamilton would want to keep himself clear of Evans altogether."

Kate picked up her phone again. She tried Jack one more time, but she was not surprised to be sent straight to voice mail. She went back to her contact list and called the school.

"Would you know where my son Jack Ford is this afternoon? He isn't answering his cell phone, and I don't have any information that he has a track meet or a club meeting. I'm getting a little worried."

"I'm sorry," the secretary, Ms. Ryder, said. "You said Jack Ford, right? He left hours ago. I was working the parking lot this afternoon and saw him leave."

Kate kept very still. "Leave? Do you mean he went home on the bus?"

"No, no," Ms. Ryder said. "He got picked up. By your father, I thought it was. At least by a man of more or less the same size. Well, he was sitting in the car, and I couldn't see him all that well. Anyway, it must have been your father or somebody he knew, because he hopped right into that car and the car drove away."

"With my father?" Kate repeated.

"I can't understand why they're not home already, unless they had something to do," Ms. Ryder said. "It wasn't more than a couple of minutes after two thirty."

"Yes," Kate said. "I'm sorry I bothered you. I should have called my father first. Let me try to get in touch with him."

"I'd appreciate it if you'd call us back as soon as you locate them," Ms. Ryder said. "It would be a very serious thing if somebody else had picked him up and it wasn't somebody you'd authorized. We take the safety of our students very seriously—"

"I'm sure you do," Kate interrupted. "If I could just get off and make a phone call to my father."

Ms. Ryder was still talking, but Kate didn't care. She hung up. Then she put the cell phone carefully down on the table and stared at it.

"What's the matter?" Tom asked.

"Probably nothing," Kate said. "The school says my father picked up Jack right after school. There's really nothing wrong with that. And I was asleep. My father probably thought that they'd be home before I woke up. But I'm not the only one around here who has episodes every once in a while. Think about the other day in the diner. I don't even know if he can drive when he gets like that. I don't think he knows either."

At just that moment, Kate and Tom heard the sound of a vehicle in the driveway. They both bolted up from the table, but Kate was faster. She was out into the garage in seconds flat, just in time to see Frank emerging from his pickup.

Alone.

★ ★ ★

It was astounding just how fast things could happen. Frank had come home alone. He was not having an Alzheimer's moment. He was entirely in his right mind. And he had not gone to the school to pick up Jack.

Kate had begun to lose it while she was still in the garage. By the time she got back to the kitchen, she was shaking all over. She could see the two of them looking at her, and she knew what they were thinking.

Tom had his own cell phone out. "Thirteen years old," he was saying. "Very slender, but also very tall. My guess is close to six feet already. Yeah. Yeah. Giving him a shot to get to six feet eight is what we're looking for here. Just a minute. I'll ask." He took the phone away from his mouth and asked Frank, "Do you have a picture of Jack?"

"There are dozens of pictures of Jack," Frank said.

"We're going to have to e-mail them a photo," Tom said. "Can I get a pencil and a piece of paper?"

Frank handed him a paper napkin and one of the pens from the little pencil holder next to the coffee maker.

"Okay," he said. "Shoot." He wrote down the number. "Why don't I hand you over to the boy's mother? She spoke to somebody at the school."

"I don't know what's going on," Kate said as Tom held out his cell phone to her.

"We're putting out an Amber Alert," Tom said. Kate blanched. "It's better to do it early rather than late. Even if he's fine and out with friends somewhere. Tell the officers what you know."

Kate took Tom's cell phone. "This is Kate Ford."

"How do you do, Mrs. Ford?" an officer said. "Please believe me when I say that I know this is a tense and even terrifying time, but almost all these alerts end well, usually because the child has gone off on his own for some reason and not thought to check in. Your son was last seen at school?"

Kate told the officer everything the school secretary had told her. Then she explained what happened when she called Jack's cell phone.

"So," the officer said, "the first time you called, it went on ringing for a long time before it went to voice mail. The rest of the times you called, it went directly to voice mail."

"Yes," Kate said. *Just the way it would have if somebody had killed him and then the phone had started ringing in his pocket and the killer turned it off so it couldn't be traced by GPS.* She put that out of her mind—well, she *tried* to put it out of her mind, even though it was near impossible.

The officer asked if there was anybody else there who might have information. Kate passed Tom's phone to Frank and then sat down. Her legs did not feel stable. Her back felt as if it were breaking in two.

After Frank gave some more information, he passed the phone back to Tom. It felt as if everything was taking forever.

Kate closed her eyes and put her head on the table and counted and counted, as if that could fix or change anything or make Jack appear out of thin air.

Tom finished the call and put his phone back in his pocket.

"As soon as Frank gets those pictures e-mailed, we'll start putting them out to the police departments and on the Internet. We've got an Amber Alert Facebook page for this county, and then—"

They both heard the sound at once. It came from the front hall, not the garage entry. The front door opened and shut, and Jack, sounding God awful, was calling.

"Mom? Grandpa? Mom?"

Kate sprang out of her seat and ran into the foyer, moving so fast and so blindly that she and Jack collided.

Jack staggered back, and Kate could see him. She gasped.

Jack had no shoes on and his feet were bloody. His clothes were torn. His hair was full of debris. He had bruises everywhere.

He looked like someone had taken him into the woods and beat him up.

EIGHTEEN

Jack's feet and lower legs looked so awful, it took Kate a minute to catch the look in his eyes, and that was so much worse. The kid was staring straight ahead, but his eyes were unfocused. He looked like the herald of one of those zombie apocalypses he talked about all the time. Kate grabbed him in an enormous hug and squeezed so hard that Jack grunted.

A second later, Frank was pulling them apart. "Let him breathe, Kate," he said. "Let him talk."

Jack staggered out of Kate's embrace and sat down. "I got home," he said. "I got home. I ran and ran, and then I wasn't sure I knew where I was going, but I got home."

Tom had taken out his cell phone and knelt down on the floor.

"What are you doing?" Kate demanded.

"I'm taking pictures," Tom said. "Of the state of his feet."

"Oh." Kate remembered. "The Amber Alert. We should cancel the Amber Alert."

"Already done it," Tom said.

"The school said you went off in a car with a man," Kate said. Now that she knew Jack was safe, her worry was turning into fury. It was so hot and white, she didn't know if she could get it to stop. "You went off with a *man*," she said again. "What's wrong with you? You know you don't get into cars with strangers. You've known that since you were *six*."

Jack stared at her blankly. Frank moved in and handed over a cup that Kate realized was full of coffee.

"Can't you see he's been drugged?" Frank demanded. "He's chock full of something or the other, and it hasn't completely worn off."

Jack started in his seat. "Drugged," he said wonderingly. "That would make sense."

Jack was drinking coffee in huge gulps. The coffee was hot and scalded his mouth a little so that after every swallow, he reared back and made a face. But he went right back to drinking the coffee.

Tom finished taking the photographs and stood up to fiddle with his phone. "I'm sending these in to my partner," he said. "I've got to report this, Kate. I've got to report it right now."

"He said he was *your* partner," Jack said accusingly, looking straight at Tom. The coffee was helping. His eyes looked distinctly sharper now. "I was walking out to the bus stop, and he pulled up and said he was your partner. He even showed me a badge. And he said Mom had had . . . that she'd had—"

"Oh, dear Jesus," Kate said. "What were you thinking? We've talked about this!"

"When I was six. Yesterday you were a mess. This guy shows up and says you're on the way to the hospital again. He shows me his badge and says Tom is on the way to the hospital with you and he's been sent to get me and bring me there. I don't know, Mom. It didn't seem all that farfetched. In fact, it seemed perfectly reasonable."

"This guy showed up and showed you a badge. Did he just show it to you, or did you take it?" Tom asked.

"No cop is going to let you take his badge," Jack said. "Don't you watch *Law & Order?*"

"Did he show you the badge up close? I presume you thought it was real."

"It looked real," Jack said.

"Yeah, I got that," Tom said. "Did he hold it out close to you or keep it near himself?"

"He kept it near himself." Jack sounded miserable. He'd also finished the coffee. Frank took Jack's cup and filled it again. Tom had started pacing around the kitchen, his hands thrust in his pockets.

"So you got into the car," he said, "and then what?"

"And then the guy took off," Jack said. He grabbed the newly filled cup of coffee like a drowning man grabs a life preserver. "And then, okay, I wasn't paying all that much attention because I was worried about Mom and I was feeling guilty because I keep thinking she makes it all up. But I was thinking maybe it was serious and she was going to die and then, I don't know, I just sort of realized that we weren't going the right way. We weren't going to the hospital. It was the wrong road."

"Do you know which road you were on?" Tom asked.

Jack shook his head. "It was out in the country some-where. I didn't recognize it at all. So I said, hey, this wasn't the way to the hospital, and he said something about it being a shortcut. Then he pulled over to the side of the road, and I was just thinking I'd jump out and take my chances. But he grabbed me and shoved this handkerchief over my face. And that's the last thing I remember before I sort of came to and I was in the trunk."

"In the trunk?" Kate repeated. "Oh my God."

"Was it the same car?" Tom asked.

"I don't know," Jack said. "I had a blindfold on, and my hands were tied behind my back, so I couldn't take it off. And I felt awful, like I was going to throw up. And we drove and drove and drove. And then the car slowed down and I could feel us pulling over, and then we stopped." Jack attacked the coffee again. "I thought he was going to shoot me. I thought he was going to kill me. I just lay there in the trunk thinking I was dead and I didn't even know why."

"But he didn't kill you," Tom pointed out.

"He didn't kill me. He opened the trunk and lifted me right out of it like I was a piece of paper. Then he put me on the ground, and that's when I realized I didn't have my shoes on. I didn't have my socks on either. I could feel the road under my feet. Road. Not dirt. But there weren't any sounds, you know, like traffic."

"And?" Tom prodded.

"And nothing," Jack said. "The guy goes, 'Give my regards to your mother.' Then he just left. He didn't peal out or anything. I heard the car leave, but it wasn't in any kind of hurry. It just went."

"'Give my regards to your mother,'" Frank said. "Kate, you can't seriously argue about getting out of here now. You've got to get out of here."

"Wait," Tom said. He kept his attention on Jack. "You're not wearing a blindfold now, and you don't have your hands tied behind your back. You must have gotten loose somehow."

"That was another one of the weird things," Jack said. His voice was almost back to normal. "I'd have realized right away if I wasn't so woozy. The stuff on my hands wasn't tied all that tight. They were just sort of hanging off my wrists, like it was some kind of a joke. Pulling at them didn't work, but twisting them around did. I got them off in no time. And then I took the blindfold off, and I knew where I was."

"You knew where you were?" Kate said.

"Did you get a look at the car?" Tom asked him. "Even a small glimpse? As it was driving away?"

Jack shook his head. "It was gone by then," he said. "But I remember it from school. It was this little silver thing, and I thought it was weird because it looked a lot like Mom's."

"Probably a coincidence," Tom said. "You didn't happen to notice the make or model or any of that kind of thing?"

Jack shrugged. "I was distracted, like I said. I was worried about Mom. I wasn't thinking about being kidnapped."

"I still say this ends the argument," Frank said. "You've got to get out of here. It's not just about your health anymore. You've got to consider the possibility that somebody out there thinks you're a threat to them."

Kate thought about Paterson out at the Fairholt Bridge and the bonfire and shuddered. "Even if somebody is," she said, "there's got to be a reason for it. And if it's just that whoever it is wants Ozgo convicted, well, they've convicted him."

"Convictions can be overturned," Tom said.

"Yes, of course convictions can be overturned, but they aren't usually, are they?" Kate said. "And if somebody thinks I know something the police don't know, they're completely addled. I don't even know what I know. I was playing detective, and I didn't find a damn thing. The whole thing sounds ridiculous and you know it."

"Ridiculous or not, we have to get the two of you out of here until we find out what's going on," Frank said. "And I think we should take seriously the idea that somebody may be following you. Somebody threw that rock through our living room window. And don't tell me that could have been any kid, because the rock they threw belonged to you. They had to get it somewhere. Somebody got access to you, Kate. They knew where to find that rock. They knew where Jack goes to school and what to say to get him to go along with them. We've got to get you two out of here and we've got to do it in a way that they don't know where you've gone—or even that you've gone—until you've been gone for a good long time."

"No," Tom said. "We've got to make them think they do know where you've gone."

"Ah," Frank said. "Smart man."

"It does help when they give you the perfect excuse," Tom said.

★ ★ ★

There were still an awful lot of loose ends, but twenty minutes later, Kate and Jack climbed into Kate's car, Frank climbed into the cab of his truck, and Tom led the way in his own car, out of Kate's driveway and down the road toward the highway.

Jack was both tense and exhausted, but he was no longer fuzzy minded. "Have any of you considered the possibility that whoever is watching us probably knows about Grandpa's cabin?"

Kate tried very hard not to bite her lip. "I've considered it," she told him. "The idea is that whoever may be watching us will think we've gone to the police station to report what happened to you, and then they'll see Grandpa leave, but not us, and they'll think we've stayed behind to finish up with the police business. This is just to buy some time to think of a better plan. This isn't a permanent fix."

"Listen to yourself," Jack said. "You can barely keep a straight face." He was right, but there were only two more turns to the police station, and she drove them without answering him.

The underground parking garage for the police station was like all underground parking garages everywhere: dark and dank and more than a little haunted. Kate pulled into a visitor spot and cut her engine. Jack got out ahead of her. Tom and Frank were already parked and waiting.

Kate got out and walked over to Tom to give him her car keys. "What are we supposed to do now?"

"Wait an hour," Frank said. "But you're not going to wait here. You're going to get in the back of Tom's car, both of you, and you're going to stay down. Way down. I need you to stay so close to the floor that nobody in another car can even guess that anybody is back there. I'll be driving."

"Every single person in this entire family has lost their screwing minds," Jack said.

But he climbed into the back seat of Tom's unmarked car. Kate watched him go—tall, yes, but still very delicate, very fine boned, almost frail. But he wasn't frail, she knew that. He was on the cusp of that growth spurt that would not only add a few more inches to his height but also fill out the muscle that was already becoming evident under the skin. He was a boy, but the man was there, waiting.

"Kate," Frank said.

Kate got into the car herself, took the vacant half of the back seat floor, and scrunched down as far as she could. Kate was smaller than Jack, but he was doing a much better job of folding himself up. That was the difference between being thirteen and thirty-six.

Frank slammed the door behind her.

If Kate could have gone to sleep, she would have. Jack did. She could hear the low hum of Frank talking to Tom, but nothing else, which did not improve her mood even a little bit.

After what seemed like forever, Frank got into the front of the car and started it up.

"See you tomorrow," he said to Tom.

Then the car began to roll, bumping and turning slowly, leaving the parking garage.

Kate knew they were out of the parking garage and onto the road again because the radio blared into life. Frank fiddled with the sound until it was at a reasonable level. He had it tuned to a local oldies station, in spite of the fact that "oldies" these days meant Metallica, not the Beach Boys.

"News on the hour," an announcer's voice said.

That's when they heard that Evans, Senate candidate and prosecuting attorney in the just-finished Ozgo trial, had just been found dead in his office.

NINETEEN

Everybody always talked about how wonderful it would be if they could just get free of technology. Almost nobody ever tried it because they knew what they wouldn't admit: off the grid was annoying and frustrating and often just plain boring.

It drove Kate nearly crazy from the moment they walked through the cabin's doors. It didn't help that there was a lot to be done. The generator had to be turned on as well as the electricity and indoor plumbing. Appliances had to be checked. Bedding had to be put on beds.

It was in the middle of all this that Kate realized they had brought no food. And a quick check of the cabinets showed that there wasn't much besides pasta, bottled water, enormous bags of tortilla chips, canned foods, and a processed cheese food that was dispensed like whipped cream from a pressure can. Frank loved tortilla chips. So did Jack. Kate hated them unless they were covered with melted cheese and accompanied by salsa.

Kate wouldn't have said she was nervous or frightened, just achy from all that time crouching down on the floor of Tom's car, but when the cabin's phone rang, she nearly jumped out of her skin.

"It's me," Tom said when she picked up. "Are you all right?"

"We're fine," Kate said. "We don't have any food, but we're fine. What have you found out?"

"I'm sorry to say that we don't have much. Someone talked to the school. Turns out they have security cameras at the front doors, but they point *at* the front doors, and that means—"

"We're not going to get a picture of the car," Kate said.

"I took down everything Jack said about where he was dumped, and we think we've identified the area. We're in between shifts. The morning guys will go out first thing tomorrow morning and see if they can get anything else useful. Oil slicks on the road. Tire tracks on the shoulders."

"Won't there be hundreds of those kinds of things out there by then? There must be cars going back and forth all the time."

"Not really," Tom said. "If it's where we think it is, it's very isolated. Not a commonly used road. Whoever dumped him wanted to scare you, but that doesn't mean that he wanted to be seen. And it gets worse. I don't know if you heard, but Evans—"

"Is dead," Kate finished for him. "It was on the radio while we were driving up here, but I only heard the last little bit of the story. Now that we're out at the cabin, I couldn't find out any more."

"It was a massive heart attack, maybe half an hour before he was supposed to give a press conference. They are doing an autopsy and will check for every known possibility, but it turns out he's had the heart condition for years."

"And I'd be paranoid to think it was anything else."

"Not paranoid, just probably wrong," Tom said.

"Listen," she said again. "I was thinking on the drive. You should go back and talk to Lucy Leeds, the woman who lives next to Flanagan. The woman I was talking to that night."

"We've already talked to her," Tom said.

"I know," Kate said. "But there's something. There really is. I can feel it."

"I'll check around first thing in the morning," Tom said. "You should go off and get some sleep."

"Right."

It was one thing to be told you should get some sleep or even to admit that you needed the sleep. It was another thing to actually get it.

Kate was exhausted, but being exhausted didn't help. Frank made the world's most peculiar dinner out of tortilla chips, canned kidney beans, and the pasteurized processed cheese food. Jack found this wretched mess absolutely wonderful. He got one of the other cans of cheese food— there were *six* of them in the cabinet—and squirted the stuff directly onto his tongue.

"Why don't we ever get this at home?" he wanted to know.

The travails of the day notwithstanding, Jack was in a good mood. Kate let him be in a good mood and even eat yet another can of cheese food. Then, when it seemed too dark to be anything but midnight, she shooed him off to bed, and Frank shooed himself.

In no time at all, Kate was alone in the cabin's small living room, staring at the blackened fireplace that had no fire in it, willing herself to fall asleep.

Several hours later, Kate gave up.

She moved herself to the small table in the kitchen area of the cabin, got paper and a pen out of her bag, and made herself write out everything she knew about the case so far. She wrote out everything she could think of about the kidnapping of Chan Hamilton and the burning down of her "cottage" and about Ozgo and his time in Afghanistan. Then she wrote a third list. This one consisted of everything she had learned that night she'd talked to Richard Hamilton.

Three lists.

She hoped that she could make a connection among these three lists and that in the connection, a solution could be found. And that solution had to be the answer to a single question: why was everybody, including the police and the prosecutor, so intent on prosecuting Ozgo for the kidnapping of Chan Hamilton and the torching of her house?

Kate was convinced, like Tom, that Ozgo was being framed. She got her cell phone from her bag and opened up her contact list. Then she picked up the receiver to the landline and placed a call.

A moment later, Mike Alexander's voice came on the line. "What the fuck?" he said. "Somebody damn well ought to be dead."

"Mike?" Kate said. "It's Kate Ford. I—"

"For Christ's sake," Mike said. "It's two thirty in the fucking morning. Are you out of your mind?"

"I'm sorry," Kate said. "I didn't realize it was that late."

"You realize it now," Mike said.

"They convicted Ozgo yesterday," Kate said. "Did you hear that?"

"I was in the courtroom when the verdict came back. You can't tell me you're surprised. A scrambled cat could have seen that coming a mile away," Mike said. "They had good evidence. I heard it. If you'd come to court more often, you'd have heard it too."

Kate closed her eyes and counted to ten. There was no point getting into that argument now. She opened her eyes again and stared at the wall.

"The last time we spoke, you were going to look into some things," she said. "Things about Almador, General Solutions, Robotix, and the whole incident where Turner died."

"Robotix?"

"The robotics company."

Mike had stopped talking. "Just a minute," he said. Kate could hear him moving around and springs creaking. He was getting out of bed. "You should be grateful I'm not married," he said when he came back on the line.

"Did you find out something new about how Turner died?"

"No," Mike said. "You were right about that. There doesn't seem to be any hard information. But that other stuff you were telling me about? General Solutions does reconstruction of army facilities and infrastructure in war zones. Something gets bombed, General Solutions goes in and builds it back up. It's the reconstruction projects that are interesting," Mike said. "They've been doing a lot of work for the US government reconstructing facilities that have been hit by enemy fire in Afghanistan and Iraq."

"Also on stuff hit by friendly fire," Kate said.

"I'm sure they work with every contract firm out there," Mike said, "but that isn't the point. Contracting generates public documents. Government bids out on anything they want to hire a private company to do. People submit bids. Those bids and the general outline of the assignments are public records."

Kate felt the bottom drop out of her stomach. "And the stuff for General Solutions is classified?" she guessed.

"Not exactly. For at least half the projects General Solutions took, there is no evidence and no reason there should be any contracts to send."

"What do you mean?"

"I can't link the construction to any military action, strategic or tactical. One day there's a bridge and the next day the bridge needs to be rebuilt. It's as if the stuff just fell down by itself."

Kate frowned. "And that's significant?"

"It's not so much significant as it is odd," Mike said. "One of the things in these records is always a set of pictures of the facility or whatever it is that needs to be repaired. The pictures are all there. And from what you can see in the pictures, the reconstructions were all justified."

"Okay," Kate said.

"But there's something else," Mike said. "On the few occasions where there is an explanation, it's always collateral damage."

"Collateral damage?" Kate said. Then she worked it out. "That would have to be friendly fire incidents, wouldn't it?"

"But that's not what's been bugging me about this. In every case where the reason has been put down as a collateral damage, there's been direct evidence from embedded reporters about the attack. Actual, live, existing reporters witnessed the attack. What do you think about that?"

"I don't know," Kate said. "I suppose it's not all that odd that the military is trying to hide friendly fire incidents. It's embarrassing for them. It generates a lot of bad publicity. How many incidents are we talking about?"

"Twenty-four in a two-year period."

"Jesus."

"That's about right," Mike said. "There weren't that many IED attacks in the same period. And what's more, I checked other contracts and other companies, and no other company is showing those kinds of lopsided stats. It's all General Solutions. Look, I really wish I understood your obsession with this," Mike said. "Not that I'm complaining.

It's a good thing I didn't brush you off completely. There's a lot of interesting information here that I can use. But it needs to be more than statistics."

"They're going to put Ozgo in prison, and he's going to go completely crazy," Kate said. "And I don't think he did it. I don't think he killed Turner or even was responsible for him being killed. I think he was framed to cover something up."

"Like what?"

"I don't know," Kate said.

"All right, all right," Mike said. "The case is over. I'm going to have some time on my hands over the next couple of weeks. I don't mind looking into this. If something is being covered up, it would be a big fucking deal for me to find out what it is and get it published first. But friendly fire incidents aren't going to cut it—unless we've been having a lot of them, more than usual, And in all the digging I've been doing, I haven't come across anything that would fit the bill."

Kate thought about the friendly fire. About the photo of the drone her father bookmarked for her. About her last day in the office. About the systems all going crazy. Her mouth was dry. "Did you check out Robotix?" she asked him.

"I did check out Robotix," Mike said. "And all I found was lots of stuff about robots that can clean your pool or vacuum your house—and one new one that's going to mow your lawn."

"What about their drones?"

"What drones? They don't have any drones."

"Then you're not looking in the right place."

"Goddamn it."

"What?"

"Fine. I'm up already; I might as well look into it."

TWENTY

Tom got to the cabin with four enormous porterhouse steaks just in time to start cooking dinner. At that time, Kate had heard from Mike four more times.

"You've got to ask yourself what would be worth all the fuss," she said as Tom and Frank put the steaks on the outdoor grill and started tussling over charcoal. Jack was standing to the side of the grill, handing over equipment whenever he was asked for it.

"A high-profile war hero died in a friendly fire attack? I'd say that was good enough reason by itself," Tom said.

"But it isn't," Kate insisted. "Look at what we've got to explain here. If you're right, and Ozgo is innocent of attempting to kidnap and kill Chan Hamilton, then you've got this vast apparatus in play to frame him. Somebody got to the police department and the prosecutor's office. They took you off the case. They hid or destroyed evidence that might have proved Ozgo innocent. They went through with an entire, elaborate trial—"

"And they got what they wanted," Frank pointed out. "They got Ozgo declared guilty. But why not just kill him like the rest of his team?"

"We've got to look at this as taking place in two layers," Kate said. "The first one is Chan Hamilton. She's convinced that Ozgo is in some way responsible for Turner's death. Why shouldn't she be convinced? It's what everybody's been telling her. It's what Ozgo himself has been telling her. She's convinced, and she wants revenge. She gets herself an accomplice, and they stage the kidnapping. Chan blames it on Ozgo, and then we're in court."

"We already know all this," Tom said.

"No, we really don't," Kate said. "Up to now, the general opinion has been that Ozgo kidnapped Chan. If you start with the assumption that Ozgo didn't kidnap Chan, then there has to be a reason for Chan to say he did. And I think this is the most plausible reason. Chan wants revenge on Ozgo, and big-time revenge. And she's got Paterson hanging around, and Paterson is—"

"What he is," Tom said.

Kate nodded. "But this is where it starts to get weird. When you start looking into the incident where Turner died, you get all kinds of things that are completely insane. Somebody gave the press false details about the attack and then erased or classified every single piece of information about how the attack really occurred. Including who was in it and when and where it happened. And they covered up more than that. Families of other members of that unit think their kids are still on active duty somewhere, and public records show that the same soldiers were all honorably discharged. What's more, I talked to one of those families, and they're getting money and letters from their soldier, even though she's listed as honorably discharged. This isn't the kind of thing you just do on Tuesday because you feel like it. You're breaking literally hundreds of laws, and you're getting yourself into the Department of Defense's secure network to commit them. Chan Hamilton couldn't have done any of that, and she wouldn't have wanted to. What would have been the point?"

Tom turned the steaks with tongs. Frank glared at him. "Maybe the two things aren't connected," Tom said. "Maybe Chan was getting her revenge on Ozgo, and the Department of Defense stuff was entirely separate."

"They've got a link," Kate said.

"What link is that?" Tom asked.

"Jed Paterson," Kate said firmly.

The steaks were done. So were the grilled onions and zucchini. Frank stepped in to help Tom take all the food off the fire and put it onto plates.

"We're only speculating that Paterson was the mystery man on the night of the fire," Tom said. "It might have been somebody else."

"Maybe it was," Kate said, "but Paterson was there when Turner was killed. That much was in the report."

"You really want to tell this to law enforcement?" Frank asked.

"What shouldn't she tell to law enforcement?" Tom demanded.

Kate sighed. "There are two cover-ups that are happening, but they're connected by Paterson. And Paterson is connected to General Solutions. General Solutions is connected Almador, Richard Hamilton, and Robotix. I think I know what could be going on that would make it worthwhile for somebody to go through all this trouble to frame Ozgo for kidnapping and attempted murder. And I keep thinking that if we could explain this to Chan, she might be willing to help. Because what she wants is revenge on the people who killed Rafael, and I'm pretty sure that Paterson has something to do with that."

★　★　★

Chan Hamilton "worked" as head of the Hamilton Charitable Trust. Kate and Tom both knew this the same way the rest of the country knew it: TMZ, *Entertainment Tonight*, *People*, and all the rest of them. Kate wanted to try to see Chan at home. Tom thought that was less likely to get them what they wanted than if they saw her at work.

"She's living in her father's house at the moment," Tom said. "There's security. A lot of security. And the man could be home or have the entire place bugged."

Kate let Tom have his way. The idea of coming face to face with Richard Hamilton didn't make her very happy.

The Hamilton Charitable Trust operated out of a refurbished antebellum mansion just a mile and a half from Almador headquarters but several planets away in terms of aesthetics and ambience. Kate had seen pictures of it, but she'd never driven by to look at it, even though she was close enough when she was still working for Almador.

"That would be nice," Kate said, staring up at the columns across the front of the mansion. "A family that could start an entire business just to give me some work."

They'd arrived at Hamilton Charitable Trust just as many of its staff was coming to work.

"Maybe she won't even be here now," Kate said. "Maybe she had a late night. Maybe she'll drift in around noon."

"There she is," Tom said. "I want to get to the front steps before she does."

Chan was making her way across a cobblestone path that led from another parking lot—probably the staff parking—to the front door. She didn't look like she'd had a long night. Her excruciatingly expensive suit was crisp and black and perfectly tailored to her body. Her enormous Coach bag hung off her right shoulder and moved like it contained half a dozen boulders. Her hair was pulled back in a French twist and her earrings didn't dangle.

Tom almost didn't make it. He had to slide in to stop her from starting up the steps, and when he did, Chan stepped back startled and then looked angry.

"I don't know what you think you're doing," Chan started.

By then, Kate had reached the two of them. Chan's attention swung from Tom to Kate, and then she looked both startled and annoyed.

"You again," Chan said. "What are you doing here? What's he doing here?"

"What I'm doing here is routine," Tom said. "I'm just doing some follow-up now that the trial is over with—"

"Oh, don't give me that horseshit," Chan said. "The police don't do follow-up after a trial. And if they did, you wouldn't be the one to do it. You've been suspended. My father told me all about it. You tried to get *this* person in to talk to Ozgo, and it ended up with a mess that cost two days of trial."

Tom rocked back on his heels.

"Ah," he said.

"Listen to me," Kate said desperately. "Ozgo didn't kill Rafael and he didn't cause his death accidentally, either. If all the stuff you've been doing has been to get some kind of revenge, you're picking on the wrong man, and you're doing just what his killer wants you to do. He screwed up. He was supposed to make sure that everybody on that raid was dead in the attack. Everybody. But everybody wasn't. One of the people who escaped alive didn't matter. That was an Afghani, and even if he told people what he saw, nobody would listen to him. But the other person who escaped alive was Ozgo. And Ozgo was too messed up to know what he'd seen, but he'd seen it, and if he started talking about it, it wouldn't take long until somebody figured out what happened."

"I've got to go in to my office now," Chan said. "If you're not in your car and on your way out of the campus by the time I get to my phone, I'm going to have security detain you."

"The person who killed Rafael was Paterson," Kate said. "And he did it because Rafael wasn't killed in the drone strike that had just taken place."

At the sound of Jed Paterson's name, Chan had gone completely still.

The silence went on and on. Kate almost started to babble. She held herself back. Then Chan said, "You don't know what you're talking about."

"I do know what I'm talking about," Kate said. "The raid happened on the outskirts of Kabul, and it wasn't just a bunch of soldiers striking at what they mistook for an enemy patrol. There was a drone, and it hit four small buildings that were being used to house computer equipment and to stockpile supplies. The drone hit that, and when it was over and the buildings were destroyed, Paterson led a group of men who were supposed to clean up anybody who was still alive. Rafael wasn't supposed to be there. Rafael's people weren't supposed to be there. They were in the wrong place at the wrong time. And therefore they all had to die."

Chan had relaxed. "They had to die because a drone went off course and hit the wrong target? Don't be ridiculous."

"They had to die because one of them might have figured out that the drone wasn't off target," Kate said. "It wasn't a mistake. It wasn't a friendly fire accident. That drone hit those buildings because that was what it had been directed to hit. You can make a lot of money in a war, hiring yourself out to the United States to reconstruct facilities that have been bombed or damaged. That's what General Solutions does. You can make more if you can make sure there are a lot of facilities that need reconstruction."

"You're insane," Chan said. She didn't sound as if she believed it.

"I think close to half of all the reconstructions General Solutions has done have been setups. Drones programmed to hit targets essential to US operations. Paterson and his cleanup crew were sent in to make sure there wasn't a trail that could get back to the people in the Department of Defense. They wouldn't have touched that target that night if they'd known Turner was anywhere near it, but they did. So they had to kill every single member of the group Turner had brought with him, and they failed. Ozgo was left alive. They were never going to be safe as long as Ozgo was alive."

"My God," Chan said.

"I think the idea was to kill Ozgo when he got back to the states," Kate said. "Paterson seems to have come back into the country at the same time. But then Ozgo came to you, and you let him live on the property, and that was too close to your father. If Ozgo had just gone out and wandered around, Paterson could have staged something. But Ozgo stayed on your property all the time. He never went anywhere. They'd have been stuck if you hadn't decided to fake your own kidnapping."

"I didn't fake my own kidnapping."

"Then Paterson faked it for you," Kate said, "because it was faked, and you know it, and I know it, and Ozgo is sitting in a cell right now guilty of nothing but being in the wrong place at the wrong time and coming out of it with a royal case of PTSD. There's a picture that was up on the Internet and in the papers of all of you standing outside the house while it was burning, and if you look at Ozgo's shoes, he was wearing high-top sneakers. If you look closely, there is an indention in the ankle parts of them, like somebody had tied him up. And somebody did, because the two of you couldn't let him wander around while he was supposed to be kidnapping you. And if you don't tell the truth and get him out of there, it's only a matter of time. They'll find somebody on the inside to get rid of him for good."

"They're good at cleaning up," Tom said. "They killed Flanagan, the head of homicide. Remember him?"

"And what was he to anybody?" Chan asked.

"They took me off the case because I asked the wrong kinds of questions," Tom said. "They put him on the case because he was willing to do things they knew I wouldn't. Like suppress forensic evidence. And not investigate the anomalies that made me think you hadn't been kidnapped to begin with. I think they told him that everybody knew Ozgo was guilty and your father was determined to see that the man who harmed his daughter was put away. But he was the head of homicide. Flanagan might have been a drunken asshole, but he wasn't a complete idiot. The more time he spent with that evidence, the more likely he was to find something. And as soon as he did, he started blackmailing the hell out your father and Evans. I don't see him buying a new house without a little help."

Chan looked from one to the other. Kate found it impossible to read the expression on her face. Then Chan straightened up and straightened her suit jacket.

"Wait here," she said. "I'll be right back."

"Do you believe us?" Tom asked.

Chan looked contemptuous.

She said, "I'm not sure." Then she turned on her heel and walked away, up the steps and to the front door.

Chan came back less than five minutes later, still looking cool and expensive and completely professional. Tom and Kate had spent the time since she'd left making uneasy comments about everything and anything.

"I've cleared my calendar," she said. "Let's get out of here."

"Where are we going?" Tom asked.

"I'm not sure where we're going in the long run," Chan said, "but right this minute, we're going to a car rental. My car's bugged, and I'd be willing to bet yours is, too."

TWENTY-ONE

The car ride started tense and got tenser. They were only minutes out of the Hamilton Charitable Trust's long driveway when Chan insisted that they pull over. She got out of the car, opened her purse, took out her own cell phone, and dropped it to the ground. Then she lifted her right foot in its elegant stiletto heel and brought that heel right down on the phone's screen. Kate thought the crack could be heard all the way to California.

Chan got back into the car and said, "Go now. Get out of here as fast as possible."

"You think your phone is bugged?" Kate asked.

"He's been bugging my phones and my rooms and my car and anything else he could get his hands on since I was sixteen years old. And maybe earlier. He had my dorm rooms bugged, Miss Porter's and Vassar's both. The man can't stand to be out of control for a minute."

"And you think he has Tom's car bugged?" Kate asked. "Because if you don't, then I don't understand why we're getting you a rental car."

"We're getting *us* a rental car," Chan said. "You and me. Mr. Abbott can go do whatever he wants. I need a place to think."

"To think about what?" Kate asked.

"To think about whether he played me," Chan said. "He almost certainly did, because he's my father, and that's the way my father thinks."

"You need to do something about Ozgo," Kate said. "You know he didn't kidnap you and you know he didn't start that fire. If he goes to prison, he'll die."

"That was the idea," Chan said. "Except that he was supposed to die in that fire."

★   ★   ★

Everything at Enterprise Rent-a-Car went almost without a hitch, except that Chan insisted they use Kate's or Tom's credit card to rent the vehicle.

"He keeps tabs on my credit cards," she kept insisting until Kate was ready to strangle her.

Kate used her card, signed the papers, and took the keys.

"Now what?" she asked Chan.

"We need to find a place where I can work this out," Chan said. "Someplace where you can tell me this whole idea you've got."

Tom and Kate looked at each other.

"We've got the perfect place," Kate said. "It's up in the mountains. There isn't any cell service."

"Fine," Chan said. "Let's go."

While Tom seemed entertained, Kate fumed all the way back up into the mountains. Talk about behaving like an entitled jerk. Chan might not be as obviously obnoxious as Brayde, but she was obnoxious enough.

She also didn't give a damn.

"Is this your purse?" Chan asked. She didn't wait for an answer. She upended the contents onto her lap and then went looking through the bag for anything that might be left inside. She found Kate's cell phone, opened the window next to her, and threw it out into the road.

"Speed up and keep moving," Chan said. She pawed through the things on her lap. They didn't amount to much. "You don't have anything to record this conversation with. And I know this car isn't bugged, because we rented it. It doesn't matter what I tell you. If you tell anybody else, I can just deny it."

"I don't understand why you want Ozgo to go to jail," Kate said. "He didn't kill Rafael. I thought that was all you cared about. And Paterson is the one who concocted the whole kidnapping scheme. And I'm willing to bet you only know the man because your father introduced you to him."

"He didn't introduce us, exactly," Chan said. "He recommended Jed for a job at the Trust."

"I'd say that was introducing you," Kate said.

"Jed was actually in Afghanistan," Chan said. "He was there when Rafael died, or just after. He actually saw what happened."

"Paterson was discharged from the Navy SEALs almost a full year before the attack that killed Turner," Kate said.

"He was in Afghanistan when Rafael died, but he wasn't in the military."

Chan went on staring straight ahead. She brushed off Kate's things from her lap and let them thump to the car's floor.

"Chan, listen to me," Kate said. "It would kill Ozgo to go to prison. It would. And you have to know that once Ozgo is dead, once they don't have anything else to worry about, they're going to go right back to those phony drone raids and other people are going to end up dead, including other American soldiers. You can't let it go on like this."

Kate tried to think of something else to say but couldn't. The narrow dirt road that led up to the cabin was just in front of her. She turned the car onto it and made it climb, complaining, toward the summit.

She was all the way to the top and in sight of the cabin itself before she noticed that things didn't look right, things didn't sound right. The cabin door was partway open and one of Frank's rifles was lying out on the stoop.

She was just pulling into the cabin's driveway when a bullet came through the windshield and lodged itself in the back seat.

Tom and Chan were faster than Kate was. They were out of the car and down on the ground before the car stopped moving.

Kate got out of the car as soon as it stopped and looked around frantically. There was no sign of Jack anywhere. But she spotted Frank. He had a camo coat on and was leaning against the spreading oak tree that stood right next to the cabin's side door.

As Kate watched, Frank raised his rifle, sighted it careful, and let out a shot.

Kate made her way to him. "What are you doing?" she demanded. "Daddy, for God's sake, what are you doing?"

Frank didn't look at her. "Jack's just like a deer, that's what he is," he said.

Just like a deer? Kate though furiously. Besides the rifle Frank held, there were two others at his feet. He had enough ammunition to take out the entire deer population of Northern Virginia.

"Don't have an automatic up here," Frank said. "Have to keep reloading."

"Daddy," Kate said. "Listen, please. Don't reload. Just stop shooting for a minute. Where's Jack? What's happened to Jack?"

Frank aimed again, sighted again, fired again. Then there was another shot, coming at them instead of going away. Kate tried to see where the shot was coming from and got nowhere.

"Daddy?" she demanded. "Daddy, does Jack have a gun, too? Is that what this is?"

Kate tried to remember all the things people had told her about Alzheimer's patients who got violent, who got delusional. That had to be what was happening here. That was the only reason Kate could think of why Frank would be shooting at Jack, shooting blindly into the woods, stacking up ammunition as if he were in a combat raid.

There had to be some way to stop him, to bring him under control.

"Daddy," she said, putting out her hand.

It was the wrong move. Another shot came out of the woods, and this one hit her—not hard, and not in any vital place, but it hit her nonetheless. She felt the bullet graze against the skin of her arm and looked down to see blood dripping, making a wide, red blur that stained her shirt and jeans.

"Get out of here," Frank yelled. "Get out of here."

"You can't do this. We've got to find Jack."

"He doesn't want Jack," Frank screamed. "Don't you get it? He only cares about Jack because he wants to get you."

Nothing made any sense. Nothing. Kate only knew that she had to stop Frank, she had to, and she made for the rifle he was holding in a sudden lurch that made the injured part of her arm hurt like hell. She tugged at the rifle one more time and got it loose, falling back onto the ground with it. The safety wasn't on—of course it wasn't on. The rifle discharged as soon as it hit the ground.

Tom approached and helped Frank get up.

"Where is he?" Tom demanded.

"Don't know," Frank said, "but he's close. He's not using a distance scope. He's *right fucking here.*"

Another bullet came from out of the woods.

"I don't have a weapon," Tom said. "Give me the rifle."

Of course he didn't have a weapon. He was on suspension. He'd have had to hand in his weapon and his badge.

"Let me up," Kate said, struggling. Her arm still hurt. Her whole body felt weak.

Then, out of nowhere, she heard Jack's voice: "Mom! Get out of there!"

That voice was the only thing that could have stopped Kate in the middle of what she was doing. It stopped her cold, and she twisted around under Tom to get a glimpse of Jack.

Jack was standing in the cabin's front doorway. There was the sound of another gunshot and Jack stepped back inside, quickly.

"Who's out in the woods?" Kate screamed. "Who's out in the woods?"

But the attacker wasn't out in the woods anymore. He stepped into the clearing right next to the tree and raised a semiautomatic handgun and pointed it right at Kate's head.

There he was, Jed Paterson, tall and lean and massive in the shoulders and thighs.

"I can clean up the rest of them later," he said. "Right now, I'm just worried about you."

Kate was still on the ground, finding it hard to move. Frank was caught in the middle of the scene and frozen in place. And Tom was unarmed.

Paterson was aiming his weapon at them when a bullet shot out of the front of his head and he dropped to the ground.

As his lifeless body fell, they saw Chan, in a professional wide-firing stance holding a Glock, her huge Coach bag lying on the ground in front of her.

TWENTY-TWO

The formal letter from Almador announcing that Kate Ford was officially fired came on the same day Chan Hamilton held her third press conference, and Kate didn't know what she considered less of a surprise.

It didn't help that the mail was late that day and that Jack, Frank, Tom, and even Mike Alexander were all in Kate's kitchen discussing whether or not it would be sensible for Kate to get a hibachi for the back patio. Alexander looked like he'd swallowed a canary along with a bottle of Scotch. He was now absolutely positive that he was about to be in line for a Pulitzer.

"It's not much of a patio," Kate told them as she headed for the foyer at the sound of mail coming through the slot. "It's more like a postage stamp."

"You can make lots of healthy food," Tom said as Kate came back into the kitchen, opening the envelope. He was unwrapping the ingredients for chili coleslaw dogs, including foot-long hot dogs and buns to go with them.

Kate dropped the letter on the table next to a two-quart tub of coleslaw from Hansom's Deli. "I knew this was coming," she said. "I'm going to have to start coming up with some way to make a living."

"At least you'll have a chance," Frank said.

"Take a look at this," Jack said.

It was Tom who had gotten them the small television set Kate now kept in the kitchen, because with so much on the news about what was happening in the cases of Ozgo, Paterson, and General Solutions, they all wanted to watch nonstop.

What Jack wanted them to watch was Chan, sitting at a long table with only her attorney beside her, a new attorney, not one bought and paid for by her father. There was no sign of Ozgo, who had been at the previous press conferences, looking absolutely awful and shaking like a leaf.

"I have talked to the new district attorney," Chan said. "He has refused to call for an investigation into the role of my father in my kidnapping, in the deaths of Bill Flanagan and Reggie Evans, or in any other matter. I have therefore launched my own investigation into these matters, and I have filed suit against Richard Hamilton for stalking, invasion of privacy, and extreme emotional distress. I have also—"

"I thought they weren't even a hundred percent sure Evans was murdered," Jack said.

"We're sure, we just can't prove it," Tom said. "There was definitely methamphetamine in his body, but how it got there, nobody can prove."

"But Flanagan they can prove?" Kate asked.

Tom nodded. "You were right about talking to Lucy Leeds. Once you get her started, she can't shut up. She saw Paterson's car over at Flanagan's house half a dozen times, and she saw it there right after we left that Sunday night. *And* she took down the license plate. Paterson and Flanagan both got into Flanagan's car, but it was Paterson who was driving."

"I bet her dad's going to be sorry he gave her that trust fund," Jack said, still staring at the television screen. "She's practically calling him a traitor on national television."

Tom sighed. "They've arrested him, and Mike's paper snagged a doozy of a picture with Hamilton doing a perp walk. But if Richard Hamilton was the head man behind that scheme, it's going to take a long time to prove it."

"Because Hamilton is an evil genius?" Frank asked.

"Because he would have known better than to touch anything that could tie him to it, even in a little way," Tom said.

"What about Paterson, though?" Kate prompted. "Hamilton introduced Paterson to Chan."

Tom said, "Paterson represented himself as somebody who had known Turner in Afghanistan. Chan was still mourning Turner. Paterson was a decorated war hero. How was Hamilton to know the man was a complete psychopath?"

"Do you honestly think that was what happened?" Kate asked.

Tom put hot dogs on the stove grill. "Of course I don't, but that's the story Hamilton's putting out, and with Paterson dead, there's no way to disprove it. Hell, Hamilton won't even have to lie much. He'll just have to leave a few things out. And he isn't doing any talking; his attorney is."

"But he did let himself be in contact with Paterson," Kate said. "If Paterson had lived, he could have blackmailed Richard Hamilton."

"Probably not," Tom said. "If I were Hamilton, there would have been somebody who dealt directly with Paterson and gave him his instructions about Ozgo. Richard Hamilton would have been represented as the contact of a contact, not anybody involved in the faked friendly fire accidents and not anybody who knew anything about them. Just someone who could be tricked into getting Paterson into Chan Hamilton's good graces and therefore in touch with Ozgo."

"I hate it," Jack said. "What's the point if you don't catch the bad guy?"

"Technically, we don't know that Richard Hamilton is a bad guy," Tom said.

"Of course not," Kate said. "Just because he owns the major interest in all the companies involved in the fake friendly fire attacks and he's the one who was making the most money from them, why should that mean anything?"

"It's not the same as beyond a reasonable doubt," Tom rebutted.

"Kate was right about just about everything, though, wasn't she?" Frank said. "I was reading a statement from that new district attorney, that Hobart Helms guy, and he presented it just the way Kate says it was, and she got to it first."

"Just be glad Hobart Helms is just a temporary district attorney," Tom said. "He's an idiot. Just about everybody in homicide hates him. But, yeah, he's not such an idiot that he doesn't know a good thing when he sees it. And Kate was substantially right about everything. The deal was that General Solutions, using Robotix military drones, was destroying United States and Afghan property, and then General Solutions got hired to reconstruct that property. And the contracts they got to do those reconstructions were expensive ones, with money falling all over the place and lots of corruption built in. When they could manage it, they got as many people out and away as they could. Sometimes they couldn't manage it. When that happened, they sent in Paterson and his people to clean up. Meaning kill everyone in sight. A lot of the time, they got away with claiming it was an enemy attack if nobody was alive who'd seen it. Other times?" Tom shrugged.

"Can't you get sued for saying things about people on television that you can't prove are true?" Jack asked.

"You've got to have malicious intent," Frank said.

"You don't call this malicious intent?" Jack gestured toward the television.

Chan was standing up. "I will prove that my father, Richard Hamilton, was the mastermind behind a scheme to defraud the United States government and murder American soldiers, all to increase the profits of major corporations of which he is the controlling stockholder and executive."

"There she goes," Tom said.

Tom brought the hot dogs to the table and sat down to start constructing them. "The incident with Turner was different," he said. "He was famous because he was dating Chan. If Paterson had been anybody else, he might have considered the possibility that he'd be safer not killing Turner, at least not right away, no matter what Turner had seen. Instead, he seems to have gone about the mission completely routinely. He gets his people down there. He sees the patrol that isn't supposed to be anywhere near the place. He starts taking people out. But other troops had seen the flash of the drone attack, although they don't seem to have recognized that it was a drone, and those troops had called in the medics. Everything happened fast. There were too many people around to do a proper mop-up job. He'd just killed a man with news value and a girlfriend who could get him lots more publicity once he was dead."

"And the unit," Kate reminded him. "There was an entire unit."

"Not an entire one," Frank said. "It was about six people of that unit that got killed in that particular attack. The military ought to be looking into the way those six soldiers were kept presumptively alive."

"They wouldn't have stayed alive forever," Kate said. "The idea was to cover the fact that they'd all died at the same time. And to make sure the families didn't have information about the real incident. I think they'd have been declared dead eventually. They'd just 'die,' if you know what I mean, individually and in places far away from Afghanistan."

"And you know that for sure?" Tom said.

Kate picked up a paper napkin and threw it at him. "Your Hobart Helms came out and said it."

"Nope," Tom said. "Really listen to the man. He's playing this as if the entire thing started when Paterson went rogue. He's hinting that Paterson himself hacked the records. That Paterson was trying to cover up an individual act of violence, a straight-out murder."

"Oh, for God's sake," Kate said. "That doesn't make any sense at all."

"Hobart Helms has a problem," Tom said. "He's got to explain this so that both a judge and the public will buy it. Now that Chan has admitted that she and Paterson faked her kidnapping and tried to blame it on Ozgo, Ozgo is out of jail, but the real perpetrator is dead. Helms doesn't want anything that might confuse anybody. It's bad enough having to explain the Byzantine plot Chan and Jed tried to pass off as that kidnapping attempt—tying up Chan, putting her in that closet, and then taping her and sending the tape to Richard Hamilton. That phone call to the police from Chan herself right before they started the fire. Then Jed kicking Ozgo in the head to knock him out so that he'd be burned to death, but that didn't work as planned."

"Ozgo came to and staggered out into the night," Mike said. "I spent all day today with a guy at the Pentagon. I think he thought he was going to die."

"Somebody over there ought to die," Kate said. "Soldiers did die because of all this. Other people died. Flanagan died, even if he wasn't much of a human being. Evans died."

"They died, but I'd be willing to bet that neither one of them knew anything about the military angle," Mike said. "They knew that Richard Hamilton was pressuring everybody in sight to get Ozgo arrested and convicted. They knew Tom here had been taken off the case because he wouldn't stop insisting on seeing the forensics. They knew those forensics implicated Chan in something. They both assumed that the deal was that Chan was implicated in her own kidnapping and that she might be liable for the attempted murder of Ozgo—the way Ozgo was tried for the attempted murder of her. They just thought Richard Hamilton was trying to save his daughter."

"So can't they get Richard Hamilton on that?" Kate asked.

"We found the paper trail for the bribes Flanagan was taking," Tom said. "They traced back to Paterson, not Richard Hamilton. And nothing in Paterson's life traced back to Richard Hamilton in any way."

"The original Teflon cowboy," Kate said glumly.

Mike reached forward and started to look through the cartons on the table. He found the one with potato salad and dragged it over.

"Don't worry," he said. "Richard Hamilton will get plenty of trouble. There's our girl Chan over there. And there's me. Hobart Helms may have to get his case out front without too many complications, but I don't have to care about his case at all. I'm focused entirely on the military thing, and thanks to you all, I've got lots to go on. I've got so much to go on, I got a call from the Chairman of the Joint Chiefs of Staff himself."

"Really," Tom said. "You have names?"

"No," Mike admitted, "but I'm not going to need them. I can prove that those drone attacks happened and that they were deliberate. I can prove that there were kickbacks, bribes, corrupt bookkeeping. I pulled a little string, and you know what? A federal judge just ordered thousands of documents about those reconstruction projects declassified. I'll have them tomorrow morning. And then it's clear sailing to a Pulitzer."

★   ★   ★

It was after eight o'clock and dark when Kate went out to the back patio and sat down next to Frank. With everything that had been happening to Frank over the last few months, Kate was afraid of what she might find. It had bothered her when he'd left the kitchen and taken a beer with him. He liked the company of Tom and Mike. Kate didn't see any good reason he'd want to leave it.

When she got outside, though, Frank was sitting at the little, round patio table with all his faculties intact.

He looked up when she came out and gestured to the other chair.

"Isn't it a little cold out here?" she asked him.

"I'm all right," he said. "You don't have to keep me company."

"I'm worried about you."

"Funny thing," Frank said. "I'm worried about *you*. About what you did at Almador."

"You mean accessing classified files when I didn't really have clearance?"

"That. And I've got an idea that it's probably worse than that. It's worse than that, isn't it?"

"I had my cell phone on me," Kate admitted. "And my cell phone has a camera."

"Jesus God."

"Daddy, it's all right, really. Richard Hamilton had a cell phone on him, too. He'd be in just as much trouble as I would be if anyone ever found out."

"Richard Hamilton probably has clearance."

"Nobody has clearance for that."

"You sounded pretty sure Richard Hamilton was the guilty party back in there," Frank said.

"I am pretty sure," Kate said. "But—oh, I don't know. There's still something odd about this. General Solutions and Robotix deliberately staged friendly fire incidents to destroy facilities that they'd then be asked to rebuild, and to keep that secret, everybody who witnessed the friendly fires had to be dead. And that time it was Turner and Ozgo, and Ozgo got out alive. So they had to find a way to get rid of Ozgo, which would have been easy if Chan hadn't let him live on the estate. So Paterson deliberately wormed his way into Chan's, well, into her everything, really, and fed her a bunch of lies so that she'd help him. Then he staged the kidnapping. And all of that's true, and we can prove it. But I don't know. It's like I'm missing something, and whatever I'm missing is specifically about Richard Hamilton."

"So maybe Richard Hamilton *isn't* the mastermind behind the reconstruction scam?"

"I don't know," Kate said, nearly in despair. "I think I'd make a terrible detective. I'd never be able to convince myself that anybody was really guilty."

"Is that what you're going to do now that you're at loose ends? Become a detective?"

"Let's go in and suggest it to Tom," Kate said. "I like to hear him scream."